Witch is The Nest Now Empty

Published by Implode Publishing Ltd

Chapter 1

(Author's note: This is the first book of season five. It picks up the story SIX YEARS after the previous book)

Winky was seated by the window, staring into space.

"I'm in love," he sighed.

"You're always in love," I said. "Who is it this time?"

"Daisy. I've never met anyone like her before."

"Shall I remind you that you said exactly the same thing about what's her name—Lily, wasn't it? And not more than three weeks ago."

"This is different. Daisy is different. She's an angel."

"I'll give it two weeks max. You, Winky, are a hopeless romantic."

"Oh dear, Jill." Jules was standing in the doorway. "Are you at it again?"

We'd been in our new offices at Washbridge Central Point for almost eighteen months, and I still hadn't got used to how quietly the doors opened and closed.

"No, I was just—err—"

"How long is it now?" she asked. "Since Winky passed away?"

"Almost two years."

"And yet, you still talk to him."

"No, I was just—"

"It's obvious you still miss him. Why don't you get yourself another cat to keep you company in here?"

"Definitely not. And besides, animals aren't allowed in this building."

"I just came in to ask if you wanted a cup of tea."

"Yes, please, I'd love one."

"Coming right up."

As soon as she'd left the room, Winky jumped onto my desk.

"She's got a cheek," he said. "Suggesting you bring another cat in here."

"Jules was just trying to be kind. She doesn't realise you're still around. How could she?"

When Winky had lost his fight against cancer a couple of years earlier, I'd been devastated, but then he'd reappeared as a ghost the following day. It had been amazing to see him looking so full of life, which was quite ironic considering he was actually dead. Even more surprising, ghost Winky had not one but two fully functional eyes. I'd suggested that we give him a new name in recognition of his ocular upgrade, but he'd insisted that he preferred to remain plain old Winky.

Winky hadn't finished ranting. "She's getting a bit too big for her boots, that one."

"You were the one who begged me for months to bring Jules back."

"She's changed. Become all uppity. I sometimes wish the old bag lady was still here."

"You're such a hypocrite. You couldn't wait to see the back of Mrs V."

A few minutes later, Jules returned with my cup of tea.

"Did you forget my custard creams?" I said.

"You gave me strict instructions yesterday that I shouldn't let you have any custard creams during working hours."

"Yes, but I didn't get a chance to have any breakfast this morning."

"You also said that I should ignore any excuses you might come up with, to try to persuade me to give you some."

"O—kay."

Sometimes, I hated myself.

"You haven't forgotten that you have an appointment with Mr Wright in forty minutes, have you?"

"Remind me again what he said it was about."

"He didn't. He wouldn't give me any details."

"Okay. Let me know when he arrives."

Winky laughed. "All of this time you've been waiting for Mr Right to come along, and here he is at last."

"I found *my* Mr Right years ago, and Jack and I are as happy today as when we first met."

"You hated him when you first met him."

"That's true, but you know what I mean."

Jules popped her head in the door and said, "I have your sister here. I told her you have a client coming in soon."

"That's okay. Send her through."

Ever since Kathy had sold her bridal shop empire, she had way too much time on her hands, with the result that she regularly dropped by for no particular reason whatsoever. She had made a small fortune from the sale, and now she spent most of her time buying designer clothes.

"I was just passing, so I thought I'd drop in and see my favourite sister." As usual, she didn't wait to be asked to take a seat.

"You were only here three days ago."

"Don't I get a cup of tea?"

"No. Jules told you I have a client coming in any

minute."

"I wish you'd get rid of that horrible old desk."

"Do we have to have this same conversation every time you come by? I told you that it has sentimental value."

"It has woodworm."

"This was the desk Dad sat at when he started this business."

"You've got this beautiful new office, and you have to spoil it with that monstrosity. You should have one like mine."

"Why do you even have a desk? It's not like you're in business anymore."

"I've told you before. I'm planning my next business venture."

"I'm not getting rid of this desk and that's final. If it had been up to me, I would still be working out of my old office. I only relocated because they decided to tear down the building."

"You can't stand in the way of progress, Jill."

"How is it progress to tear down a perfectly good building and replace it with another multi-storey car park?"

"Have you heard from Florence?"

"Not for a few days."

"I still can't believe you and Jack decided to send her to boarding school."

"I'm not having this conversation with you again, Kathy. Florence wanted to go there."

"But she's only eleven. A kid that age needs—"

"Enough!" I stood up. "You need to leave now."

"I was only saying."

"I know what you were *only* saying. You've *only* said it

at least a dozen times. Now, if you don't mind, I have a client to see."

"I'm sorry." She stood up. "I didn't mean to upset you. Are you and Jack still coming over for Pete's birthday this Saturday?"

"As long as you promise not to bring up the subject of boarding school again."

"I promise."

"Okay, we'll see you on Saturday."

"Someone touched a nerve," Winky said, after Kathy had left.

"There's nothing wrong with this desk."

"That's not what I meant, and you know it. It still hurts, doesn't it? Florence going to CASS."

"Of course it does. I never wanted her to board there. And Jack certainly didn't. She's still my little girl." I dabbed my eyes. "It's what she wanted, though, and I know she's really happy there."

"When is she coming home next?"

"I'm not sure. Half-term, obviously, but she might manage a weekend before then."

Jules popped her head around the door again. "Are you okay, Jill?"

"I'm fine."

"It looks like you've been crying."

"No, it's just a bit of hay fever."

"Mr Wright is here."

"Send him in, please."

Incredibly, Mr Wright was very normal. I mention that only because I was beginning to think that every client who walked through my door was destined to be weird in one way or another: ridiculous name, crazy attire, you get the picture. But not Mr Wright. He was average height and weight, dressed quite conservatively, and had a sensible name.

"Hi, I'm Kevin Wright." He placed his briefcase on my desk.

"Jill Maxwell."

"Would you mind if I took Cecil out of the case?"

"Sorry?"

"He's a little agoraphobic."

Something told me I had spoken too soon.

Before I could ask who Cecil was, Mr Wright had opened the briefcase and taken him out.

"Why do you have a weasel in your briefcase?"

"Cecil isn't a weasel, although that's a common mistake to make. He's a ferret. Say hello to Jill, Cecil."

Cecil didn't say hello, but unbeknown to his handler, he did have something he wanted to get off his tiny chest, "Will you tell this one that my name is Guy?"

"*Guy*?" I repeated.

"Sorry?" Mr Wright gave me a puzzled look.

"I was just saying that Cecil is a nice *guy*. Very handsome."

"Thank you."

"My name is *Guy*," Guy insisted.

"What brings you here, Mr Wright?"

"Please call me Kevin. Or Kev."

"Which would you prefer?"

"Err, Kevin. No. Kev. No. Kevin, please."

"Okay, Kevin it is. How can I help you today?"

"I need some help with F-O-F. It stands for Friends Of Ferrets. I'm the treasurer. Or at least I used to be until—"

He hesitated. "I can hardly bring myself to talk about it."

"I'm afraid I'm not going to be able to help you unless you do."

"Okay. I have to be strong. I owe it to Cecil and all the other ferrets."

"It's Guy!" The ferret rolled his little ferret eyes.

"Take your time, Kevin. Maybe a cup of tea would help?"

"No, thank you. I'm allergic to hot drinks."

"See what I have to put up with?" Guy said.

Ignoring the ferret, I offered Kevin a glass of water.

"That would be very acceptable, but I'd prefer it in a cup. I can't bear the feeling of glass against my lips."

"Okay." I buzzed Jules. "Could you bring Mr Wright a cup of water, please?"

"You'd like water in a cup?"

"That's right."

Once Mr Wright had his drink, I tried again to get him to open up.

"You were saying that you are—err—used to be the treasurer of F-O-F."

"And had been for eleven years."

"I take it you didn't resign the position?"

"Certainly not. I loved that job."

"Was it your fulltime job?"

"No, it wasn't a paid position. F-O-F is run by volunteers. None of us are paid, other than expenses, obviously."

"Right. If you didn't resign your position as treasurer, what happened? Why were you removed?"

"I was accused of misappropriating the organisation's funds. A totally outrageous accusation with no basis in truth."

"Did some money go missing?"

"Yes. Just over a thousand pounds."

"From where, exactly?"

"The safe."

"And where is that safe?"

"In the F-O-F office."

"Which is where?"

"In my back garden. In a shed to be precise."

"Let me make sure I have understood this correctly: the F-O-F office is in the shed in your back garden?"

"Correct."

"And the safe is in that shed?"

"Also correct."

"Right, and you were accused of pocketing the money?"

"Yes, they said I'd faked the theft and I was summarily dismissed."

"That seems rather harsh after you'd spent so long in the job."

"It's an absolute travesty, particularly as I'm one of the founders of F-O-F."

"Were the police involved?"

"Yes. They took a note of the theft and gave us a crime number, but I don't expect to hear any more from them."

"How exactly can I help you?"

"I want you to find out who really took the money, in order to clear my name. Can you do that?"

"Possibly, but here's the thing: I charge by the hour, and it won't take long for my bill to rise above the amount of money stolen. Even if I was to find the money, which isn't guaranteed, you would still be out of pocket."

"Money isn't the issue here. My integrity is what's at

stake."

"I understand that, but you could end up with a very large bill."

"Fortunately, I'm independently wealthy thanks to a generous inheritance."

"And you understand that you may end up paying considerably more than the amount stolen?"

"Absolutely. Are you in?"

"I'm in."

"Excellent. How do we begin?"

"First, I'll need you to sign my standard contract."

"No problem, then maybe we can arrange a date for you to visit the F-O-F office, so I can tell you everything you need to know."

"Sounds like a plan."

"Every time," Winky said after Mr Wright had left. "Without fail."

"What?"

"Another case. Another nutter. How do you do it?"

"I wouldn't call Mr Wright a nutter."

"Not to his face, maybe, but you know it's true. The man is a ferret short of a business."

"This case is not about ferrets. A man's integrity has been called into question."

"It's not his *integrity* that's in question. It's his *sanity*. Who walks around with a ferret in his briefcase?"

"A case is a case. I'm not going to turn away a man just because he has some unusual habits."

"Especially if he's stinking rich."

"That certainly helps."

Chapter 2

Being the consummate professional, I had searched online to find as much information as I could on Friends Of Ferrets.

"Have you ever seen a sorrier looking bunch?" Winky said.

"Do you mind? You shouldn't be looking at my computer screen. This is confidential client business."

"Yeah, but just look at the state of that crowd. I bet they haven't got a girlfriend between the lot of them."

He was referring to the group photograph of the members of F-O-F, taken at the previous year's annual dinner.

"Maybe their girlfriends had their photographs taken separately."

"Yeah, right. Bunch of losers."

My phone rang.

"Jill, it's Amber. Are you busy?"

"I'm doing some research for a case I've just taken on."

"We're holding a family meeting. Can you come over?"

"What's it about?"

"I'd rather not say on the phone. You never know who might be listening in."

"Okay. Where are you? Aunt Lucy's or Pamber?"

"How many times do we have to tell you not to call it that?"

"Sorry."

"We're in the function room."

"Okay. Give me a couple of minutes and I'll be there."

When the twins had expanded Cuppy C, they'd added a restaurant and function room, above the original tea room. Before reopening, they'd decided that the place needed a new name. At the time, I'd thought changing the name was a terrible idea—I still did—but they wouldn't listen to reason. Decision made, there had followed the great debate about the new name. Amber had wanted to call it Amber & Pearl's; unsurprisingly, Pearl had wanted to call it Pearl & Amber's. Neither of them had been prepared to back down, but they'd eventually agreed to abide by the result of a coin toss. Pearl had won, and so the new name was declared to be Pearl and Amber's. What neither of them had foreseen was that a lot of customers would find the new name to be too much of a mouthful, so had taken to shortening it to Pamber. That had infuriated the twins, which is why I took great pleasure in calling it that.

Petty? Maybe, but also very funny.

Juliet, their manager was behind the counter downstairs in the tea room.

"The twins are upstairs in the function room, Jill."

"I was hoping I might be able to grab a latte before I go up there."

"No problem. How's your daughter taken to boarding at CASS?"

"She seems to be enjoying it so far. Fingers crossed."

"My Pauline started there last month, but she isn't boarding." Juliet handed me my drink.

"Thanks. I'd better get upstairs before Grandma sends out the search party."

"Your grandmother isn't up there. It's just the twins and your Aunt Lucy."

"Oh? Okay." Why would the twins and Aunt Lucy hold a family meeting without Grandma?

"Here she is," Pearl said. "We had already got you a coffee."

"Ah, sorry." I took a seat at the table, next to Aunt Lucy. "Where's Grandma?"

"It's just the four of us," Amber said.

"I thought you said it was a family meeting?"

"It is."

"I don't understand."

"We're planning Grandma's surprise birthday party," Pearl announced.

"You're doing *what*? Does she know about it?"

"Duh? It wouldn't be a surprise if she knew about it, would it?" Amber rolled her eyes at me.

"But why throw her a party this year?" I said.

"Because she'll be a thousand years old."

"No, she won't."

"She will," Pearl insisted. "We've checked and double-checked."

"It's a terrible idea." I turned to Aunt Lucy who had yet to speak. "What do you think about this?"

"I'm with you on this one, Jill. I've already tried to talk them out of it, but they won't listen."

Despite Aunt Lucy's warning, I felt I had to try to make the twins see sense.

"There are two things Grandma hates: being reminded how old she is and surprises."

"Yes, but a surprise birthday party is different," Amber said. "We think she'll love it. Now, are you willing to help or not?"

"What would I have to do?"

"We're going to provide the venue, obviously."

"Where?" I asked.

"Where do you think? You're sitting there now."

"Right, sorry."

"We'll also be providing all the catering except for the birthday cake."

"You surely don't want me to bake the cake?"

"Of course not. We're not crazy. Mum is going to make it."

"So, what's left for me to do?"

"You have to get Grandma here on the day without letting on what's going on."

"How am I supposed to do that?"

"You'll have to figure that out. The important thing is that when she walks through that door, she mustn't have any idea what's waiting for her inside."

"Even if I agree to do it, she's bound to find out what you have planned long before the day. You know what she's like. She has eyes and ears everywhere."

"No, she won't. We're going to be super secretive."

"When is it?"

"Two weeks on Sunday, so we have plenty of time."

I still wasn't convinced, but I could see the twins had made up their minds, so reluctantly I agreed to play my part in this ill-fated charade.

***

These days, I often arrived home before Jack, which meant I was the one who had to get dinner ready. It was also why we ate far more takeaways than we used to.

Several years ago, we'd come into some money when one of my clients, a Ms Lockjaw, had given me a percentage of the money she'd made from the sale of jewellery, which I'd recovered for her. We'd put that money towards the purchase of the village store, which the Stock sisters had put up for sale when they'd decided to retire. Now called Maxwell's Convenience Store, it was Jack's pride and joy. There were times when I thought he loved that place more than he loved me; he certainly spent more time there than he did with me. Still, I didn't begrudge it because it was probably the first time in his life that he'd been truly happy in his work.

After parking the car outside the old watermill, I walked over to the store where I expected to find him hard at work. He wasn't the one behind the counter, though.

"Jack is in the back," Mr Ivers said. "He's just checking the delivery that arrived an hour ago."

Although Jack was clearly a natural when it came to retail, I still had my doubts about his decision to employ Mr Ivers as his assistant. But to be fair, he'd been in the role for almost two years now, and Jack reckoned he had no regrets.

"Okay, I'll go through and see him."

I found Jack counting cans of beans.

"They've done it again," he said. "We're one pallet short."

"I love it when you talk beans to me."

"Sorry. I'm losing patience with that new supplier of ours." He walked over and gave me a peck on the cheek. "Let me guess. You fancy another takeaway?"

"It's ages since we last had one."

"It was three days ago."

"I can't bear the thought of making dinner, and I really fancy a pizza."

"Pizza is fine by me."

"What time will you get done here?"

"I'll be back by six-thirty."

"I'll order it for a quarter to seven, just to be safe."

An hour later, we were seated at the kitchen table, tucking into pizza.

"How much pizza did you actually order?" Jack said. "We'll never eat all this."

"It was on a buy three, get one free, offer."

"There's only two of us here now."

"I still haven't got used to that."

"I wonder what Florence is up to." Jack sighed.

"Having a great time, I'm sure."

"Do you think she might be homesick?"

Florence leaving home had hit us both hard, but it had affected Jack much more than me.

"I very much doubt it." In an effort to distract him, I told him about the surprise birthday party for Grandma.

"One thousand years old? Really?"

"That's what the twins reckon, but I don't think anyone really knows how old she is. And that includes Grandma herself."

"I can't get my head around the idea that you're going to live forever too."

"I won't live *forever*."

A couple of years ago, I'd finally bitten the bullet and told Jack that as a witch I would age differently to humans. I'd expected it to freak him out, but at the time he'd taken the news quite calmly. It was only much later, after he'd had time to fully digest the information, that he'd realised what the implications were.

"No, but you'll outlive me by a few hundred years."

"Not necessarily. It's not like I'm immortal."

"I just hate the thought of you being with someone else after I die."

"I've told you a hundred times. There won't be anyone else."

"That's a stupid thing to say. You can't be alone for hundreds of years."

"Can we not talk about this again, please? We only end up arguing."

"Sorry. What do you think of the idea of a surprise birthday party?"

"I think it's a terrible idea. I told them so, but they've made their minds up. It's never going to happen, anyway."

"Why do you say that?"

"Because Grandma will find out long before the day of the party. You know what she's like; she doesn't miss a thing."

I was just about to take another bite of pizza when my phone rang with an unknown number.

"Is that Jill Maxwell?"

"Speaking."

"This is Mrs Littledo."

Mrs Littledo was the headmistress of CASS. She'd taken over from Hildegard Bogart who had retired just over a year ago.

"Is Florence alright?"

"Your daughter is absolutely fine, and from what I hear, she's settling in as a boarder very well."

"What's wrong?" Jack said.

I covered the phone and reassured him. "Nothing.

Florence is okay."

"I'm sorry to call you out of the blue like this, Jill, but I was wondering if you might be able to spare me a few minutes sometime."

"Sure. When did you have in mind?"

"This is a bit cheeky, but I don't suppose you're free right now, are you?"

I glanced down at the half-eaten pizza. "Yeah. Give me ten minutes, and I'll be with you."

"Great. I'll tell the receptionist to expect you."

"Okay, see you in a few minutes."

"What was that all about?" Jack asked when I'd ended the call.

I shrugged and then shoved a huge slice of pizza into my mouth.

"Is it about Florence?" Jack pressed.

Unable to speak, I simply shook my head.

"What is it about, then?"

After I'd managed to swallow the last of the pizza, I said, "I've no idea, but she said that Florence was fine and that she'd settled in well."

"Come here." Jack took out a tissue and wiped my mouth.

"I'll be back in a few seconds."

"Hello, Jill," Miranda said. She had been receptionist to Hildegard Bogart and had remained in the post when the new headmistress joined the school. "Mrs Littledo said you should go straight in."

The headmistress' office looked nothing like it had when I'd last visited Hildegard Bogart. I wasn't sure I approved of the modern minimalist look.

"Thank you for coming over, Jill. Please, take a seat. Can I get you a drink?"

"No, thanks. I've just had dinner."

"In that case, I'll get straight down to business. Last week, we had an inspection by SupEd. Are you familiar with them?"

"They're the body that inspects schools, aren't they?"

"That's correct. CASS has always been awarded the highest rating, but on their last visit, a couple of weeks ago, the chief inspector told me that we had only just managed to retain that level. A couple more marks lost would have meant that we would have been downgraded. That simply cannot be allowed to happen. Not on my watch."

"I see. And you're in the process of telling all parents about this, I assume? Is that why you asked me to come over today?"

"No. I asked you here because I want you to help us to reverse the decline."

Chapter 3

"Have you made a decision about CASS?" Jack asked the next morning over breakfast.

"I'm going to tell Mrs Littledo that I'll do it. It's only one day a week for an hour. I can manage that."

"What about Florence?"

"She'll be thrilled when I tell her."

"Hmm."

"What does that mean?"

"Think back to when you were Florence's age. Would you have wanted your mother to be a teacher at your school?"

"I wouldn't have minded."

"Then you're the only kid in the world who wouldn't."

"Why should it bother her?"

"Because parents are embarrassing."

"I wouldn't do anything to embarrass her."

"You won't need to. Just being there will be enough."

"I think you're wrong. I reckon she'll be chuffed to bits when I tell her."

"We'll see. What exactly will you be doing, anyway?"

"Mrs Littledo wants me to run lessons on using magic in the human world. No one else on the teaching staff lives over here."

"How long will you do it for?"

"I told you: one hour, on one day per week."

"I meant how long is your contract for?"

"We didn't discuss that. I suppose she wants to see how it goes."

Jack checked his phone. "I'd better be making tracks."

"Already? It's only six-thirty."

"I have an early delivery this morning."

"Couldn't Mr Ivers deal with that?"

"No, he worked the late shift yesterday."

"I never see you these days."

"It'll be better when I get a replacement for Grace."

"Have you made any progress with that yet?"

"I'm interviewing a few people today. Fingers crossed that one of them will be okay. Replacing Grace isn't going to be easy, though."

"I still can't believe she left you in the lurch like that."

"She's going to live in France with her new husband."

"She could have commuted."

"Yeah, right. I'll see you tonight." He gave me a quick peck on the lips and then left.

I still loved the old watermill, but it seemed so empty these days: Florence was rarely here, and Jack spent as much time at the store as he did at home. I didn't even have the goldfish for company since Wanda and Mabel had gone to the great goldfish bowl in the sky.

I had just stacked the dishes in the dishwasher when there was a knock at the door. Before answering it, and just in case it was some overeager salesman, I glanced out of the front window, only to see Goldie standing there.

Goldie Barr had moved to the village some years ago with her then husband, Liam Locks, but he'd run off with his secretary about nine months ago. After he'd moved out, she had reverted to her maiden name.

"Jill, I'm really sorry to trouble you at this time of the morning."

"That's okay. Are you alright?"

"Not really." She began to cry. "I'm sorry."

"Come on in." I helped her into the lounge, made her take a seat on the sofa, and handed her the box of tissues.

"I'm sorry." She wiped her eyes and blew her nose.

"What's happened?"

"Someone has been in the house."

"Are they still there?"

"No."

"Are you sure?"

"Yes, I've looked all around."

"What did they take?"

"Nothing, as far as I can tell."

"Why don't we go over there, and you can tell me exactly what happened?"

"Don't you have to go to work?"

"That can wait. Do you feel okay to walk?"

"Yeah." She got to her feet and the two of us took a walk down to her house, which was still called Goldiam.

"Would you like me to go in first and take a look around?" I offered.

"No, it's okay."

I'd been in her house a couple of times before, but not since Liam had moved out. From what I could see in the hallway and lounge, nothing much had been changed since his departure.

"Why don't we have a cup of tea, and you can tell me all about it," I said.

"Okay, but I'll make it. You take a seat. I have some of those biscuits you like. Would you like one?"

One?

"Thanks, that would be nice."

My mood improved considerably when she returned with the tea and the packet of custard creams.

"I'm feeling a little embarrassed for knocking on your door, Jill."

"There's no need to. Why don't you tell me what happened?"

"This is going to sound ridiculous."

"Never mind that. Just tell me."

"The milk was in the fridge when I came downstairs."

"Okay?"

"I had my shower and got dressed as usual, then came downstairs to get breakfast. That's when I saw it." She hesitated.

"The milk?"

"Yeah. In the fridge."

"Sorry, Goldie, but I think I must be missing something here. Why does seeing the milk in the fridge make you think someone was in the house?"

"Because I hadn't brought it in."

"You have your milk delivered?"

"Yeah, the milkman leaves it on the doorstep."

"How often?"

"Every other day."

"Is it possible that the milk in the fridge was delivered yesterday morning and you brought it in then?"

"No, because I remember thinking, yesterday, that it was a good job the milk was being delivered this morning because I was all out."

"Are you sure you didn't fetch it in this morning and then forget you'd done it? I do that kind of stuff all the time; it drives Jack mad."

"No, I'd only just come downstairs when I saw it in the fridge. I hadn't stepped foot outside. And that's not the only thing. There were three fresh bottles of milk in the fridge. I only have one bottle delivered at a time."

"Have you contacted the milkman?"

"That was the first thing I did. He said he delivered one pint as usual this morning."

"And left it on the doorstep?"

"Yeah."

"That is strange. What do you think happened?"

"You'll think I'm cracking up if I tell you."

"I won't. I promise."

"I think this house might be haunted."

"A ghost?"

"See, I told you that you'd think I was mad."

"I don't think that, but I do think there could be another explanation. Does Liam still have a key for this place?"

"*Liam*? Why would he do something like this?"

"I'm not saying he did. I just wondered if he could gain access to the house."

"He gave me his keys when he left."

"Could he have made copies?"

"I guess so, but this is not down to him."

"How can you be so sure?"

"Because he has no interest in me or our past life together. And besides, he and that new woman of his moved to Newcastle a few weeks ago."

"Have you heard from him since then?"

"No. Don't feel you have to hang around, Jill, I'll be okay now."

"Are you sure?"

"Positive. Thanks for listening to my crazy ramblings."

Although Goldie was trying her best to put on a brave face, I could tell the incident had upset her. She'd half-jokingly mentioned the possibility that a ghost was behind the unusual goings-on, but I hadn't sensed the presence of any ghosts in the house.

***

If it had been up to me, I would never have moved out of my old office building, but I'd had no choice. The move hadn't been all bad: the new building had underground parking which meant I didn't have the trek back and forth from the car park. It also had a gym that was available to all tenants of the building. I'd used it twice in the first week that I moved in, but since then I'd been too busy to take advantage of it.

My office was located on the ninth floor, which gave me a good view over Washbridge. It was just as well that Winky was now a ghost because if he'd tried jumping in and out of the windows like he used to in the old building, it wouldn't have been long before he was splattered all over the pavement below.

"Hi, Nancy," I called to one of the women who manned the main reception that was based on the ground floor.

"The lift is out again, Jill."

"Great."

The view from the ninth floor might be good, but that was slim consolation for having to trek up nine flights of stairs. By the time I reached my office, I was red in the face and gasping for air.

"Are you alright, Jill?" Jules hurried out from behind her desk and took my arm.

"Water. Need water."

"Sit down and I'll get you some."

I did as she said and took a seat on the new couch I'd

purchased when we moved into the new office. The stupid thing made an unfortunate noise every time anyone sat on it, which could be a source of some embarrassment.

"Thanks, Jules." I took a long drink. "That lift will be the death of me."

"What's wrong with it?"

"It's out again. Was it working when you got here?"

"I don't know. I always take the stairs. It keeps me fit."

Of course she did.

"Right." I got to my feet and started towards my office.

"There was a call for you just before you got here. A Mr Sneeze."

"Another wind-up?"

"I don't think so. This guy sounded genuine."

"*Mr Sneeze*? Really? What did he want?"

"I don't know. He wouldn't say over the phone. I've made an appointment for him to come in tomorrow morning at ten. I hope that's okay."

"That's fine. You'd better make sure we're stocked up with tissues, though."

"Sorry?"

"Mr Sneeze. Tissues. Get it?"

"Oh yeah, right. That's funny."

My comedic talents were wasted.

"No, it wasn't," Winky said.

"What wasn't what?"

"That quip of yours. On a scale of nought to not funny, it was awful."

"You shouldn't be listening in on my conversations."

"I have to do something to relieve the boredom. Do you

know how tedious it is to be stuck in this office twenty-four seven?"

"There's no reason for you to be stuck in here. You always have the option of moving to GT."

"Why would I want to go to Ghost Town? It's full of dead people."

"You are dead."

"Wash your mouth out. You're only as dead as you feel and right now, I feel as alive as I've ever been."

"If you don't want to go to GT, you can still move around in this world. You don't have to stay in this office."

"How am I supposed to do that? We're nine floors up. I could do myself a serious injury."

"Which part of being dead don't you get? Now that you're a ghost, you can move around the building freely. It's not like anyone else can see you."

"I know that. How do you think I met Angel? Speaking of which, she promised to drop by later, so I hope you have plenty of salmon in."

"That's another thing I don't understand. How come I still have to feed you, even though you're dead?"

"I'd explain, but I doubt you'd understand. It's very complicated."

Just then, Jules came through and closed the door behind her.

"You were doing it again, Jill, weren't you? Talking to that dead cat of yours."

"Absolutely not. I was on the phone to my sister."

"Hmm." She looked unconvinced. "Mr Petty would like a word with you. Shall I tell him you have a client with—"

She was interrupted by the door behind her opening.

"It's only me, Jill," Peter Petty said. "I told Julie that it was very important that I speak to you."

Peter Petty was true to his name. Ever since he'd moved into the next office, he'd been a pain in my backside, with his constant complaining, usually about nothing. That was bad enough, but for reasons I had yet to work out, the man always smelled of fish.

"Actually, Peter, I'm expecting a—"

"This will only take a minute." He walked over to my desk and took a seat. "Do you think you could get me a tea, Julie?"

"It's Jules," she snapped.

"Of course. Milk and five spoons of sugar. There's a darling."

Jules looked at me for guidance, so I gave her a nod.

"What is it, Peter?" I said once Jules had brought his tea. "You'll have to make it quick because I have an important meeting in a few minutes."

"Look at this." He held out his hand, palm up, with only his index finger extended.

"What am I supposed to be looking at?"

"The dust." He pushed the finger closer to my face. "This is off the skirting boards out there." He now used the dusty finger to point in the general direction of the door, through which he'd just walked. "Amongst other things, we tenants pay the management company to keep the common areas clean."

In my previous office building, the common areas had been cleaned once a flood, so although I wasn't thrilled at having to pay a service fee in this building, I'd never had reason to complain about the cleanliness of the common areas. The availability of the lift, though, that was a whole different matter.

"The common areas always look clean to me," I said.

"Clean?" He scoffed. "The cleaners were here earlier this morning and yet look at this." He held out his finger for my inspection again.

"My client will be here any minute, Peter."

"I intend to write a letter of complaint. No doubt you'll want to co-sign it."

"I—err—"

"They think they can walk all over us, but they haven't accounted for Peter Petty."

"Okay, time for you to go." I walked over to the door, opened it, and ushered him out.

"What did he want this time?" Jules asked after he'd left.

"He isn't happy with the job the cleaners are doing in the common areas."

"It always seems clean to me."

"It is. The man is just a nasty little busybody. It was the drinks machine last month if you remember."

"Oh yeah." She grinned. "Didn't he say the tea tasted of Marmite?"

"He's an idiot."

Jules had just walked out of the door when I got an eerie feeling that someone was watching me. I turned around to find Grandma sitting behind my desk.

Chapter 4

"Who was that funny little man?" Grandma said.

"He works in the office next door."

"Doesn't he have more important things to worry about than a bit of dust? What's his job?"

"He's an accountant, I think."

"Figures."

"What are you doing here? And would it kill you to come through the door like everyone else?"

"I would have done, but that lift is out of order again. I can't imagine what possessed you to move your business here."

"I didn't have any choice. They were knocking down my old building."

"But nine floors up?"

"It was the only office I could afford. Did you want something because I'm actually quite busy."

"With Ferret man?" She laughed.

"How do you know about—never mind. What do you want?"

"I'm here on WHS business."

WHS stands for Witch Heritage Society, something which until a couple of years ago I'd never heard of. If only that were still true. Just over two years ago, Grandma decided, seemingly out of the blue, to retire. Now don't get me wrong—if the woman really was a thousand years old, as the twins would have me believe, then she was certainly entitled to retire. Her decision, however, had also had serious implications for yours truly. After divesting herself of all her business interests, she had decided to devote herself to a number of charities and societies. Chief amongst them was WHS which, as its name suggests, was involved in collecting, restoring and displaying important pieces related to the history of Candlefield witches. As she'd done with all of her business ventures, Grandma had thrown herself into the work of the society, and within six months of joining, she'd been named the new chairwoman.

"If you're collecting money again, I only gave you a donation last month."

"Relax, I'm not after your money. I'm recruiting volunteers to help with—"

"I'm busy that day."

"I didn't say when it was."

"I just meant I'm pretty busy for the foreseeable future."

"Do you have any idea how important the work of WHS is?"

"I should do because you've told me often enough." Whoops, I didn't mean to say that out loud.

"Then, I won't need to tell you again. WHS has outgrown its current home, and we've been lucky enough to be offered a new one at Candlefield Science Park."

"Isn't that the brand-new building on the site of the old cheese factory?"

"That's the one."

"That's going to cost you a fortune in rent."

"That's where you're wrong. We've been offered three rooms there rent-free."

"What? How did you wangle that?"

"The manager of the Science Park, Roland Rossburger, is an old friend of mine."

"Rossburger? Where have I heard that name before?"

"I've no idea. Now, are you going to help us with the

move to the new premises or not?"

"What would I have to do? Some of those exhibits are enormous, and I have a bad back."

"No, you don't. Anyway, you needn't worry because all the large exhibits are being moved by a firm of professional removers."

"Why didn't you get them to do it all?"

"For two reasons: First, the cost; moving the smaller stuff ourselves will save quite a bit of money. And second, I don't trust them to put everything where it should go. I've spent a lot of time planning where everything should be placed in its new home."

"When is this happening?"

"Sunday."

"That's a shame. I already have something on this Sunday."

"That's okay. It's a week on Sunday, and don't worry, you won't be working alone. The twins will be helping too."

"How on earth did you get them to agree to that?"

"I haven't yet. I'm going over there as soon as I've finished here."

"What if I have something planned for a week on Sunday too?"

"Cancel it."

And with that, she disappeared, and Winky came out from under the chair.

"You let that woman walk all over you," he said. "I don't know why you're so scared of her."

"That's rich coming from you. You're a ghost, but you're still terrified of her."

"Rubbish."

"You were hiding under the chair."

"No, I wasn't. I was just having a nap."

A few minutes later, Jules came through to my office.

"Marcy is here. Can you spare her a few minutes?"

"Sure, send her through."

Marcy Bowkoo worked as a marketing executive (whatever that was) for Slade Marketing, who were located on the top floor of the building. Not long after I'd moved in, she and I had been stuck in the lift together. It had taken almost an hour for someone to free us, during which time we'd become firm friends. Larger than life, and with a tendency to speak her mind, she often dropped by for a chat and/or a cuppa. Unlike Grandma and Peter Petty, though, I was always pleased to see her.

"Hey, Jill," Marcy walked in on heels so high they would have given me vertigo. Her green blazer and orange trousers were typical of the outfits that only she could pull off. "I've asked Jules to make us a brew, I hope that's okay."

"Of course. Having a bad day?"

"Same old, same old. I had to come out before I strangled Victor."

Victor Slade was the founder of Slade Marketing.

"Is he giving you a hard time again?"

"Nothing I can't handle." She took the tea that Jules had just brought through. "Thanks, Jules, you're a lifesaver."

"Have you had a visit from your friend and mine: Mr Petty?" Marcy asked me.

"Yeah, just now. He came in especially to show me the dust on his finger."

"He did the same to me. The man is a liability. Do you

reckon he's married?"

"I doubt it." I grinned. "Why, are you interested?"

"Oh yeah. I've definitely got the hots for him."

"Did he ask you to co-sign a letter to the management company?" I said.

"Yeah, I told him I'd have to run it past our legal people first." She laughed.

"If he's going to write to the management company about anything, it should be that lift. It's out again this morning."

"It's useless, but if it hadn't been for the lift breaking down, you and I would never have got to know each other's life stories." She grinned.

"Have you had any more trouble from Leonard?"

"Not for a while, thank goodness. I think he's got the message at last, thanks to your Jack. I hope I'll get the chance to meet him and thank him in person someday."

"There's really no need. Jack was happy to do it."

During the time we'd been stuck in the lift together, Marcy had told me that she'd been having a lot of trouble from her ex-husband, Leonard. He was an engineer of some kind who spent long periods working away from home. Marcy had discovered that he'd had a series of affairs while on the road, so she'd thrown him out and then divorced him. Leonard had been unwilling to accept the divorce, and he had been stalking her ever since. She had become quite tearful when unburdening herself to me, and it was clear that it was causing her a lot of stress, so I'd offered to ask Jack to get one of his ex-colleagues to have a word with Leonard, in order to get him to back off. As far as Marcy knew, that's what had happened. In fact, I hadn't said anything to Jack because I knew what his reaction would be—he would have refused point blank to get involved. Instead, I'd turned up at Leonard's door, dressed as a policewoman. I'd been the one to order him to steer clear of Marcy.

Her phone rang.

"Yeah? I'm in the ladies if that's okay with you. I'll be there in five." She ended the call. "I'd better go. His highness is after me." She necked the rest of the tea and then headed out of the door.

"When are you going to do something about your fitness?" Winky said, out of the blue.

"What are you talking about? I'm at the peak of fitness."

"Yeah, right. You were on the point of collapse when you took the stairs earlier. You could start by addressing your diet."

"What's wrong with it?"

"Custard creams and muffins does not a healthy diet make. I'll get Daisy to draw up a healthy diet for you."

"I don't need advice on my diet from a cat."

"Daisy is a fully qualified dietician. She usually charges a small fortune for her services, but I'm sure I can persuade her to help you free of charge."

"I suppose it couldn't do any harm to hear what she has to say."

I couldn't put it off any longer, so I took all the paperwork out of the bottom drawer and spread it out on my desk.

"What's that lot?" Winky said.

"Bills, invoices and bank statements for the last six months."

"Great filing system you have there."

"Be quiet. I'm thinking."

Since my accountant, Arthur Bacus, had decided to retire just over six months ago, all the paperwork had accumulated in my bottom drawer. I was supposed to be looking for someone to replace him, but what with one thing and another, I'd never got around to it. I had been keeping my own records, which were in pretty good shape, even if I do say so myself, but my year-end accounts would have to be filed soon, so it was essential that I found myself a new accountant quickly. When Peter Petty moved into the next office, and I realised he was an accountant, I thought my prayers had been answered. But then I met him.

"You need an accountant," Winky said.

"Brilliant suggestion. I never would have thought of that."

"I could do it for you. For a small fee."

"I need a *qualified* accountant."

"I'll have you know I'm a member of the Association of Chartered Certified Feline Accountants."

"Yeah, and I'm a neurosurgeon. No, thanks, I'll find my own accountant." I buzzed Jules and asked her to come through.

"What's all that, Jill?" She stared at the pile of papers on my desk.

"That's what I wanted to talk to you about. I need to find a new accountant, so I'd like you to do some research, to see which of the local ones get good reviews."

"What about Mr Petty?" she grinned.

"I trust that's a joke."

"Obviously. The man's not the full shilling."

"A what?"

"It's what my great-grandmother used to say."

"I definitely don't want Petty anywhere near my books."

"Okay, I'll get straight on it."

With Jules on the case, I figured I might as well put the papers back into the drawer.

"I still don't see why you won't let me—"

Winky's words were drowned out by the sound of sirens coming from down on the street. It was most likely another car crash. The speed that some people drove around the streets in this part of Washbridge was crazy.

The door to my office flew open and Jules rushed in; she was clearly distressed.

"Have you seen what's happened, Jill?"

"I heard the sirens. Has there been another crash?"

"No. Someone has fallen from the building."

"This building?" I stood up and started towards the window.

"I think so."

On the street were an ambulance and a number of police cars. Several of the police were busy keeping the crowd away. Two others were standing next to the body of the person who had fallen to their death. At first, my view of the body was obscured by one of the policemen who was bending over it. Only when he stood up, did I see that the person on the ground was dressed in orange and green.

As I rushed down the stairs, I said a silent prayer that it wasn't Marcy but, deep down inside, I knew it must be her.

As I approached the scene, a young police officer blocked my way.

"Sorry, madam, you can't go through there."

"I think that might be my friend."

"What's your name?"

"Jill Maxwell. My office is on the ninth floor."

"Wait there. I'll just talk to my gaffer."

He disappeared, leaving one of his other colleagues to make sure I didn't move. A few minutes later, he returned, accompanied by a familiar face: Detective Archie McDonald, AKA Big Mac. He and I had a long history. Let's just say he wasn't my favourite person, and I certainly wasn't his.

"Hello, Maxwell. This officer tells me you think that the deceased might be a colleague of yours."

"I believe it's Marcy Bowkoo."

"Does she work with you?"

"No, she works on the top floor. What happened?"

"We're still trying to establish that. When was the last time you saw her?"

"No more than an hour ago."

"How was she then?"

"Perfectly fine. We had a cup of tea and a chat."

"She didn't seem upset or agitated?"

"Definitely not. You can't possibly think she jumped, do you?"

"As I said, we're still trying to establish what happened. Do you happen to know who her next of kin is?"

"Err, no. She's divorced and I don't know any of her family."

"Not to worry."

"Can I see her?"

"No. It's probably best you go home. You've had a nasty shock."

***

Jack came home to find me sitting in the lounge.

"Haven't you started dinner?" he said.

"Sorry, I—err—"

"Jill, what's wrong?" He took a seat beside me. "Have you been crying? Is Florence okay?"

"It's Marcy."

"Who?"

"She worked on the top floor of my building. We were stuck in the lift together once."

"I remember that. What's happened to her?"

"She's dead."

"I'm so sorry." He put his arm around my shoulder. "What happened?"

"She was having a cup of tea in my office, and then an hour later, she fell."

"Fell? Did she bang her head or something?"

"She fell from the building."

"What? How?"

"I don't know. Big Mac was there." I stood up. "I'd better start on dinner."

"Sit down. I'll make it tonight."

"Okay, thanks."

"Are you feeling any better?" Jack asked over dinner.

"A little. I just can't get my head around what's happened."

"Do you think she might have jumped?"

"No! It must have been an accident of some kind."

"But what was she doing on the roof?"

"I've no idea. Do you mind if we change the subject?"

"Sure. Goldie came into the store this morning and said I should thank you for helping her. She didn't say what it was you'd done, and I didn't like to ask because she looked terrible."

"I didn't do much, really. Just listened to what she had to say. She was upset about the milk."

"*Milk*?"

I told Jack all about the mysterious milk bottle situation.

"Who does she think put the milk in the fridge?"

"She doesn't know. She says she checked with the milkman, and he insisted he only left the usual one pint on the doorstep, but there were three bottles in the fridge."

"That's just weird."

"I know, and I hate to say this, but Goldie has been acting a little strange lately. I don't think it's beyond the realms of possibility that she did it herself."

Chapter 5

I had the most awful nightmare in which I saw Marcy standing on a window ledge. I ran to try and grab her, but she stepped off the edge just before I reached her. I woke up in a cold sweat, and I was unable to get back to sleep for several hours. Then, when I did eventually manage to nod off, I didn't wake up until seven-thirty. Why hadn't Jack woken me? Where was he?

There was no sign of him in the kitchen, and I was beginning to think he must have gone into the store early when I heard the television. I found Jack seated on the sofa, glued to the TV.

"Why didn't you wake me?"

"Shush." He pointed to the TV, which I realised was tuned into the local news.

On screen was an image of Washbridge Central Point, then the picture switched to the police station, outside which Big Mac was being interviewed.

"Detective McDonald, do you have any more information about the deceased?" the interviewer asked.

"Yes, we do. Her name was Marcy Bowkoo. She was a thirty-six-year-old woman, employed by Slade Marketing, whose offices are located on the twelfth floor of Washbridge Central Point."

"Do you know what happened?"

"We believe the deceased may have jumped from the roof of the building."

"No suggestion of foul play, then?"

"None."

"That's rubbish!" I yelled at the TV.

"They said a couple of people from the building across

the road saw her," Jack said.

"I don't care what anyone says. I was talking to her an hour before. There's no way she would have killed herself."

Jack turned off the TV. "I ought to be going to the store. Will you be okay, or would you prefer I stayed with you for a while longer?"

"I'm fine. You get going."

I showered and got dressed, but I couldn't face any breakfast. All I could think about was Marcy. I still couldn't believe she'd gone.

I had a meeting with a man, who was supposedly called Mr Sneeze, at ten o'clock. When I arrived at the office building, I expected to see some kind of police presence, but there was no sign of them, or anything that might suggest something untoward had taken place there.

Amazingly, the lift was working again, so I avoided the long trek up nine flights of stairs.

"Good morning, Jill." Jules was behind her desk; she was wearing a pretty, yellow sundress.

"Morning."

"Have you seen the news? They're saying Marcy jumped."

"That's rubbish. You saw her when she came to see me yesterday. Did she look suicidal to you?"

"No, she seemed quite chipper, but if she didn't jump, what do you think happened?"

"I have no idea."

"You haven't forgotten you have a meeting with Mr Sneeze this morning, have you?"

"No, but I still refuse to believe that's his real name."

"That's what he said, honestly. I even asked him to repeat it."

"Hmm, we'll see."

Winky wasn't alone in the office. Sitting next to him, on my desk, was a cute white cat. I'd met quite a few of Winky's lady-friends over the years, but this one certainly stood out from the rest.

"Jill, this is Daisy. Daisy, this is Jill Maxwell."

"I'm very pleased to meet you, Jill." She offered her paw. "Winky has told me so much about you that I feel I know you already."

"Nice to meet you, too. I just—err—I didn't realise you were—" I gestured to the wings on her back.

"Didn't Winky tell you?"

"No, he—"

"I did tell you," Winky insisted.

"You did, but when you said Daisy was an angel, I didn't realise you meant she was *actually* an angel. Sorry, my bad. How did you two meet?"

"It's a funny story." Daisy laughed. "You tell her, Winky."

"No, you tell it so much better than I do."

"Okay, then. It was at Zulie's birthday bash."

"Zulie?"

"She's one of the biggest feline celebrities in GT."

I turned to Winky. "I thought you said you didn't like GT?"

"I said I don't want to live there, but I'm always up for a good party. Go on, Daisy, tell her what happened."

"Zulie is absolutely minted, so no expense was spared for her birthday bash. Halfway through the evening, a huge cake was wheeled in, and Zulie asked for a volunteer to cut it for her."

"And I stepped forward," Winky chipped in.

"The thing is, Jill." Daisy giggled. "It wasn't really a cake. It was hollow inside, so as soon as Winky tried to cut the cake, it ripped open, and guess who popped out?"

"You?"

"That's right. I'd been in there for almost an hour, so I was glad to get out. Winky offered to get me a drink."

"And, as they say, the rest is history." Winky planted a kiss on her cheek.

"Where do you live, Daisy?" I asked.

"In GT, at the moment."

"I'm trying to persuade her to move back here," Winky said.

"Hold on," I interrupted. "I can't have another ghost cat living in here. No offence, Daisy."

"None taken, Jill," she said. "And, anyway, I'm not ready for us to move in together yet. Winky tells me you'd like some help with your diet."

"It's actually pretty healthy for the most part, but I guess it wouldn't do to get a little advice."

"Pretty healthy?" Winky scoffed. "Yeah, right."

"Winky!" Daisy shushed him.

"Sorry."

I was pleased to see this angelic little cat took no nonsense from Winky.

"Why don't you talk me through a typical day for you, Jill? What did you have for breakfast this morning?"

"I didn't actually eat breakfast today."

"That's really not good."

"I usually do. I overslept."

"What would you typically have for breakfast?"

"Cereal, usually."

"That's good. What kind of cereal?"

"Chococandy pops."

"Oh dear." She shook her head.

"I don't always eat those."

"Oh?"

"I sometimes have Strawberrycandy pops."

"That's no better."

"But I thought strawberries were good for you."

"Strawberries are, but there are very few strawberries in that cereal. What there is, though, is lots of sugar. What about lunch?"

"We try and have a traditional Sunday lunch every week."

"What about during the week?"

"That's more difficult because I'm working, so I usually have to eat on the move."

"And that would normally be?"

"It varies from day to day. I might pick up a salad."

"Yeah, right." Winky laughed but soon stopped when Daisy shot him a look.

"What else?" Daisy asked.

"I eat a lot of sandwiches."

"Such as?"

"All kinds. Mostly healthy stuff."

Winky was shaking his head, but he refrained from passing further comment.

"What about your evening meal, after work?"

"Jack, that's my husband, makes most of the dinners, and he's obsessed with healthy eating."

"That's good."

"Yeah. Lots of white meat, salads and pastas."

"Okay, and what about snacking in between meals?"

"Hardly ever."

"Okay, that's enough!" Winky said. "How do you expect Daisy to help you if you're going to tell such blatant lies." He jumped off the desk. "Just look in here." He pulled open the bottom drawer of my desk to reveal my cache of custard creams.

"Jill?" Daisy gave me what I can only describe as a disappointed look.

"Okay, I admit that I do have a bit of a custard cream problem."

"A *bit*?" Winky laughed. "Eating half a dozen a day is a *bit* of a problem. Eating four packets a day is a *major* problem."

"I do not eat *four* packets a day."

"You need to cut out the biscuits, Jill," Daisy said. "Or at least bring down your consumption to a sensible level."

"Which would be?"

"Two a day."

"Packets?"

"Two biscuits."

"Right."

"Any other snacking that I should know about?" Daisy's interrogation continued.

"Not really."

"What about the muffins?" Winky said.

"Jill?"

"I am partial to the occasional muffin, but I always eat the blueberry ones. That's healthy, right?"

"If you want to eat blueberries, you should do so minus the muffin."

"Right."

"Here's what I suggest," Daisy said. "Why don't I go away and draw up a diet that will help you to turn your life around?"

"I wouldn't want you to go to all that trouble."

"It's no trouble. I'm happy to do it, but I will need a commitment from you that you'll stick to it."

"Err, yeah. Sure."

"Don't worry, Daisy," Winky said. "I'll keep an eye on her to make sure she doesn't cheat."

"It's agreed then," Daisy said. "I'll get that diet to you in the next couple of days."

"Great. Can't wait."

After giving Winky a kiss, Daisy disappeared.

"This is going to be fun." Winky grinned.

"You're enjoying this, aren't you?"

"You should be thanking me. I'm trying to put you back on the path to health."

"You don't think I can do it, do you?"

"I know you can't. You won't make it through the first twenty-four hours."

"Rubbish. When I put my mind to something, I have a will of iron."

"In that case, you'll be willing to put your money where your mouth is and have a small wager."

"I would, but I don't see how it could work. You'll have no idea what I eat when I'm not in the office, so I could cheat, and you'd never know."

"True, so why don't we just wager on the custard creams? I bet you eat more than two custard creams while you're here in the office."

"You're on. How much do you want to wager?"

"How about a tenner?"

"Make it twenty."

"Okay. So, if you eat more than two custard creams while you're in the office, you pay me twenty pounds."

"Yep. This is going to be easy money."

"We'll see."

Jules came through to my office.

"Jill, your ten o'clock appointment is here."

"Send him in, please."

The man, who looked to be in his thirties, was dressed in a white polo shirt and light blue chinos. He'd no sooner walked through the door than he sneezed.

"Excuse me. I seem to have picked up a sniffle this weekend."

"Please take a seat, Mr Sneeze."

"Sorry? What did you just call me?"

Oh bum! I should have known Jules had misheard his name.

"I—err—"

"Did you say sneeze?" He grinned.

"I might have done. Sorry, what is your name?"

"Sonny Ease."

"Right. Sorry about that, Mr Ease. I imagine you get that a lot?"

"Actually, no. This is a first. Please call me Sonny."

"What is it I can do for you, Sonny?"

"I believe you find missing persons?"

"That's correct."

"What about animals? Can you find missing animals?"

"It's not something I get a lot of requests for. Although, I did track down some missing chickens some years ago."

"My father is Dez Ease. You may have heard of him?"

"I don't think so."

"He's one of the most successful horse trainers in the UK. Our stables are twenty miles north of Washbridge,"

"Right, sorry, I'm not much of a horseracing fan."

"Anyway, the reason I'm here today is one of our top horses has gone missing."

"When you say *missing*?"

"Stolen. Some evil swine has taken him."

"Is the horse valuable?"

"His name is Majestic Tears, and yes, he's worth a small fortune."

"Has there been a ransom demand?"

"Not yet, but we're expecting one at any time."

"I assume you've informed the police."

"No, and it's essential they know nothing about it."

"Why not?"

"If word gets out that a horse was taken from our stables, no one will ever trust us to train their horses again."

"Let me get this straight: Is Majestic Tears your horse or does it belong to someone else?"

"He's ours, but we also train horses for lots of other owners."

"I see. Can I ask what prompted you to contact me about this?"

"May I be honest?"

"I would prefer that."

"We were worried if we used one of the bigger investigation agencies, word would get out. We figured that was less likely if we worked with someone no one has ever heard of."

Charming.

"You won't be disappointed if you decide to hire me."

"I'm sure, but I plan on interviewing a number of other investigators before making a decision."

"Of course, but if it helps you to decide, I should mention that I do have extensive experience in the equine world."

"Really?"

"Oh yes. I was raised in the countryside and learned to ride when I was just a child."

"Interesting. Do you still ride?"

"Oh yes. As often as my work allows."

"Hmm." He sat back in his chair, stroked his chin, and then said, "Damn it, you strike me as the right person for the job."

"I'll fully understand if you want to check out other investigators first."

"There's no need. I have a good feeling about you, Jill. Where do I sign?"

Before he could change his mind, I took out my standard contract and slid it across the desk.

"Thanks, Sonny, you won't be disappointed."

"Would you be able to pay a visit to our stables this week?"

"I'm free on Friday."

"Excellent." He took out a business card and handed it to me. "Shall we say ten-thirty?"

"That works for me."

He stood up and shook my hand. "I'll see you on Friday, Jill."

"You never learn, do you?" Winky said.

"What are you talking about?"

"*Raised in the countryside*?" He scoffed. "*Learned to ride as a child*."

"I used to go on the donkeys when we went to the seaside."

"Have you forgotten what happened that time when you pretended to be an expert skier?"

"It'll be fine. I won't actually need to ride any of the horses. I just need to get up to speed with all the horsey jargon."

Chapter 6

It was early afternoon and I was starving, but I'd had two custard creams in the morning, and if I had any more, Winky would claim his twenty pounds. On reflection, that wager probably hadn't been such a good idea.

Twenty minutes later, and the hunger pangs were getting worse, so I magicked myself over to Pamber where I'd be able to enjoy a muffin, away from Winky's prying eyes.

What do you mean I have no willpower? I didn't have Daisy's diet yet, so muffins were still fair game. Obviously, once she presented me with the diet, I would stick to it religiously.

"I don't know how you dare show your face in here," Amber said.

"Yeah, you've got a cheek," Pearl chipped in.

"What do you mean? What did I do?"

"As if you don't know."

"I don't have the first clue."

"Why did you volunteer to help Grandma with the WHS move?"

"I didn't volunteer for anything. She turned up at my office and strongarmed me into agreeing to do it."

"That's not what she told us," Pearl said. "She said it was your idea to volunteer and that we were honour bound to do the same."

"She lied. Did you agree to help?"

"We had no choice. She doesn't seem to realise we're trying to run a business here."

"It's not that she doesn't realise. She just doesn't care. That woman has always been selfish, but she's got much worse since she retired. It's about time someone set her right."

"Did someone mention my name?" Grandma appeared beside the counter. "My ears are burning."

"Not me." Amber shook her head.

"Nor me," Pearl said.

"It must have been you, Jill." She fixed me with that super-evil look of hers.

"I was just asking the twins what muffins they have."

"Hmm, strange. I must have been mistaken. I trust the three of you are still eager to help with the WHS move."

"Absolutely," the twins chorused.

"Jill?"

"Of course. I'm looking forward to it."

"Excellent." And with that, she disappeared.

"You sure set her right, there, Jill," Amber said.

"Shut up and give me a blueberry muffin and a caramel latte."

Once I had my drink and muffin, the three of us took a seat by the window.

"Is this how it will always be?" Amber said.

"What do you mean?"

"Will Grandma always boss us about and have us running around after her?"

"She's been doing it for a thousand years." I took a bite of muffin. "I can't see her changing anytime soon."

"She'd better appreciate the party we're throwing for her," Pearl said. "After all the trouble we're going to."

"I still think that it's a mistake."

"You just don't like parties. She'll love it. You'll see."

"How has Florence taken to boarding?" Pearl asked.

"Fine, and I've got a big surprise for her that'll make it

even better."

"What's that?"

"The headmistress has asked if I'll teach there for an hour, one day a week."

"Will you be teaching Florence's class?" Amber said.

"Yeah."

The twins exchanged a glance, and then Pearl said, "Are you crazy, Jill?"

"What do you mean?"

"Florence is going to hate you."

"No, she won't. What are you talking about?"

"Don't you realise how uncool it is for one of your parents to be a teacher at your school?"

"You're wrong. Both of you. Florence will be thrilled."

I was starting to have doubts about my decision to accept the teaching post at CASS. I'd felt sure that Florence would be thrilled at the news, but so far everyone I'd told about it had been convinced I'd made a terrible mistake.

"You have crumbs on your blouse," Winky said.

I instinctively made to brush them off before I realised there were none there.

"Gotcha." He laughed. "I knew it. You've been eating muffins."

"If you must know, I had one. A very small one. And, anyway, it doesn't count because I don't have Daisy's diet yet."

"Like that will change anything." He scoffed.

"Of course it will. Once I have it, I'll stick to it religiously."

"I'll believe that when I see it."

Jules came charging into the office. "Guess who's here, Jill?"

"It had better not be my sister again."

"It's Mrs V!"

To say I was gobsmacked would have been the understatement of the year. Mrs V and Armi had gone on vacation to Australia almost six years ago. Despite her reservations about the deadly spiders there, she and Armi had fallen in love with the place, and they'd decided to make their home there. Naturally, I'd been disappointed to learn she wouldn't be returning, but I was happy that they'd be able to live out the rest of their lives somewhere they loved so much. Jules and Mrs V had kept in touch, so when Jules learned Mrs V would be staying down-under, she'd contacted me to see if I'd be needing a replacement.

But what was Mrs V doing back in this country?

"Show her in and make some tea, would you. Best cups."

"Will do."

Mrs V didn't look a day older than she had when I'd last seen her six years earlier. Although, to be fair, she'd looked old and decrepit then.

What? I'm only joking. Sheesh!

"This is all very posh." Mrs V looked around the office and nodded her approval. Although, I'm not sure I like the idea of being this high off the ground."

"It's so lovely to see you again, Mrs V." I came out from behind my desk and gave her a hug—just a gentle one.

"It's lovely to be back. You're looking very well. How is the family? Has Florence settled in at her new school?"

Since Mrs V had moved to Australia, we'd kept in touch with the occasional letter (she didn't do email or any of the social *mania* thingies, as she put it). It was a few months since her last communication, in which she'd given no hint that she was thinking of returning for a visit.

"She seems to be enjoying it, but we're both missing her terribly, as you can imagine. Please, have a seat."

"I don't want to keep you if you're busy. I should have rung before I came."

"It's fine. I don't have any meetings for the rest of the day."

"Do you like it here, in your new offices?"

"It's okay, but I still miss the old place."

"I can't believe they demolished it to build that monstrous car park."

"Me neither. But never mind about that. What are you doing here? Why didn't you write and tell me you were visiting?"

"I'm not. Visiting, that is. Armi and I are back to stay."

Before I could respond, Jules came through with the tea.

"Best cups, I see." Mrs V beamed. "I'm honoured."

"Did I hear you say you were back to stay?" Jules said, as she handed us our drinks.

"That's right, dear, but don't worry, I'm not after my old job back."

"I wasn't thinking about that," Jules said. "It's just nice to have you back."

"How is she doing?" Mrs V asked after Jules had left us alone.

"Really well, but she had some very big shoes to fill. So, come on, tell me, how come you've decided to return?"

"There was no *one* reason. Australia is lovely and we were both very happy there, but it isn't home. Even after six years, I still felt like I was on an extended holiday. I started to get the itch to come back about eighteen months ago."

"You never mentioned it in your letters."

"That's because I didn't really expect us to return. I thought Armi was happy to live out his life there, so it didn't seem fair for me to say anything to him. Then, one day, totally out of the blue, he said he was missing *home*. That got us talking about the possibility of coming back, and so here we are."

"Where are you living?"

"We managed to rent a house in your old stomping ground: Smallwash. It's nothing special, but it'll do until we find something more permanent. That toll bridge is a pain in the bum, though."

"Tell me about it. I certainly don't miss it."

"Are you feeling okay, Jill?"

"Me? Yeah, fine. Why do you ask?"

"It's just that it's not like you to have a drink without a custard cream."

"I'm on a new healthy diet."

"Since when?"

"Since now. I'm rationing myself to two custard creams per day."

"Hmm." She grinned.

"I'm not surprised you don't want your old job back. I imagine you've got used to retirement by now."

"I'm not sure I'll ever fully get used to it. I helped out with a few local charities in Australia. Anything to get me out of the house, really. I'll probably do something similar back here. And, of course, if at any time you need a hand—say if Jules is off ill or on holiday—, just give me a call. I'll be more than happy to step into the breach." She took a slip of paper out of her handbag. "That's my temporary address and my phone number. Just in case."

"Thanks, that's very kind of you."

"I'll not keep you any longer." She stood up. "Give my regards to Jack and Florence."

"I will. Take care of yourself, Mrs V."

***

Every now and then, I tried to spend a few hours in the store with Jack. I found working behind the counter quite relaxing, and I sometimes thought I wouldn't have minded doing it full time. But, there were two problems with that idea, though: We needed my income to cover all our outgoings. Plus, if Jack and I had worked together, we would have killed one another within a week.

As there was nothing much spoiling, I told Jules I was leaving early, so that I could surprise Jack. In the event, though, I was the one who got the surprise. When I stepped into the store, I could hear him talking to a woman, who I assumed to be a customer. I was wrong. The attractive young woman, who looked to be in her early twenties, was standing behind the counter. Leaning on one elbow, she was staring into Jack's eyes, and giggling at whatever he'd just said. It was then that I remembered he'd told me that he would be interviewing candidates for the vacant assistant position.

I cleared my throat as I approached the counter.

"Jill," Jack took a step away from the woman. "I didn't see you there. Finished early?"

"Yeah, I thought I'd come and give you a hand, but I see you already have some help."

"This is Kiki. She was one of the people I told you I'd be interviewing today."

"Nice to meet you, Jill." Kiki flashed me an altogether too perfect smile. "I love this little store of yours. I can't wait to start working here."

"Right. I'm sure Jack will want to discuss all the candidates with me tonight."

"Actually, Jill," Jack said. "I've just offered Kiki the job. She can start tomorrow morning. Isn't that great?"

"Amazing."

"I should be going." Kiki, and her long legs, stepped out from behind the counter. "I'll see you in the morning, Jack. Bye, Jill."

"Bye, Kiki," Jack called after her, then he saw my expression and said, "What?"

"You were a bit eager to set her on, weren't you? What's the hurry?"

"I didn't want to risk her finding another job somewhere else."

"What about the other candidates?"

"One was a no-show and the other two were pretty useless."

"What was it sold you on *Keekee*? Other than her legs and boobs, I mean?"

"You're being ridiculous. I didn't even notice—"

"Liar."

"Okay, yeah, she's very attractive, but that's not why I gave her the job. She has a ton of retail experience, and she has a fantastic personality. I think she'll be a big hit with the customers."

"How come she can start tomorrow?"

"What do you mean?"

"If she's all that, how come she doesn't have a job at the moment?"

"Kiki explained that. Her boss, at the last place she worked, kept coming on to her, so she was forced to leave."

"Right. What about her CV? References?"

"She hurried out of the house this morning and left them on the kitchen table."

"Really?" I rolled my eyes.

"She has promised to let me have them, though."

"It's a bit late for that, isn't it? You've already given her the job."

"You're overreacting, Jill. Kiki is going to be a real asset to this business. You'll see."

"Hmm."

Chapter 7

The next morning, over breakfast, you could have cut the atmosphere with a knife.

"I can't believe you're still in a huff," Jack said.

"I'm not in a *huff*." I most certainly was. "I just thought you would have consulted me before setting someone on."

"I didn't consult you when I set Grace on."

"That was different."

"Why? Because she was fifty-three?"

"That's got nothing to do with it. When you set Grace on, I hadn't had much experience of working in the store, but now I feel like I'm better able to judge someone's suitability for the job."

"Right." He scoffed.

"What does that mean?"

"You work in there two or three hours a week. Six tops."

"Because I'm busy with my own work."

"Exactly, which is why I should be the one to make decisions regarding the store's employees. Answer me this: Have you ever consulted me over *any* decision you've ever made regarding your business?"

"No, but—"

"And I wouldn't expect you to. You're just going to have to trust me on this, Jill. Okay?"

"But she didn't even have references."

"So?"

"So, you'd better keep a close eye on her because I still think there's something fishy going on."

"Can we please change the subject? I still can't believe

Mrs V is back."

"Me neither. You could have knocked me down with a feather when she walked through the door. I don't think I told you last night, but they're renting a house in Smallwash until they can find something more permanent."

"Is Armi okay?"

"I think so. She didn't say otherwise. She doesn't look any different to the day she left. She even said she'd be willing to stand in for Jules if I needed her to."

"How old is she now?"

"I'm not actually sure, but she looks as fit as a fiddle."

Jack glanced up at the kitchen clock. "I'd better be making tracks. I want to be there for when Kiki arrives, so I can introduce her to Monty."

"Say hello to *KeeKee* for me."

"Jill!"

"Sorry. Have a good day."

I was loading the dishwasher when I sensed someone else was in the room. I assumed Jack must have forgotten something, but when I turned around it wasn't him standing there.

"Florence? What's wrong? Are you ill?"

"I'm fine, Mother."

The only time she ever called me mother was when we were falling out, so I knew something was amiss.

"Why are you here? Did you get permission to leave CASS?"

"No, I didn't, but it's not like anyone will know. Old Mumbledown is too slow to catch a cold."

Florence's form teacher was Miss Tumbledown who

was a dear old thing.

"You mustn't call Miss Tumbledown that. I've told you before."

"Whatever."

"What are you doing here?"

"You can't do it, Mother. You just can't."

"Can't do what?"

"Mrs Littledo said you're going to be teaching us."

"That's right. Starting this Friday."

"You have to tell her that you can't do it. That you've changed your mind."

"I can't. I've made a promise. I just don't understand what you're so upset about."

"Do you have any idea how much stick I get already from the other kids because my mother is *the most powerful witch in the world*?"

"Why haven't you told me about this before? I'll talk to the headmistress about it."

"No, you won't. I can fight my own battles. I just don't need you making it even worse by becoming a teacher. Why didn't you ask me before you agreed to do it?"

"I—err—it never crossed my mind to. I just assumed you'd be pleased."

"Well, you were wrong, so are you going to tell Mrs Littledo you can't do it?"

"I can't, Florence."

"Right, I guess I'll see you in class, then. I'll be the one causing all the trouble."

"What do you—?"

It was too late; she'd disappeared, presumably back to CASS. It seems Jack and the twins had been right, and I'd got it spectacularly wrong.

Again.

***

This wasn't turning out to be a great week. So far, I'd managed to fall out with Jack over his new assistant who, by the way, I still had my doubts about. And I'd upset Florence by agreeing to teach at CASS. Hopefully, throwing myself into my work would take my mind off issues at home.

I had a meeting with Kevin Wright in his shed, which doubled as the admin centre for F-O-F. As I didn't have to be there until ten o'clock, I decided to drop in at the office first. Nancy was on the main reception desk again.

"Have the police still got the top floor sealed off, Nancy?"

"No, haven't you heard?"

I walked over to the desk. "Heard what?"

"They've finished their investigation. They've concluded Marcy committed suicide."

"That's insane. There's no way she would have done that. Aren't there any cameras on the roof?"

"Apparently not."

"Is Victor Slade in, do you know?"

"Yeah, I saw him arrive about twenty minutes ago."

"Okay, thanks."

I couldn't believe that the police had dropped their investigation. Who was I kidding? There never was an investigation. Someone decided that Marcy had killed herself and that was that.

I was the only one in the lift, so I punched the button for the top floor. Surely, I couldn't be the only one who saw how ridiculous this thing was. Victor, her boss, must realise that there was no way Marcy would have jumped.

"I'd like to see Victor," I snapped at the young man on reception at Slade Marketing.

"Do you have an appointment?"

"No, but I want to see him, and I want to see him right now."

"I'm not sure if—"

"Tell him Jill Maxwell wants a word with him."

He hesitated for a moment, but then picked up the phone and punched a couple of numbers.

"Mr Slade, it's—yes, I know you said you weren't to be disturbed. Yes, I'm sorry but I have a woman out here who insists on seeing you straight away. Her name is Jill Maxwell. Just a moment—I'll ask her. Who are you?"

"I work on the ninth floor."

"She says she works on the ninth floor. I don't know—oh, okay, I'll bring her through." He put down the phone, stood up and came from behind the desk. "This way, please."

I followed him down a short corridor, at the end of which he stopped outside a door. After taking a deep breath, he found the courage to knock.

"Come!" bellowed a voice from within.

"Jill Maxwell for you, Mr Slade."

He stepped aside to allow me to enter the room, and then he beat what seemed to me to be a hasty retreat.

Although I'd listened to Marcy talk about her boss on numerous occasions—mostly to moan about him—I had never actually met him until now. He was a giant of a man, at least six-six, and with a physique that suggested he spent a lot of time in the gym.

"When Toby told me your name, it rang a bell, but it took a minute for me to place you," Slade said. "But then I remembered seeing your sign. I've often wondered what a real life P.I. does." He offered his hand and shook mine with a firm, almost crushing grip. "Please, have a seat, Jill. Is it okay to call you Jill?"

"Sure."

"Great. And you must call me Victor. Can I get you something to drink?"

"No, thanks."

"How can I help you today? Are you looking to market your agency? If so, I already have a few ideas."

"That's not why I'm here. I wanted to talk to you about Marcy Bowkoo."

"Oh." His expression changed in an instant. "Such a tragedy."

"Apparently, the police are saying it was suicide."

"Poor Marcy. I knew she was having a hard time, but I never expected her to—"

"Hold on. You don't actually believe that she killed herself, do you?"

"I don't want to." He shrugged. "But I don't see what other explanation there can be. She'd been very down lately."

"That's rubbish. She was in my office no more than an hour earlier, and she most certainly wasn't suicidal."

"You never can tell, though, can you?"

"While she was with me, she received a call from you, which sent her scurrying back up here. What was it about?"

"I—err—have no idea. I make a lot of calls."

"Think. It could be important."

"Err, oh yeah. I'd had a call from one of our clients, Jade Holdings, they were annoyed because they hadn't received the proposal that we'd promised them. I asked Marcy why it was late. She said she'd come and sort it out."

"That's it?"

"Yeah, it was nothing out of the ordinary. It's the sort of thing that happens all the time."

"And did you see her after that call?"

"No, I didn't. In fact, the next thing I knew was when someone told me what had happened. I couldn't believe it. I still can't." He made a show of checking his watch. "I'm really sorry but I have an important meeting in five minutes."

"Something doesn't smell right about this."

"I know you're upset. I am too. But sometimes we don't know people as well as we think we do." He started to walk towards the door, which was clearly his not too subtle way of telling me the meeting was over.

As I walked back downstairs, I became angrier and angrier. Not only had Victor Slade shown little or no emotion over Marcy's death, but he also seemed way too keen to accept that she'd committed suicide.

"Are you okay, Jill?" Jules said. "You look—"

"I'm fine. Just angry. Can I get a quick cup of tea before I go and see Mr Wright."

"Sure."

I made straight for my desk and opened the drawer in which I kept my custard creams, only to find it was empty.

"What the—?"

"It's for your own good." Winky jumped onto my desk.

"What have you done with my biscuits?"

"I know we had a bet that you couldn't stick to only two a day, but I got to thinking about it. What's important here is your health, so I've confiscated the custard creams. From now on, I'll give you your allowance of two per day."

"How dare you take my custard creams?"

"It's for your own good, and besides, you agreed to this."

Whatever had possessed me to go along with this?

"Okay, well I want my two biscuits now."

"Are you sure? It's still early, and you'll have the whole—"

"Right now."

"Okay, okay. Close your eyes."

"What?"

"Close your eyes and turn around so you can't see where I've hidden them."

I did as he said but only because I needed those custard creams. "Hurry up."

He handed me the biscuits, which I gobbled, and then washed down with the cup of tea Jules had made for me. Then I headed out.

"I'm going to see Mr Wright, Jules. I should be back this afternoon."

Chapter 8

Kevin Wright had told me that he was independently wealthy, so I was a little surprised to discover that the address he'd given me was for a mid-terraced house in one of the less desirable neighbourhoods on the outskirts of Washbridge. I was half expecting someone to tell me that I had the wrong address, but it was Kevin who answered the door.

"Hi, Jill, did you find me okay?"

"Yeah. No problem at all." I glanced around the small hallway, which had framed photos of what I assumed to be ferrets on the walls.

"That one is Charlie." Kevin pointed to the photo closest to the door. "He's the first ferret I ever owned. I still miss that guy."

"Have you lived here long, Kevin?"

"All my life. After Mum died, she left me the house."

"Right."

"The year after she died, her brother, my uncle Winston, sadly passed away too. He was the Winston in Winston Shaving Cream. You might have heard of it? His death was in all the national papers."

"Doesn't ring any bells."

"Anyway, it turned out I was his only living relative, so I inherited his fortune."

We had moved into the lounge by now where the framed photos of ferrets had been replaced by the real things. On top of a V stand was a sizeable wooden cage, from inside of which a ferret was staring out at us.

"You've met Cecil, haven't you, Jill?"

From that, I gathered that this was the same ferret he

had brought to my office. I wouldn't have known because to me one ferret looks much like another.

"Oh yes, I remember."

"How many more times? My name is Guy!" the ferret once again insisted.

Ignoring Guy, I said, "Do you just have the one?"

"Goodness, no, but only Cecil gets to live in the house with me. The others are out the back. Shall we?"

"Lead the way."

I expected him to take me through the back of the house, but instead, we went out through the front door, and then walked down the gennel that ran between his house and the one next door. The back garden was tiny, and I could see why we hadn't exited through the back door. Standing in front of it, was a cage, which was at least three times larger than the one in the lounge. Peering through the wire netting were another four ferrets. That wasn't the only cage in the back garden, though. There were another two identical ones, each containing more ferrets. The remaining space in the garden was taken up by a sizeable wooden shed.

"Is that where you keep the safe?" I gestured to the shed.

"My office, yes. Why don't we talk in there?"

Thankfully, the shed was a ferret-free zone, and it did actually resemble an office, furnished as it was with a desk, two chairs, a filing cabinet and a small safe.

"Have a seat, Jill, please." He went and sat behind the desk.

"Please don't take this the wrong way, Kevin, but I can't help wondering why you haven't used some of the money you inherited from your uncle to move somewhere—err—

bigger."

"This is my home. It's where I've lived since I was born. The thought of living anywhere else simply holds no appeal for me."

"Right, but you'd have more room for your ferrets. The back garden is a little cramped."

"That's true. I probably should think about it, but right now, the only thing that concerns me is being able to clear my name."

"Hopefully, I'll be able to help you do that. Why don't you tell me everything about the theft. Start at the beginning."

"Okay. The problem with ferrets is that they look too cute."

Cute? Those horrible little things? Was he trying to wind me up?

"Sorry, did you just say *cute*?"

"Yes, and because they are so cute, lots of people buy them as a pet, without realising that they are actually quite demanding animals. Unfortunately, that results in lots of these poor creatures being rejected. That's where F-O-F comes in."

"I assumed the society was just ferret owners who got together to discuss their pets."

"Not at all. Our primary aim is to raise money to fund resources that will educate people about these wonderful creatures. We hold collections from time to time. You may have seen someone with one of our collection boxes at your local supermarket."

"I—err—possibly." I would have given them a wide berth if I had. "When did you discover the money had been taken?"

"On the first day of each month, I do a quick audit of the F-O-F funds. When I opened the safe, the cash had gone."

"Was the safe still locked?"

"Yes."

"Are you absolutely sure about that?"

"Positive."

"I can see it's a combination lock, so whoever stole it must have known the combination."

"I guess so."

"Who apart from you knows it?"

"No one. Only me."

"What's that?" I pointed to a yellow post-it note on the side of the safe.

"That's—err—" He blushed. "In case I forget it."

"Was that there the night the money was taken?"

"Yeah."

"So, basically, anyone could have got into the safe and taken the money."

"I suppose so, but how would anyone guess there was a safe in a garden shed?"

He had a point.

"What did you do once you realised the cash had gone?"

"Telephoned Gordon."

"Who's he?"

"He's the chairman of F-O-F. He said I should call the police, which I did."

"What did they do?"

"They sent someone to see me, but not until three days later. He looked at the safe, asked me a few questions, and gave me a crime incident reference number."

"Any follow-up?"

"I got a phone call a few days later to say that they'd been unable to identify the thief, and that they'd closed the incident. I don't think they actually did anything."

"What I don't understand is why you lost your post at F-O-F."

"That's simple. Because Gordon and the others, but mainly Gordon, decided I must have pocketed the cash. He said it must have been me because I was the only one who knew the combination."

"Was the F-O-F money the only cash in the safe? Didn't you have any of your personal money in there too?"

"No, that's all in the bank. I never take out large amounts."

"I have to ask: Is there anyone who holds a grudge against you? Anyone who you might have fallen out with?"

"No, not really. I wouldn't call myself Mr Popular, but I don't have any enemies as such."

"Do you work, Kevin?"

"Of course. I work at Stamp Beauty in Washbridge."

"What's that?"

"We buy and sell rare stamps."

"Do you own the shop?"

"No. I just work there. I've been there for just over fifteen years."

"Weren't you tempted to leave when you received your inheritance?"

"Certainly not. What would I do all day? After ferrets, stamps are the passion of my life. I have several albums in the house if you'd like to see them."

"Err, thanks, but I don't really have the time right now.

Tell me, do the members of F-O-F get together or do they just communicate with one another online?"

"There's a meeting every Tuesday evening at seven o'clock, in the old chapel on Tontine Road."

"Do you still attend those?"

"No, they made it very clear I wouldn't be welcome."

"Okay, I think we've covered as much as we can for now. If I think of any more questions, I'll give you a call."

"Do you think you'll be able to find out who took the money, Jill?"

"I don't know, but I promise you I'll give it my best shot."

***

"What's that you're reading?" Winky said.

"Nothing." I'd deliberately placed the book on the desk in such a way that he couldn't see the cover.

"Come on. Let's have a look." He jumped onto my desk.

"Get down."

"The Idiot's Guide to Horse Racing?" He laughed.

"It's research."

On my way back from F-O-F, I'd called in at Washbridge library. I was due to pay a visit to Sonny Ease's stables the next day, and I was beginning to worry that I might have oversold my knowledge of all things equestrian.

That's why I was studying the book. Or at least I would have been if Winky wasn't distracting me so much.

"Do you mind? I'm trying to read."

"That book isn't going to do you any good. You told that guy that you'd grown up around horses and that you were an accomplished rider. How long do you reckon it will take him to figure out that your full of it."

"It'll be fine. He's only concerned with whether or not I can find his missing horse."

"Don't you have some kind of horsey spell in that spell book of yours? There's all kinds of weird stuff in there."

He had a point.

"I suppose it wouldn't do any harm to check." I brought up the spell book app on my phone and searched for horse. "The never-full clothes horse spell. Hmm, that could come in handy."

"Focus, Jill," Winky snapped.

"Sorry. Wait a minute, this one might be helpful: The 'horse riding made easy' spell. It says this spell will let you become an accomplished horse rider instantly. Brilliant. I won't be needing this now." I closed the library book. "That was a good idea of yours, Winky."

"In return for which, a small reward is called for, I believe."

"Red not pink?"

"Obviously."

When Winky had returned as a ghost, I had foolishly thought that I would no longer have to fork out for salmon and full cream milk. Boy, was I wrong. It turns out that ghost cats eat and drink just as much if not more than their living counterparts. Now, though, I had the added problem of having to smuggle in the salmon and milk. It was either that or try to explain to Jules why I had developed such a weird craving.

Winky was still tucking into the salmon when his new squeeze, Daisy, appeared in the office.

"I hope you aren't going to eat all of that salmon,

Winky," she said. "What have I told you about portion size?"

"Err, right, yeah. I'll leave the rest until later."

Some chance. As soon as she left, he would have his head straight back in the bowl.

"I have your personalised diet here, Jill, as promised." She passed me a sheet of paper.

"Great, thanks."

"If you want to see results, you have to take it seriously. No cheating."

"Absolutely. You can trust me."

"Yeah, right." Winky scoffed.

"That's enough of that," Daisy snapped at him. "You should be encouraging Jill."

"Sorry, my angel. I will. I promise."

"Good. I can't stay because I have a spinning class in ten minutes." And with that, Daisy disappeared.

A spinning class for ghost cats? My mind was boggled.

"You've got no chance of sticking to that diet," Winky said.

"You promised Daisy you'd be supportive."

"There's supportive and then there's delusional."

"We'll see. I might surprise you."

"Yeah, and I might save the rest of this salmon until later." He put his head back into the trough.

***

Despite what Winky thought, I was determined to give the diet my best shot. It took only a quick glance at it for me to realise that none of the food I had in the house would pass muster. At least, nowadays, I didn't have to fight my way around the supermarket because I had my very own store back in the village.

After parking outside the old watermill, I made my way to the store, diet sheet in hand. There were no customers inside, nor was there any sign of Jack. Instead, it was Kiki who greeted me from behind the counter.

"Good afternoon, madam." She beamed. "Is there anything I can help you with?"

"It's me. Jill."

"Nice to meet you. I'm Kiki."

"We met yesterday. I'm Jack's wife. Remember?"

"I'm so sorry. I never have been very good with faces, Jean."

Or names, apparently.

"Is Jack around?"

"He's just checking a delivery in the back." She turned around and yelled, "Jacky! Your wife is here."

Jacky?

Moments later, Jack appeared. "Hey, sweetie. Everything okay?"

"Fine, yeah. I just dropped by to pick up a few bits and bobs."

"Custard creams?"

"No, actually, I want to get some of the stuff on here." I held out the diet sheet.

"I didn't know you were going on a diet."

"I told you." I hadn't.

"I must have forgotten. Who's Daisy?"

"She's—err—a friend."

"My mum says diets are for losers," Kiki said. "No offence, Jean."

"It's Jill," Jack corrected her.

"Sorry."

"Why don't you go and finish checking the delivery, Kiki?"

"Sure."

I waited until she was out of earshot and then said, "*Jacky*?"

"She's taken to calling me that for some reason."

"She didn't even remember who I was."

"She has only met you the once. How come I've never heard you mention this Daisy before?"

"Because Daisy is a cat. Or to be precise, an angel cat. She's Winky's new girlfriend."

"And she's drawn up this diet for you?"

"Yes."

He skimmed the diet sheet. "You'll never stick to this."

"Of course I will."

"It's basically just salads, pasta and the like."

"So?"

"What about fry-ups?"

"I won't be having them for the foreseeable future."

"Are you honestly trying to tell me that you're going to be chewing on a stick of celery while I eat sausage, bacon, eggs and all the works?"

"No, because you're not allowed to have a fry-up while I'm on my diet."

Chapter 9

It was the next morning, and I was staring at a bowl of fresh fruit, wondering how that was supposed to sustain me through the morning.

"You're still planning on going through with the CASS thing, then?" Jack said as he bit into a sausage.

"I promised the headmistress I would. I can't very well back out on the first day that I'm supposed to be giving a lesson, can I?"

"What about Florence?"

"She'll be okay. I think she was just upset because I hadn't told her myself."

"From what you've told me, it sounds like she was more than a little upset. I did warn you this might happen."

"Thanks for the reminder, Mr Know-It-All. And do you have to savour that sausage quite so much?"

"You mean *this* sausage?" He took another bite. "It's deee-licious!"

"I thought you might at least try to be supportive of my diet."

"I am supportive, but that doesn't mean I have to change my eating habits, which by the way have always been much healthier than yours."

"Rubbish."

"I don't eat cake and biscuits all day long for a start."

"You could at least have had muesli this morning, seeing as it's my first day at this. That would have made my fruit bowl look appetising."

"I fancied a fry-up."

I popped a handful of blueberries in my mouth and

tried to pretend it was a slice of bacon. It didn't work.

"Is Flirty McGee on duty today?" I said.

"I assume you're referring to Kiki."

"Oh, is that her name? I'd forgotten."

"For your information, Kiki hasn't once tried to flirt with me or any of the customers. She's very professional."

"I still say she's untrustworthy. Has she let you have her references yet?"

"No, but then I didn't think to ask for them. I was too busy showing her the ropes."

"I'll bet."

"That's enough, Jill. Just because this diet of yours is making you irritable, there's no need to take it out on me. Or Kiki."

He was right. The stupid blueberries, raspberries and strawberries were making me irrational. But that wasn't the only thing that was causing my bad mood.

"I'm sorry. I can't stop thinking about Marcy. I don't believe she killed herself, no matter what the police might say."

"Didn't you tell me that her boss said she'd been depressed and acting weird?"

"That's nonsense. Remember, she was in my office less than an hour before it happened. She was no more suicidal than I am."

"If the police and everyone else says it was suicide, there's nothing much you can do."

"We'll see about that."

"Don't get involved."

"Relax, I have to work on the Majestic Tears case anyway."

"That's the missing racehorse, isn't it?"

"Yeah."

"Aren't you worried that they're going to realise you're not the equestrian you made yourself out to be in order to get the case?"

"No, because I've found a spell that will let me ride a horse like a seasoned pro."

"Oh? I guess you'll be okay, then."

***

I was ravenous when I left the house. There was no way that a few berries were going to get me through the day, so I decided to grab a snack from somewhere where I knew no one would grass on me.

Mad Hour had been open for just over three years now. When Mad had been passed over for the position of head ghosthunter, she'd handed in her notice and, as far as I could tell, had never looked back. That's when she and Brad had made the decision to expand what was then Vinyl Alley, to include a retro café. Both sides of the business had flourished, and they had soon outgrown their small premises. Fortuitously, around the same time, Mad's mother, Deli, had decided she was ready to retire. Not long afterwards, Mad and Brad had taken over the lease to Deli's shop. Although a lot had happened in their lives, one thing hadn't changed: they still weren't married.

"Hey, Jill." Brad waved to me from the other side of the shop, from where he still ran the vinyl record section of the business. "How are you?"

"Hungry."

"How's Jack? I haven't seen him in a while."

"He's fine. He set on a new assistant yesterday."

"The store is doing well, I assume?"

"Yeah, but not as well as this place. Is Mad in?"

"She's over there somewhere."

I walked over to the other side of the shop where the café was located. The café had the same vinyl record theme, with images of cover sleeves of classic rock and pop records on the walls. There were a few customers seated at the tables but no sign of Mad behind the counter.

"I won't be a minute, Jill."

I could hear her, but I still couldn't see her. Then, suddenly, she popped up, seemingly from under the counter.

"What were you doing under there?"

"I've lost one of my contact lenses."

"Did you find it?"

"Not yet. What can I get for you?"

"It's okay. Find your lens first."

"That could take hours. It's alright. I can see okay with one eye. Coffee?"

"Yes, please, and a sausage cob."

"Coming right up. Grab a seat and I'll bring it over."

A few minutes later, she brought over my food and drink, and joined me at the table. She still had one eye open and the other closed.

"Thanks." I took a bite of the sausage cob. "I'm ready for this."

"We don't usually see you first thing in the morning."

"You haven't seen me today."

"Sorry?"

"If Jack happens to come by, I wasn't here. And I definitely wasn't eating a sausage cob."

"Okay." She grinned. "Got it."

"And tell Brad to keep schtum too, would you?"

"No worries. Want to tell me what this is about?"

"Best I don't. That way you have plausible deniability. Business is still booming, I see."

"Absolutely. Moving onto the high street was the best decision we ever made."

I glanced around to make sure no one was in earshot. "Don't you ever miss the ghost-hunting?"

"Not for one minute. You know how devastated I was when they screwed me over, but with hindsight, they actually did me a huge favour. I'm happier than I ever could have been if I'd stuck with the ghost hunting. And I'm definitely making much more money."

"I assume you still see them? The ghosts, I mean."

"Of course I do. All the time. But as long as they aren't doing me or mine any harm, I let them be. They're someone else's problem now."

"And what about Lizzie? Do you still see her?"

"Yes, but not as often as I used to when she was younger."

"Same here. It's weeks since I last saw her, and I haven't seen Mikey since he went away to Uni. I was going to ask you if Lizzie is still ghost-hunting."

"As far as I know, but it was only ever a part-time thing for her. After what happened to me, she no longer sees it as a viable career option."

"Last I heard, she was studying physics, but then she always was the brainy one of that family. She definitely doesn't get it from Kathy, that's for sure."

"How is your rich sister?"

"To tell you the truth, I think she's bored. She doesn't know what to do with herself since she sold the shops.

That's why she's always calling around and annoying me. What about your mum? How is Deli enjoying her retirement?"

"She's loving it. She and Nails seem to be trying to set the record for the number of cruises you can take in one year. They're on the high seas now somewhere or other. I've lost track."

***

I'd spent so long jabbering to Mad that I only just had enough time to drive the fifteen miles to Ease Stables for the meeting with Sonny Ease and his father.

"Hi, this is Jill Maxwell," I said into the intercom, which was on the post next to the tall metal gates. "Sonny Ease is expecting me for a meeting at ten-thirty."

"I'll buzz you in," said a female voice. "Come straight up the driveway. I'll meet you outside the house."

As I drove towards the house, I could see a number of horses being put through their paces in the field beyond the building. As I got closer, one of the double doors opened, and out stepped a young woman, who gestured that I should park in front of the house.

"Hi, I'm Honey." The young woman shook my hand. "Sonny's sister. And yes, before you ask, my parents thought it would be funny to give us rhyming names."

"Nice to meet you. I'm afraid I'm a couple of minutes late."

"Don't worry about it. My father is never on time for anything, so we probably won't see him for a while. Sonny should be with us any minute, though. I thought we could go through to the boardroom. I've asked

Kathleen to make us drinks. Is tea okay for you?"

"Tea would be lovely."

We'd no sooner got our drinks than Sonny joined us in the boardroom, which I suspected doubled as a dining room. Although the business operated out of this building, it was clear that it was primarily a family home.

"Sorry I'm late." He took a seat next to his sister, and opposite me. "Dad?"

"Late as usual." Honey sighed.

"I say we start without him."

The words were no sooner out of Sonny's mouth than the door opened again, and in walked a tall, silver-haired man who was wearing a tweed suit.

"I bet they told you I'd be late," he addressed his comments to me. "I'm Derek Ease but everyone calls me Dez."

"Jill Maxwell."

He had a firm handshake and a smile that I would have wagered could still charm the ladies.

"Sonny tells me that you're something of an equestrian yourself, Jill."

"I have spent a lot of time around horses."

Mainly the My Little Ponies that Florence used to love so much, but he didn't need to know that.

"Excellent. That should be useful with your investigation. How much has Sonny told you?"

"Just that one of your horses, Majestic Tears, has been stolen."

"That's right as far as it goes, but Majestic is not just one of our horses. He's by far the most successful horse I've ever bred, and I've been at this game for over thirty years."

"I assume by that he's valuable?"

"Extremely. He's due to retire at the end of this season and we'd expect him to earn a small fortune in stud fees."

"When and how was he taken?"

"I was abroad on business at the time," Dez said. "Honey, would you like to tell Jill what happened?"

"Sure. I oversee all the stable hands. I normally drop by the stables at around eight in the morning, to make sure they've all turned up, and that there have been no problems overnight. This particular morning—it was a Thursday—I got down there to discover Max hadn't turned in."

"Max?"

"Sorry. That's Maxine Westlake. She's one of our stable hands. She'd gone down with a stomach bug overnight and wasn't well enough to come in."

"Hadn't she called to let you know she wouldn't be in?"

"She'd called Thomas—he's our stable manager. Thomas was going to cover Max's work, but he hadn't got around to checking on Majestic by the time I got down there, so I said I'd do it. But he was gone."

"What did you do?"

"At first, I just assumed one of the other stable hands must have taken Majestic out for a run, but it soon became obvious that no one had. To be honest, I was in a state of utter disbelief. A horse can't just disappear. But he had. I rang Sonny."

"And I called Dad," Sonny said.

"And I jumped on the next plane and came straight back."

"I assume you haven't received any kind of ransom demand?"

"Not a word."

"That surprises me."

"Why do you say that, Jill?" Dez said.

"I'm just trying to figure out what motive someone might have for taking Majestic. Presumably, they can't race him or put him out to stud because he'd be recognised. So, as far as I can make out, the only way they stand to gain financially is if they can extract a ransom from you."

"You're right."

"Do you have CCTV here and at the stables?"

Although neither Sonny nor Honey spoke, they both turned to look at their father.

"Why don't you come out and say it?" Dez snapped at them. When they didn't react, he turned to me. "They've been pushing me to have CCTV installed for some time, but I've always vetoed the idea."

"Any particular reason?"

"I hate this big brother state that we live in at the moment, where you can't go anywhere without someone watching you. And, the truth is, I never believed something like this would happen. Obviously, I was wrong."

"Okay, so no CCTV. Can you talk me through the logistics of what someone would have to do to steal a horse from your stables. It can't have been easy."

"I'll take this," Honey said. "First, there are only two ways onto the estate. There's the way you came in—the front gate. There's another one at the other side of the estate. We always use that entrance when bringing horses to and from the stables."

"How secure is the other gate?"

"Entrance is by intercom similar to the front gate."

"Is there a way to override the intercom?"

"You can gain entry by entering the correct combination on the keypad."

"Who has that combination?"

"The three of us, obviously."

"Plus most of our clients," Sonny chipped in.

"How many people are we talking about?"

"A lot."

"From that, I have to conclude that gaining access to the stables won't have been an insurmountable problem. How would they have taken the horse away? They would have needed a horsebox, I assume."

Dez and Sonny both nodded, but Honey said, "Not necessarily."

"Not this again, Honey," her father snapped at her.

Ignoring his outburst, I asked what she was going to say.

"Someone could have ridden Majestic off the estate."

"That's ridiculous," Sonny said.

"Why so?" I addressed both father and son.

"Majestic is an incredible horse," Dez said. "But he's also notoriously hard to ride. Very few jockeys have been able to get the best out of him. The idea that someone could just waltz in here, saddle him up and ride him away is ridiculous."

"I disagree," Honey said, somewhat meekly.

"Okay, I think I get the picture," I said.

"What happens now?" Dez asked.

"I still think it's likely that you'll receive a ransom demand. If you do, you must inform me straight away. Agreed?"

"Agreed."

"In the meantime, I assume you'll grant me full access to the house, stables and all the people who live or work here."

"No problem."

"I'll also need a list of all your clients, current and past."

"You can't tell any of them about Majestic," Dez said.

"I understand that. I'll be very discreet in what I say."

"I'll email the info to you later today," Sonny said.

"Great." I stood up. "Thanks for your time."

"Is that it?" Dez said.

"For now, yes, but I'll need the combination to the gate so I can come and go as needed."

"I'll give you that on your way out," Honey said.

Chapter 10

I left Ease Stables with more questions than answers, but the thing that was perplexing me the most was the *why*. What possible reason could there be to steal Majestic other than to demand a ransom payment? If I could figure out the answer to that question, I would be a lot closer to finding the stolen horse.

Right now, though, I had a much bigger problem: I'd just finished my tuna salad, and I was still ravenous. I was beginning to question why I'd agreed to follow Daisy's diet. It might have been suitable for cats because they just lazed around all day, doing nothing much of anything. In contrast, I was on the go all the time, so I needed something much more substantial. As far as I could see, there were only two possible solutions to my predicament: Call upon my renowned powers of self-control and ignore my hunger. Or find the nearest fish and chip shop. No prizes for guessing which of those options I chose.

I'd just eaten the last chip when I got a call from Aunt Lucy.

"Are you busy at the moment, Jill?"

"Nothing that can't wait. Is everything okay?"

"Yes, everything is fine, but there's something I'd like to talk to you about. Do you think you could pop over for a few minutes?"

"Sure, I'll be right there."

"Great. I'll put the kettle on."

"Hey, Jill." Barry came bouncing over to greet me. He'd calmed down a little over the last few years, but he was still always pleased to see me.

"Hi." Buddy was still as unenthusiastic as ever, and just about managed to nod to me from his favourite spot on the armchair.

"I hope you two have been behaving yourselves."

"They're as good as gold," Aunt Lucy assured me, as she handed me my cup of tea. "Help yourself to a cupcake."

"I shouldn't. I've just—"

"I've tried something new: Mango flavour."

"In that case, I ought to give them a try. Mmm, that's delicious. So, what is it that you wanted to talk to me about?"

"Magic Or Not."

"Sorry?"

"The TV gameshow. Don't tell me you haven't seen it."

"I've never heard of it. I take it that it's on here in Candlefield?"

"Yes, it's been the most-viewed show for a couple of years now."

"I rarely watch TV in Washbridge, and I never watch it over here, unless you happen to have it on when I visit."

"I love that show. I've only ever missed one episode and that was when your grandmother went down with her tummy problem a couple of months back. Do you remember?"

"How could I forget? She insisted on giving me all the gory details."

"Anyway, on a whim, I applied to take part in the show. Thousands of people apply every month, so I didn't really think I'd have a chance, but then, this morning, I got a letter to say I'd been accepted."

"You must be thrilled."

"I am."

"So why don't you look like you are?"

"The game consists of two teams of two people."

"You and Lester?"

"He hates that program so I couldn't put his name forward."

"So who did you—hang on. You didn't—you did, didn't you?"

"You were the first person I thought of. You being so smart and all."

"Why didn't you ask me?"

"I should have done, but like I said, I never thought there was a chance that we'd be accepted."

"Why didn't you put one of the twins' names forward?"

"They'd be hopeless, and besides, if I chose one of them, the other one would only sulk. It's okay. I should never have put your name down without asking you first. I'll tell them that I'll have to withdraw."

Now I felt terrible. It was obvious that this meant a lot to her, and I owed her so much.

"No, don't do that. I'll take part in the gameshow."

"Are you sure?"

"Positive. I want to."

"Thank you, Jill." She threw her arms around me. "It'll be such fun, I promise."

"When is it?"

"Two weeks tomorrow, but you'll need to swot up on the game format between now and then. I can help you with that."

"Okay, but I'd better get back now."

"Take a cupcake with you."

"Thanks."

"What's that in your hand?" Winky said.

Oh bum! Without thinking, I'd magicked myself straight back to the office with the cupcake still in my hand.

"Err, nothing." I put both hands behind my back.

"Show me your hands."

I put out one empty hand. "See. Nothing."

"Now, show me the other one."

I did as he asked. "See, there's nothing there either."

"Show them both at the same time."

I quickly cast a spell to make the cupcake invisible.

"See, I don't have anything."

"You made it disappear."

"I don't know what you're talking about."

"I'm not stupid. I know what I saw. You couldn't even get through one day without breaking the diet. I warned Daisy you were a lost cause."

"That's not true." I reversed the spell, and the cupcake reappeared. "If you must know, Aunt Lucy insisted that I take it, and she wouldn't take no for an answer."

"That's no excuse."

"If you'll let me finish. I was going to say that I didn't want to upset her, so I took it with the intention of giving it to Jules."

Speak of the devil: Jules came walking into my office.

"I thought I heard your voice, Jill. I didn't see you come back in."

"You must have been in the loo."

"Who were you talking to? Not that dead cat again?"

"Of course not. I was on the phone to Jack. I've got something for you." I held out the cupcake.

"That's so very kind of you. Thank you. Aren't you having one?"

"No, I'm on a bit of a diet at the moment."

She took a nibble. "It's delicious. What flavour is it?"

"Mango."

"Mmm, thanks very much, Jill."

"You should see your face," Winky said once we were alone again. "Giving up that cupcake was really painful, wasn't it?"

"Rubbish. I keep telling you that I have iron willpower."

Five minutes later, I was still mourning the lost cupcake when Jules came back through to my office and closed the door behind her.

"Jill, there's an Ivor Payne out there. He wonders if you can spare him a minute."

"Did he say what it was about?"

"He works on the top floor. He said he wanted to talk to you about Marcy."

"You'd better send him through."

The man, who looked to be in his mid/late twenties, came hobbling into my office.

"Are you okay?" I said.

"It's nothing. I just picked up an injury playing football last weekend."

"Take a seat."

"I won't, thanks. My leg tends to seize up if I sit down."

"Jules said you work at Slade Marketing?"

"That's right. I'm a junior account executive; I worked under Marcy. She was a brilliant boss." He looked for a moment as though he might well up, but then he continued. "She often spoke about you."

"Me?"

"Yeah, she said what a cool job you had and that she wished she'd done something more interesting with her life."

"She was a great lady. Her death must have hit you hard, Ivor."

"It did. I'm still in shock. May I call you Jill?"

"Of course."

"The thing is, Jill, I just don't believe she would have killed herself."

Although I felt exactly the same way, I decided to play devil's advocate.

"People can do all kinds of things when they're upset or depressed."

"Not Marcy. She was tougher than that."

"Victor Slade seems to believe it was suicide."

"You've spoken to him?"

"Briefly, yes. Did Marcy say anything to you in the days leading up to her death that might have suggested she was worried about anything?"

"There was one thing, but I don't see how—"

"Tell me."

"A couple of days before it happened, she told me she was going to get a locksmith in because she thought someone had been in her apartment."

"A burglar, you mean?"

"I don't think so. She said nothing had been taken, but a couple of things weren't where they should have been. It had freaked her out a bit, I reckon."

"She never mentioned anything about that to me."

"You won't tell Victor Slade that I've been talking to you, will you?"

"No, of course not. What made you decide to come and see me?"

"I'm not really sure. I suppose I was hoping that you might be able to find out what really happened to Marcy."

"I don't have anything to go on. Nothing solid, I mean."

"Surely, it must be worth a try," he said.

"Could you get me the contact details for Jade Holdings?"

"Why do you want that?"

"According to Victor Slade they'd telephoned to complain about Marcy just before she died. It might not be connected at all, but I'd like to check it out."

"Okay, I can do that."

"And Marcy's home address."

"No problem."

"Okay, I'm not making any promises, but I'll do a little sniffing around and see what I can turn up."

"Thanks, Jill."

***

It was ridiculous how nervous I was feeling about my visit to CASS. It's not like it was my debut as a teacher; I'd taught there for a while before Florence was born. When Mrs Littledo had first approached me, I'd been quite excited at the prospect of returning there. It was only since Florence's outburst that I'd begun to have doubts as to whether or not I'd made the right decision. In my experience, though, things never turned out as badly as you expected them to. The anticipation was almost always worse than the event itself, and I was sure that would prove to be the case this time.

I arrived at the appointed classroom several minutes ahead of time. As was the practice when a teacher takes a class for the first time, I wrote Mrs Maxwell in big letters on the whiteboard at the front of the class. A couple of minutes later, a bell sounded, and shortly afterwards, the kids came walking down the corridor and piled into the room. For a horrible moment, I thought Florence had decided not to attend, but then I spotted her chatting with two other girls. I tried to make eye-contact, but either she was too engrossed in her conversation, or she was deliberately blanking me. Either way, she took a seat at a desk on the back row of the classroom. The students, who were an almost equal mix of girls and boys, were quite rowdy and seemed in no hurry to begin the lesson.

"Okay, everyone," I said in my normal voice, to no effect. Somewhat annoyed, I raised my voice until I was almost shouting, "Quiet!"

The room fell silent, and all eyes were on me. All eyes except for Florence's that is. She appeared to be staring down at her desk.

"As you can see from the whiteboard, my name is Mrs Maxwell, and I'm going to be taking you for this lesson every Friday from now on."

Florence's hand flew up immediately.

"Yes, Florence?"

"There isn't a name on the whiteboard."

A ripple of low-level laughter spread around the classroom, as I turned around to find the whiteboard was blank. Judging by the expression on Florence's face, I didn't need two guesses to work out who'd erased my name.

"How strange," I said. "Perhaps, Florence, you'd like to

come out here and write my name on the board again."

"Me?"

"Yes, after all, if anyone should know how to spell my surname, it would be you."

"But—"

"Now, please."

The last thing I'd wanted to do was embarrass my daughter, but she was the one who'd thrown down the gauntlet, and if I was to maintain any level of authority, I couldn't simply let it go.

"There you are." I handed her the board marker.

After writing my name, she handed back the marker, and returned to her desk, all the time glaring at me.

"Thank you, Florence. You're probably all aware that Mrs Littledo has asked me to teach a lesson, once a week, on the use of magic in the human world. Hands up all those who live in the human world."

"Duh! None of us live there," Florence shouted out. "We all board here."

Another ripple of laughter.

"Thank you for stating the obvious, Florence, but I'm sure you and the rest of your classmates understood what I meant. Whose home is normally in the human world?"

Less than a quarter of the children raised their hands.

"What about you, Florence? Don't you normally live in the human world?"

"I guess."

And that pretty much set the tone for the rest of the lesson. At every possible opportunity, Florence did her best to disrupt the flow of the lesson, by making some kind of smartass quip. The bell to mark the end of the lesson came as something of a relief. As the children filed out of the classroom, I decided to address the problem.

"Florence, would you stay behind, please?"

"I'll be late for PE."

"No, you won't. I'll only keep you for a minute." Once all the other kids had left, I closed the door. "Okay, what was that all about?"

"What?"

"You know what. You were doing your level best to disrupt my lesson."

"No, I wasn't."

"Why would you act like that? It's just not like you."

"I told you I didn't want you teaching here."

"And I told you that I couldn't go back on my word to Mrs Littledo."

"You should never have agreed to do it without talking to me first. Do you know how much of a hard time I've been getting from the rest of the kids in my class. They've been calling me teacher's pet ever since they found out."

"So, you decided to prove them wrong?"

"Something like that."

"I let it go this time, but if you do it again next week, I'll be forced to take some action."

"Like I care."

"Florence!"

"Can I go now, or I'll be late for PE."

"Okay."

Chapter 11

The next morning, Jack and I were at the breakfast table. Fortunately, today, he was eating muesli, which made even my bowl of bran flakes look delicious.

"You have to let it go, Jill," he said.

"That's easy for you to say. You didn't see how she carried on in class."

"No, I didn't, but you've told me enough times that it feels like I was in there with you."

"Pardon me if I'm boring you."

"I didn't say you were boring me but to keep reliving it isn't helping you."

"What do you think I should do, then?"

"My advice would be to forget it. She's probably got it out of her system now. Next week will be much better, you'll see."

"It had better be or I'll be forced to put our daughter in detention."

"Let's hope it doesn't come to that."

"Shouldn't you be at the store by now?"

"There's no need for me to go in today; Mr Ivers and Kiki have it covered."

"Nice one. What shall we do all day?"

"It's Peter's birthday party this afternoon. You hadn't forgotten, had you?"

"Of course not." I most definitely had. "Where did you put his card?"

"What card? I assumed you'd bought it."

"Why me? He's your brother-in-law too."

"Yes, but he's *your* sister's husband."

"Well, I didn't get one."

"Neither did I. What about a present?"

"We all agreed not to buy one another presents, remember?" I said.

"Oh yes, I remember now. You came up with that idea the day after your birthday, as I recall. Incredible timing that, Jill."

"That was just a coincidence. Anyway, we all agreed, so we only have the card to worry about. You could nip over to the store and get one while I do some stuff around the house."

"By *do some stuff*, I assume you mean laze around on the sofa."

"I meant change the bed and put the washing on, actually."

"I changed the bed on Monday, and the washing basket is practically empty. And, besides, I don't want to go to the store because I might get dragged into something."

"Fine, I suppose I'll have to go, then."

"Be careful when you pick his card. Remember what happened when you bought Kathy's birthday card."

"I explained that at the time. It wasn't my fault that someone had put grandmother cards in amongst the cards for sister, was it?"

"The wording on the front did rather give it away, though."

"Do you want me to go to the store or not?"

"Yes, please, darling." He blew me a kiss which I batted away.

As I walked to the store, I was still reliving my CASS experience from the day before. When I'd got home yesterday, I'd seriously considered calling Mrs Littledo and telling her that I quit, but that would have been to send all the wrong messages to Florence. And, as Jack had reminded me last night, I hadn't exactly been an angel when I was a kid in school. I was determined to stick it out and if Florence didn't like it, then she would just have to lump it.

Although I was still a little miffed that Jack had forgotten to buy Peter's birthday card, I was actually interested to see how the dynamic duo, Mr Ivers and Kiki, were coping. If my hunch about Flirty McGee was correct, I suspected she'd be letting Mr Ivers do all the work while she sat around doing her nails. If so, and if I caught her in the act, I would tell Jack he needed to get rid of her.

Just as I thought, when I walked into the store, there was no sign of Kiki. Mr Ivers was all alone behind the counter.

"Good morning, Jill." He beamed. "Run out of custard creams again?"

Why did everyone associate me with custard creams?

"No, I'm here to buy a birthday card for my brother-in-law. Jack should have got it yesterday, but he forgot." I glanced down each of the aisles to make sure Kiki wasn't there. "Hasn't Kiki turned in?"

"Oh yes. She was here before I was. Very keen."

"Has she nipped out?"

"No, she's in the back."

"On a break already?"

"No, she's doing a stock check. Jack said he was going to try and find time to do one next week, but as we were quiet, Kiki decided to make a start on it today. I can go and get her for you if you like?"

"Err, no that's okay. I'll just pick out a card."

Adding greetings cards into the store had been one of the many changes Jack had introduced since we bought the business. Since the change of ownership, turnover had increased by almost forty percent. If I'd so desired, I could have given up the PI work, and joined him fulltime in the store. We'd discussed the idea several times over the years, but each time we'd both concluded that working together in such a confined environment would be a recipe for disaster.

As I looked through the cards, I couldn't help but wonder whether Kiki was actually doing a stock check, or if that was just an excuse to put her feet up. I was sorely tempted to go and check on her, but in the end, I decided against it. Instead, when I got back home, I would casually mention to Jack about the 'stock check' and watch his reaction.

I hated choosing birthday cards. Or Christmas cards. Or any cards for that matter. They were such a waste of time and money. That's why I'd made the mistake when purchasing Kathy's card. I'd just picked a card at random, and I hadn't spotted that it was in the wrong section.

Peter was a fishing enthusiast, so the card which featured a fishing rod was an easy choice. And, yes, it did say Brother-in-law, not Granddad. After paying Mr Ivers—still no sign of Kiki—I made my way back home.

"Did you get one?" Jack called to me, as soon as I walked into the house.

"Yeah, I got the perfect card." I walked through to the kitchen and handed it to him.

"Oh." He frowned.

"What's wrong? It says brother-in-law."

"Yeah, I can see that."

"What then?"

"Don't you remember Kathy told us Peter had given up fishing. It was about a year ago."

"Oh bum! I don't remember that. I'll have to go and swap—"

"Gotcha!" Jack laughed. "You should see your face."

"You're hilarious. Not."

"Are my staff hard at work over there?"

"Mr Ivers is behind the counter. Kiki is in the back, stock checking, *supposedly*."

"Stock checking?"

"That's what she reckons."

"That's great."

"It is?"

"I mentioned that I needed to do a full stock check this week, but I wasn't sure how I was going to find time to do it. Kiki told me that she'd had experience of doing them at the last place she worked, and—"

"The one she hasn't provided references from yet?"

"Anyway, she said she'd be pleased to lend a hand, but I never expected her to make a start on her own. I knew I'd made the right choice when I hired her."

***

My idea of a birthday party is a gathering of close friends and relatives. Okay, that's a lie. My idea of a birthday party is no party at all—I hate parties. Yeah, yeah, I know, I'm a terrible person.

Anyway, Kathy's idea of a birthday party is, apparently, to invite the whole of Washbridge (and surrounding districts). I'm pretty sure there were fewer people at

Middle Tweaking's summer carnival than there were at Kathy's house. I say house, but it was more of a mansion—bought with some of the proceeds of the sale of her bridal shop empire.

"Cracks me up every time." I chuckled as we drove through the gates.

When Kathy and Peter had moved into their new place, she'd decided the house deserved a name. It's common practice for couples to combine their names to create a house name. For example, if Jack and I were to do it, we'd end up with something like Jacill or Jillack. Obviously, Kathy being Kathy, she'd insisted her name came first, so they ended up with Katheter. It was only after the sign had been installed on the wall next to the entrance that someone (me) had pointed out the obvious. Since then, Kathy had insisted that the house name was pronounced: *Kay-theeter*. Yeah, right. Snigger.

"Don't you dare bring that up again," Jack said. "You know how sensitive Kathy is about it."

"Spoilsport. If I can't even do that, why did we bother coming?"

"How could we not come? It's Peter's birthday. Kathy would have killed us if we hadn't turned up."

"How would she have known? Just look at this crowd."

"Peter's obviously a popular guy."

"Freeloaders out for a free lunch, more like."

"Jack, Jill, there you are." Kathy appeared through the throng. "I was beginning to think you weren't coming."

"Don't be ridiculous," I scoffed. "I was just saying to Jack that we wouldn't have missed this for the world."

"Where is the birthday boy?" Jack asked.

"Over there. Look. By the chocolate fountains."

Fountains? Plural? The last time I'd seen one of those was when the twins had installed one in what was then Cuppy C. That hadn't ended well, as I recall.

"I'll go and give him his birthday card." Jack was quick to offer, most likely because he was keen to avail himself of the chocolate fountains.

"No Florence?" Kathy said.

"You knew she wouldn't be able to come."

"I thought she might have been able to get a weekend pass under the circumstances."

"They don't give out passes willy-nilly. Her uncle's birthday party would hardly qualify."

"You must worry about her."

"Not really. She's doing just fine." I glanced around. "What about Mikey? Is he here?"

"No, he has a rugby match this weekend."

"I didn't think he was very sporty?"

"He isn't, but he seems to have taken to rugby for some reason."

"What is it he's studying again?"

"Horology."

"Right? And what's that again?"

"The study of time." She must have seen the puzzled expression on my face. "Don't ask. I don't really understand it either, but he seems to be enjoying it, so that's all that matters."

"What about Lizzie? Is she here?"

"She will be when she manages to drag herself out of bed. I swear that girl gets lazier and lazier. Anyway, I'd better circulate. A hostess' duties are never done. There's plenty of booze and cakes in the Velvet Room."

Velvet room. One of the first things Kathy had done

when they bought the new place was to give all the reception rooms and bedrooms names. She was so far up her own backside, that one. Still, cakes sounded good. And, before you lot chime in, the rule of diets is that they do not apply to birthday parties. I thought everyone knew that.

I was halfway through a very small slice of lemon drizzle cake when Lizzie, looking very pale and bleary-eyed, joined me on one of the many sofas that were scattered around the huge room.

"Hey, Lizzie. Your mum said you were still in bed. Aren't you feeling very good?"

"I'm fine. I was working until four am, but I couldn't tell Mum that, could I?"

In little more than a whisper, I said, "When you say working, I assume you mean ghost hunting?"

"Yeah. Washbridge library has been overrun by them for a couple of weeks now, but I think we got rid of them last night. I hope so, anyway."

"You're not letting the *you-know-what* hunting affect your schooling, are you?"

"I try not to. It's not usually as bad as it has been recently. I really wish Mad was still working with us. She would have had this lot under control long ago. Her replacement is pretty useless."

"If you didn't get in until gone four, you really should have stayed in bed a little longer."

"Any other weekend, I would have done, but I'd never hear the end of it if I wasn't around for Dad's birthday party. Not from him, he wouldn't have minded. But you know what Mum's like."

"I sure do. Why don't you have some cake? That might

get you going."

"Yuk." She screwed up her face. "I couldn't face cake. I'll go and make myself a couple of slices of toast."

"Okay, I'll catch up with you later."

I was just wondering if I dare grab another slice of cake when the birthday boy himself came into the room.

"Jack said I might find you near the cakes." He grinned.

"That husband of mine is such a wit. Happy birthday, Peter. You've drawn quite a crowd here today."

"Hmm. That wasn't my idea. If it had been up to me, I would have invited just you, Jack and a few other close friends. But you know what your sister is like."

Before I could agree, the woman herself joined us.

"Should my ears be burning?"

"No, my darling." Peter gave her a quick peck on the cheek. "I was just thanking Jill for my card."

"I don't know why you're thanking her. Jack will have chosen it. Jill *doesn't do* cards."

"That's where you're wrong. I picked that card."

"Hmm. Come on, Pete, I want to introduce you to the Lance-Millers. He's something important in the city."

"Must I?"

"Yes, come on." She turned to me. "And try to leave some cake for the rest of us."

I was so annoyed by that quip that I had to eat a raspberry cupcake to calm myself down.

Chapter 12

After Saturday's ordeal (AKA Kathy's social gathering of the year), it had been nice to enjoy a lazy Sunday, doing nothing much of anything. Jack had needed to work in the store in the morning, but then we'd met for lunch, after which we'd had a drive out into the countryside. Much as I missed Florence, when she wasn't doing her St Trinians' impression, it was nice to have some time just for the two of us.

When Monday morning came around, I was feeling rejuvenated and ready for whatever the week had to throw at me.

"I'm impressed that you've managed to stick to your diet so far." Jack took a bite of his sausage cob, which I desperately wanted to snatch out of his hand.

"It's just a question of mind over matter. When I put my mind to something, nothing can shake me."

"What are you up to this morning?"

"Buying a ferret."

"What? I thought we'd agreed that we wouldn't have any more pets."

"Relax, I need it for one of the cases I'm working on. I'll give it back afterwards."

***

Before going shopping for a ferret, I called in at work. As soon as I walked into the outer office, I was met with the most awful, ear-piercing noise, causing me to put my hands over my ears.

"Are you okay, Jill?" Jules appeared confused by my

actions.

"Can't you hear that?"

"Hear what?"

Only then, did the penny drop. Whatever the noise was, Jules couldn't hear it, otherwise she too would have been trying to block it out.

"Err, nothing. I must have imagined it."

I hurried through to my office, to find Winky and three other ghost cats, dressed in white waistcoats, black bowties and straw hats. They were singing, and I use that term in its loosest possible sense, some awful song about catching mice.

"Stop! Stop that awful noise."

"*Awful noise*?" One of the cats huffed indignantly.

"Who is this two-legged?" a second cat demanded.

"I must apologise for this unseemly interruption, gentlemen," Winky said, and then turned to me. "Can't you see we're rehearsing?"

"Not in my office you aren't. I've never heard such an awful racket."

"Well!" The first cat shot me a look. "I have never been so insulted in my life."

"I think we should leave," said the third cat.

"I really am sorry, gentlemen," Winky was in full-on grovel mode now. "I'll be in touch to arrange another date."

"Just make sure this person isn't around next time," said the first cat.

And with that, the three of them disappeared.

"That was rude," Winky said. "How dare you burst into the middle of our rehearsal like that?"

"Do I have to remind you that this is my office?"

"Yes, but I distinctly recall you saying you wouldn't be in until later this morning."

"Did I? Well, even if I did, that doesn't give you licence to invite your friends around for a singalong."

"I'll have you know that those three gentlemen are the GT Feline Barbershop Choir, and I'm honoured to say they've invited me to join their troupe."

"You? Haven't they heard you sing?"

"I auditioned for them, and I was chosen from thirty other applicants."

"I dread to think what the others sounded like."

"You're only jealous because you can't sing to save your life."

"I'll have you know that I have an amazing voice, but that's irrelevant. I'm not having you disturb all my neighbours with that dreadful cats' chorus."

"No one except you can hear us. We're ghosts, remember?"

"Oh yeah."

"Which means we're not doing anyone any harm."

"You're doing my eardrums serious harm. They're still ringing now."

"We have to practise because it's the annual barbershop choir competition this weekend."

"In Ghost Town, I assume?"

"Yes, in the Spirits' Central Hall. Now, can we practise here or not?"

"Only if you do it at nighttime when I'm not here."

"But we—"

"Nighttime or never. Take it or leave it."

Twenty minutes later, Winky was still sulking, but I

didn't care. There were limits to what anyone could put up with for their pet, alive or dead, and being subjected to that awful cat's chorus went way beyond that limit.

Jules popped her head around the door. "Ivor Payne is here to see you again. He says it will only take a couple of minutes."

"Send him in, please."

If anything, Ivor seemed even more nervous than he had on his first visit.

"I have the information you requested, Jill." He handed me a sheet of paper. "I didn't want to send it via email or text, just in case."

The note contained the contact details for Jade Holdings, and Marcy's home address.

"Thanks, Ivor, that's very helpful."

"There's something else you should know, Jill."

"I'm listening."

"Someone started work yesterday in Marcy's old job."

"It's rather soon, but I suppose they had to replace her sometime."

"Yes, but here's the weird part. Her replacement's name is Rhonda Elpme, and until two months ago she was head of marketing for guess who?"

"I have no idea."

"Jade Holdings."

"That is weird."

***

My pet shop of choice in Washbridge had long been Rue Pets, but it seemed this time they would be unable to help in my quest to purchase a ferret.

"I'm really sorry, Jill," Rupert said. "I made a decision a few years ago not to sell them."

"Any particular reason?"

"I probably shouldn't say this, but the truth is I'm not fond of the little blighters. They're too cunning and devious for my liking."

"I had no idea."

"Oh yes. Never trust a ferret. That's the golden rule."

"I don't suppose you know where I might be able to get one, do you?"

"I'm afraid not. To the best of my knowledge, no other pet shops in the area sell them."

"That's a blow."

"Would you like some more fish instead? I know you were hit hard when yours died, but maybe it's time to try again."

"I'm too busy with work, and now Jack is out of the house most of the day, it wouldn't be fair. I don't want any more pets."

"Why did you ask about a ferret, then?"

"It's connected to a case I'm working on. I don't want to keep the animal, just borrow it. But I may have to come up with another plan."

"Not necessarily. I don't know any shops who sell them, but I do have the contact details for a local guy who rescues them. He left his card with me in case anyone came to the shop wanting to offload them. Just wait there while I nip to the office and see if I can find it."

I began to walk down the aisle of fish tanks, but I had to turn back because I found it too upsetting. Although Wanda and Mabel had been the bane of my life while they were alive, I still missed them.

"Here it is." Rupert reappeared, brandishing a business card. "If anyone can help you, it will be this guy."

"Ricky Hits?"

"Yeah, but if I remember correctly, he goes by Rick. If you like, I can give him a call to see if it's worth your while going over there."

"Yes, please, that would be great."

He took out his phone and punched in the number on the card. "Rick? Hi, it's Rupert from Rue Pets. Good, thanks. What about you? Good, good. Look, the reason for the call is I have a young lady here with me. She's a private investigator and she needs the loan of a ferret to help with one of the cases she's working on. What? I don't know the details. I didn't like to ask. I was just wondering if you might be able to loan her one from your menagerie. I can vouch for her as a responsible pet owner. Okay. When? Just a minute and I'll check with her." Rupert turned to me. "Rick says he can spare you some time now if you pop over."

"Great. Tell him I'm on my way."

The Ferret Sanctuary was located on a farm on the outskirts of West Chipping. The hand-painted wooden sign featured a drawing of what I assumed to be a ferret, but which could just as easily have been a squirrel or a rabbit.

The sanctuary was based in one of the stone outbuildings, whose walls had been whitewashed. As I got out of the car, a tall, slim, weaselly-looking man appeared in the doorway and waved to me.

"Jill?"

"That's me."

"Come inside and meet the guys."

"Okay, thanks."

The building was jam-packed with cages, most of them occupied by ferrets of all colours.

"Sorry about the noise," Rick said. "They get quite excited whenever someone new comes into the building."

"What are you doing here?" shouted a ferret in the cage close to my shoulder.

"Who's she?" asked another one.

"No idea. Never seen her before."

I found all the chattering quite distracting, but I did my best to focus on Rick.

"I had no idea you would have so many of them," I said.

"The numbers have grown every year. People think that keeping a ferret as a pet is easy, but they require a lot of attention. When it becomes too much, people just want to be rid of them. That's when they end up here."

"How long have you been doing this?"

"Coming up for ten years. When I started, I kept them in a shed in my back garden, then I moved to a much bigger shed on an allotment. Two years ago, my friend, Jimmy, who owns this farm, was kind enough to offer me the use of this building for free. It's been a lifesaver. Literally, as far as the ferrets are concerned."

"Do you manage to rehome many of them?"

"Yes, but never quite enough to keep pace with those handed in. Rupert said you're a private investigator."

"That's right, and I really need the loan of a ferret to help with a case I'm working on."

"I'm very particular about who I allow to adopt a ferret, and that would apply in this situation too. Can you tell me what the case is about and why you need a ferret?"

"Sure, but before I go into detail, can I ask if you've heard of F-O-F?"

"Friends Of Ferrets? Of course. They often raise money in support of this place."

"Are you a member?"

"No, but only because I simply don't have the time. I have a fulltime job—I'm a tig welder—so what with that and looking after these guys, it's impossible."

"Do you know a man called Kevin Wright?"

"No, I don't think so."

"Kevin is my client. He was treasurer of F-O-F until recently when he was accused of stealing money from the organisation. Something he emphatically denies. He's hired me to clear his name, but to do that I need to gain access to F-O-F."

"For which you would need a ferret?"

"Yes, plus I need to know as much about the little creatures as possible."

"Do you really believe this guy, Kevin, is innocent?"

"I do, otherwise I wouldn't have taken on the case."

"I do hate to see injustice of any kind. How long would you need the ferret for?"

"The meeting is tomorrow evening, so I could have it back with you first thing, the next day."

"Okay."

"I can take one?"

"Yes, but first, why don't we have a cup of tea and I'll tell you everything you need to know about ferrets."

"Thank you. That's very kind."

It took just short of an hour, and you might have

expected that I would be comatose by the time he'd finished, but Rick Hits had a way of making ferrets sound like the most fascinating animal alive.

"Thanks for taking the time to do that, Rick," I said.

"My pleasure. I love educating people about these wonderful animals. Now, I guess it's time for you to choose one to take away with you. Before you do, though, I assume you have somewhere suitable to keep him overnight?"

"Err, yes, we have a hutch that we used to keep rabbits in," I lied.

"That should do just fine. Now, which of this fine bunch would you like to take?"

"Do you have any suggestions?"

"Actually, I do. Given the reason you need it, I think it would be best if you were to take one with a laidback disposition. Over here." He led the way to one of the cages halfway down the building. "This here is Sandy, on account of his colour. He's very chilled out."

"Bored out of my brain, more like," Sandy said.

Oblivious to the ferret's comments, Rick continued, "I get the feeling that he loves being here amongst so many friends."

"*Friends*? This lot? They don't have two brain cells amongst them. Please, get me out of here."

"Yeah." I nodded. "Sandy sounds like just the ticket."

Rick was kind enough to loan me a ferret basket, which looked remarkably like a cat basket, in which to transport Sandy.

"Freedom!" Sandy called out as we left the farm. "Where are we going?"

"I'll need to take you back to my house until the F-O-F

meeting tomorrow night."

"What's F-O-F?"

"It stands for Friends Of Ferrets. They're a group of people who like ferrets."

"They sound like a bunch of losers."

"Why would you say that? From all accounts they spend a lot of their time raising money to help ferrets."

"All very admirable, but if that's all they can think of to do in their spare time, they must be a pretty sad crowd. Do you have cable?"

"Sorry?"

"At your place. Do you have cable TV?"

"Yeah, but you—"

"Brilliant. That Rick guy's heart is in the right place, but wouldn't you think that he would have installed TVs in that barn of his?"

"I—err—"

"I need to catch up on all my soaps."

"Actually, you'll be outside in the garden."

"Are you kidding me right now? Do you honestly think I would have agreed to help you if I'd known you were going to leave me outside? I'd be better off back in Rick's barn. Turn around. Take me back."

"It's okay. I guess it wouldn't hurt for you to stay in the house just for a couple of nights."

"Will there be TV in the room?"

"Yes."

"Excellent. Let's go."

Chapter 13

I drove to Middle Tweaking and parked in front of the old watermill. I'd just lifted the basket, containing Sandy, out of the car when a familiar voice made me jump.

"Another pet?" Grandma said. "I thought you'd have more sense now Florence has left home."

"Florence hasn't left home. She's at boarding school."

"Why another cat, though? Isn't that ghost one of yours enough?"

"It isn't a cat. And it isn't a pet."

She leaned forward to get a better look. "A ferret?"

"Yes, he's helping me with my case."

"Oh yeah." She cackled. "I'd forgotten about that."

"I'm Sandy," my newly acquired ferret introduced himself.

"Why would you think I care what your name is?" Grandma said.

"There's no need to be so rude to him, Grandma."

"Did you hear that someone has bought the hotel?"

"What? No, I hadn't. Who?"

"It doesn't matter. I can see you're far too busy with your ferret to talk to me." And off she went.

When Grandma had divested herself of all her businesses, she'd been unable to sell the hotel as a going concern, so the building had been put up for sale. That was almost two years ago, and I had begun to think it would never be sold. Seems I was wrong.

"Come on," Sandy said. "The TV awaits."

"Have a little patience. There's something I need to do first."

When I'd told Rick that I had a rabbit hutch, I'd been

lying. If I'd told him the truth, I didn't think he would have let me borrow Sandy. I now had to pin my hopes on being able to magic one up from somewhere.

"Hurry up!" Sandy snapped.

Were all ferrets this bolshy or had I just drawn the short straw?

I brought up the spell book app on my phone and searched on ferret, but it returned no results, so I tried again this time with the search term: rabbit. That was just as unhelpful, but for the opposite reason: there were hundreds of spells related to rabbits. Finally, when I refined the search to the terms: rabbit and hutch, I hit pay dirt. The pop-up rabbit hutch spell was exactly what I needed.

"Okay, let's go." I took Sandy through to the kitchen where I used the spell to make the hutch appear. I was just about to transfer him from the basket to the hutch when he pulled back.

"Where's the TV?" he said.

"It's in the lounge."

"Then that's where I need to be."

I wasn't happy with the idea of having a ferret in there, and I was sure that Jack wouldn't be, but it was only for a couple of nights, so we'd just have to suck it up.

"Okay, okay, keep your wig on."

I reversed the spell, causing the hutch to disappear, then I went through to the lounge, and recast the spell. Only when I'd turned on the TV, and handed Sandy the remote control, was he happy for me to transfer him to the hutch.

"I have to get back to work now."

"What about something to eat and drink?"

"I didn't think to ask Rick for any of your food."

"I don't like the muck he feeds us anyway. Do you have any biscuits?"

"Err, yeah, but—"

"What kind?"

"Custard creams."

"My favourite. Bring the packet through."

Once I'd given Sandy the milk and biscuits, I took my leave. I was rapidly beginning to regret taking on the ferret case, but I couldn't back out now.

***

Before getting into my car and heading back to the office, I decided to surprise Jack, by dropping in on him, but when I walked into the store, there was only Mr Ivers behind the counter.

"Hi, Jill. We've moved the custard creams to—"

"I'm not here for biscuits. Where's Jack?"

"He's in the back with Kiki." I guess Mr Ivers must have seen the look on my face because he quickly qualified that. "They're stocktaking. Shall I go and get him for you?"

"No, that's okay." I hurried behind the counter and through the door to the stockroom.

The first thing I heard when I stepped inside was the sound of laughter: Jack's and Kiki's. She wouldn't be laughing after I had turned her into the rat she most clearly was.

I found them in the second aisle of shelving; Jack was sitting on a sack of potatoes while Kiki was standing in front of him with a clipboard in her hand. The two of them were laughing so much that neither of them noticed me.

I cleared my throat loudly in an attempt to get their attention. When that didn't work, I shouted, "Hello, Jack!"

"Jill." He stood up. "I didn't see you there."

Clearly.

"Hey, Jill." Kiki beamed. "I never realised that stocktaking could be such fun. This hubby of yours is so funny."

"Oh yeah. Jack's hilarious. Do you think you might give us a couple of minutes in private?"

"Sure, I'll go and see what I can help Monty with."

I waited until she'd left the room and closed the door behind her, then turned my glare on Jack.

"So, what was it that Kiki was *helping* you with?"

"We're just stocktaking."

"Really? You always told me that you hated stocktaking because it was so boring."

"It is."

"It didn't sound like it."

"Kiki found a box of VHS videos under one of the shelving units. It must have been there from when the Stock sisters had the store. I reckon they must have sold them back in the day."

"So?"

"One of them was a Norman Wisdom movie. Kiki had never even heard of him; can you believe that?"

"Easily. She can't be more than twenty-five."

"I did my Norman Wisdom impression for her. That's what she was laughing at. Would you like to see me do Norman Wisdom?"

"Definitely not."

"Are you okay, Jill? You seem annoyed about something."

"I'm fine."

"Hang on. You're not jealous of Kiki, are you?"

"Don't be ridiculous."

"There's really no need to be."

"I've just said I'm not."

"Okay. How come you're in the village?"

"I—err—left something behind this morning."

"What?"

"It doesn't matter. I've got it now. I just popped in to say hello."

"Why don't you stay and have a coffee?"

"I can't. I need to get back."

"Okay, I'll see you tonight."

I stormed out of the shop without a word to Mr Ivers or Kiki, but I'm not sure they noticed because both of them were in hysterics. As I left the shop, I heard her say something about Mr Grimshaw. Whoever he was.

***

"Can I get a cup of tea, please, Jules?"

"Sure."

"Any calls?"

"Just a wrong number. A Mrs Nought wanted to order a board game. When I told her she had the wrong number, she got really cross."

"I have a bone to pick with you," Winky said.

"This really isn't the time. I'm not in the mood for your nonsense."

"You embarrassed me in front of my friends this morning."

"Did I? I'm so very sorry."

"And so you should—"

"Wait a minute. Correction: I actually meant to say that I don't give a flying fig."

"Charming. You should encourage the performing arts."

"I *was* being encouraging. I was encouraging you all to give it up before you embarrass yourselves any further."

"I'm not speaking to you ever again."

"Don't get my hopes up."

He skulked off to the other side of the room and turned his back on me. That gave me the perfect opportunity to sneak a few custard creams without him noticing. I opened the bottom drawer, only to find it empty except for a scribbled note that read: *I heard you had given up custard creams for your diet, so it seemed criminal to let these go to waste. Edna.*

How could she? I would strangle that fairy the next time I saw her.

"Are you okay, Jill?" Jules said, as she handed me my tea.

"Never been better."

I'd had my fill of ferrets, so I decided to turn my focus to the case of the missing racehorse—an altogether more majestic creature (pun intended). I still hadn't received the list of Ease Stables' clients from Sonny, and I suspected that Dez was still resisting giving up that information. It might not matter, though, because if I could find out how the horse had been taken from the stables, I was convinced that I would be much closer to identifying the abductor.

I made a call to the stables.

"Ease Stables, Honey Ease speaking."

"Hello, there," I said in my best upper-crust accent. "My name is Camilla Horton-Williams. I'd like to speak to someone about the possibility of stabling a number of horses with you."

"I can help you with that Mrs Horton—err—"

"Williams."

"You said horses. Plural?"

"That's right, my dear. You should know that I'm acting for my client, Sheik Atayl Fether. He has asked me to look at a number of stables and yours was one on his list."

"I'd be only too happy to show you and the sheik around, and to answer any questions you may have."

"It will just be me. The sheik is a very busy man, but he trusts my judgement."

"I understand. When would you like to pay us a visit?"

"The earlier, the better. How about tomorrow?"

"That's fine. What time?"

"Shall we say two o'clock?"

"I'll see you then."

***

Jack was already home by the time I got back to the old watermill and, judging by the smell that met me when I walked into the house, he'd made a start on dinner.

"I wasn't expecting you to be home yet," I said.

"Mr Ivers volunteered to do another shift, so I finished early."

"Did you get your stocktaking done?"

"Not quite. We should get it finished tomorrow."

"I'm sorry if I was a bit off when I came into the store."

"Forget it. You really don't have to be jealous of Kiki, you know."

"I've already told you that I'm *not* jealous."

"Good because you have no reason to be." He came over and gave me a hug. "You're the only woman I have eyes for."

"I know." I gave him a peck on the lips.

"And besides, Kiki's boyfriend is built like a tank."

"She has a boyfriend?"

"Yeah. Orlando. He came to pick her up this afternoon. He was friendly enough, but you wouldn't want to meet him down a dark alley."

Dinner was delicious, made even better because Jack decided we should open the bottle of wine that had been in the cupboard since Christmas. To show my gratitude for his making dinner, and because I was still feeling a little guilty about the way I'd acted at the store earlier, I volunteered to clear up and stack the dishwasher while Jack went and put his feet up in the lounge.

I'd barely made a start when he came charging back into the kitchen.

"Care to explain why there's a ferret in there, Jill?"

Oh bum! I'd completely forgotten about Sandy.

"Because that's where the TV is and Sandy likes watching soaps."

"I wasn't asking why it's in that room specifically. Why do we have a ferret in the house at all?"

"I need it for the F-O-F case I'm working on."

"The *what* case?"

"F-O-F. It stands for Friends Of Ferrets. The ex-treasurer has hired me to prove he didn't steal funds from the organisation."

"I'm not having a ferret in the lounge."

"I was going to put him in here, but like I said, he insists he wants to watch the TV. It's only for a couple of nights and then I'll take him back to the ferret sanctuary."

"Fine, but you can sit on the side of the sofa nearest to his hutch."

"Thanks, Jack. You're the best."

Chapter 14

As Mr Ivers had worked late the previous day, Jack had agreed that he would take the early shift. He was up and out of the house by six o'clock, leaving me to have a lie in. I was just enjoying a lovely dream about a giant jammy dodger when something tickled my nose. I assumed it was a fly, so I tried to swat it away, without opening my eyes. It didn't do any good because moments later, its tiny feet were back on my nose.

"Happy birthday to you. Happy birthday to you."

What the actual—?

I opened my eyes to find three teeny fairies perched on my nose, singing happy birthday.

"Happy birthday, dear Suzy. Happy birthday to you."

I sat bolt upright in bed, causing them to tumble onto the duvet.

"What's going on?" I demanded.

"Happy birthday, Suzy. From your friend, Jasmine."

"First, my name isn't Suzy. And second, I don't have a friend called Jasmine."

"Are you sure?"

"That my name isn't Suzy? Yeah, I'm pretty sure."

"Is it your birthday?"

"No, it isn't."

The three of them looked at one another, clearly non-plussed.

"Is this the Old Waterworks, Farnham?" One of them asked eventually.

"No, it's the Old Watermill, Middle Tweaking."

Two of them turned on the third one. "You've done it again, Jackie!"

"I was sure I'd got the right place this time," Jackie said, rather sheepishly.

"I'm really sorry about this," said one of the others. "We are greetings fairies, but we must have got the wrong address."

"You don't say."

"We'd better get going. We need to track down Suzy before she wakes up. Bye."

"Goodbye."

So much for my lie in.

I thought the morning couldn't get any worse, but as always, I was proved wrong.

"I was beginning to think you were never going to get up," Grandma said.

She was seated at the breakfast table, cup of tea in front of her, and a slice of toast in her hand.

"Make yourself at home, why don't you?"

"Do you always get up so late?"

"It isn't late, and I wouldn't be up yet if it wasn't for those stupid greetings fairies. They woke me up by singing happy birthday."

"It isn't your birthday."

"I know that. They got the wrong address. Anyway, never mind them. What makes you think you can just let yourself in whenever it takes your fancy?"

"I didn't let myself in. Jim did on his way out."

"How long have you been here?"

"Too long, but it's okay because I watched Greenfield Place with Sandy."

"Watched *what*?"

"Don't tell me you haven't heard of Greenfield Place.

It's the best soap on TV here in the human world."

"I don't have time to watch soaps."

"Your loss."

"Did you make any toast for me?"

"I would have done, but I didn't want to wreck your diet."

"How do you know—never mind. I assume you want something or is this yet another social call?"

"I was going to update you on the hotel sale, but if you're not interested." She made to stand up.

"I am interested. Who bought it?"

"I knew if I waited long enough, someone would come along who recognised the value of such a prime location."

"So, who is it?"

"A company called CCI."

"What are they going to do with it?"

"Use it as a combined convention centre and hotel, apparently."

"Who are CCI, anyway?"

"I haven't had many dealings with them directly. The solicitors took care of most of it. All I care about is that they have the money and that they can act quickly. If all goes to plan, the sale should be finalised within a few weeks."

"Congrats, I suppose."

Curiosity got the better of me, so after Grandma had left, I looked up CCI, and what I discovered left me speechless.

What do you mean you find that hard to believe?

Before setting off to the office, I decided to drop by the store to share the news with Jack who was alone behind the counter.

"No Kiki?"

"It's her day off. Monty will be in this afternoon. You okay?"

"Yeah, I just heard some interesting news about the hotel from Grandma."

"Did she tell you who's bought it?"

"She did." I held out my phone to show him the article I'd found. "It's these people."

"Cosplay Conventions International? Is that what I think it is?"

"Yeah. Shades of Clare and Tony."

Clare and Tony had been our next-door neighbours when we'd lived in Smallwash. To say they were cosplay fanatics would have been an understatement. Very few weekends went by when they didn't attend one cosplay convention or another.

"I don't understand." Jack looked confused. "Why would anyone want to hold a convention in an out-of-the-way place like Middle Tweaking?"

"I was wondering the same thing, so I did some research on them. They're building a network of relatively small locations all around the country, where they can hold small scale conventions, in addition to the larger national ones they run. Judging by their results so far, it seems to be a winning strategy."

"I suppose there are worse things that could have happened to the hotel."

"I agree, although I'm not sure the residents of Middle Tweaking are ready for what's about to hit them. Can you remember some of the outfits that Clare and Tony wore?"

"How could I forget?"

"I can't wait to see the vicar's face when he sees dozens

of hotdogs walking around the village."

"Or toothbrushes." Jack laughed.

***

I'd just parked in the basement of my office block when I got a phone call from Aunt Lucy asking if I could go over to Pamber because the twins wanted another meeting about Grandma's surprise birthday party.

"Sure, I'll come straight over."

The twins and Aunt Lucy were waiting for me in their function room. In the centre of the table was a huge birthday cake with the number 1000 iced in big red letters.

"That looks amazing, Aunt Lucy." I took the seat next to her.

"Thanks, Jill. I wanted to write happy birthday on it, but the twins insisted I did this."

I turned to the twins. "Are you sure that's a good idea? I think Aunt Lucy is right. A plain old happy birthday might be better."

"Rubbish." Pearl scoffed. "It's not every day that you're one thousand years old."

"Grandma will love it," Amber insisted.

"I hope you're right."

"We called this meeting to get an update," Pearl said. "Mum has done her bit as you can see. We've ordered in all the additional catering supplies, and we'll have this room trimmed up on the day."

Amber turned to me. "That just leaves you, Jill."

"I thought all I had to do was to get her here on the day?"

"That's right, but obviously that will need careful

planning ahead of time. What have you done so far?"

All eyes were on me, so I didn't think I could tell them that I hadn't given it a moment's thought since our last meeting.

"Don't worry. I've put a lot of careful planning into it."

"Good." Amber nodded her approval. "Care to share?"

"Probably best I don't. The fewer people who know, the less chance there is of it getting back to Grandma and spoiling the surprise."

"Fair enough," Pearl said.

Phew! I couldn't believe they'd bought it.

"Okay." Amber stood up. "It sounds like we have all our ducks in a row, so we'll all be back here a week on Sunday, at one o'clock, for the biggest party Candlefield has seen for years."

"A thousand years," Pearl quipped.

Back in the human world, the enormity of what I was expected to do hit me. How on earth was I going to get Grandma to go to Pamber for her surprise birthday party? That woman didn't do anything she didn't want to, so she was bound to insist on knowing why I wanted her to go with me to Pamber. If I lied, she would know—Grandma could smell a lie a million miles away. But if I told her the truth, she was bound to refuse to go. Contrary to the twins' wishful thinking, Grandma hated birthdays, surprises and being reminded of her age.

"Jill, I have those names you asked for," Jules said.

"What names?"

"You asked me to find possible accountants for you."

"Oh yeah, I'd forgotten about that."

"I spent a lot of time reading through the reviews and

the three names I have listed come out best. I've put the list on your desk."

"Thanks, Jules. Good job."

"I don't know why you're wasting your time with those," Winky said. "I told you that I'm a member of the Association of Chartered Certified Feline Accountants."

"I don't believe that for a minute, but even if you are, how would it look if I trusted my accounts to a cat?"

"No one need know. I could use my accountant name."

"Which is?"

"Donald Addemup."

"Forget it. I'm going to use one of these on this list."

"Your loss."

The three names on the list were: Sylvia Silver, Phillip Philmore and Laurence Enger. All my previous accountants had been men, so I decided I would give Sylvia Silver a call.

"Sylvia Silver Accountants, how may I assist you today?"

"Hi, my name is Jill Maxwell. I'm looking for a new accountant."

"You're very lucky because Sylvia has recently decided to take on a couple of new clients. May I ask the nature of your business?"

"I'm a private investigator."

"That sounds exciting."

"Not always."

"Sylvia likes to visit new clients at their premises for the first meeting. That way, she's able to get a feel for your business, and any particular requirements you may have. Would that be okay?"

"Sure."

"Let me just check her diary to see when she's free. Are you okay to hold for a minute?"

"Yeah."

Why did people choose such horrible hold-music? Where did they even get it from? Awful Hold Music Ltd?

"Sorry to keep you waiting. Sylvia could do Thursday morning if that works for you."

"That's fine."

"Excellent. Is ten o'clock okay?"

"Perfect."

***

The address that Ivor Payne had given me for Marcy Bowkoo was a flat on the third floor of an apartment block, just around the corner from where Kathy's first bridal shop was located.

I gained access to the building without any problems. I had intended to use magic to get inside her flat, but before I could cast the spell, I heard movement inside, so I rang the doorbell. Moments later, Leonard, Marcy's ex-husband, answered the door. I'm not sure which of the two of us was the most surprised.

"I wasn't doing anything wrong," he blurted out before I'd even had a chance to speak.

It was only then that I realised he must have remembered me from when I posed as a policewoman and warned him off.

"You shouldn't be here. I told you to stay away."

"How come you aren't in uniform?"

"I'm working plain clothes, but never mind that. What are you doing here?"

"I didn't go anywhere near Marcy after you came to see me, I promise. I assume you heard what happened to her."

"Yes, I'm aware."

"I still can't believe it." He was close to tears. "I know I was a bit of a prat, but I still loved her, you know."

"What are you doing in her apartment?"

"I don't really know." He looked down at his feet. "I just wanted to be near her things."

"Have you taken anything?"

"No, I promise. I was just looking around."

"Stand aside."

I pushed by him and walked into the unfamiliar apartment.

"You didn't say what you were doing here," he said.

"I'm part of the team investigating Marcy's death."

"I read that it was suicide."

"That's the official line for the moment, at least. Why don't you come inside, and we can talk."

I led the way into the lounge, which had Marcy written all over it: bold colours and the weirdest collection of furniture I'd ever seen. And yet, somehow, it seemed to work.

"Take a seat." I pointed to the faux-leather armchair.

"I really ought to be getting back."

"Sit down, Leonard!"

"I only wanted a small memento," he said. "Something to remember her by. I wasn't going to take anything of any value."

"Where were you last Tuesday?"

"*Tuesday*?"

"A week ago today. Where were you in the morning?"

"I—err—I'm not sure."

"Think."

"Tuesday. Tuesday." He tapped his forehead with his finger. "Hang on, yes, I remember. I was at the dentist." He opened his mouth as though that would somehow confirm what he was saying. "I had a root canal treatment. It took over two hours."

"I assume you can prove that."

"I can show you the tooth."

"No, thanks, but you can give me the name and address of your dentist."

"No problem." He took out his wallet from which he handed me an appointment card for the dentist.

"What did you think when you heard about Marcy?" I asked.

"I couldn't believe it. I still can't get my head around it."

"When you two were together, did she ever try to harm herself?"

"No, but she threatened to harm me a few times." He managed a smile. "She didn't mean it, though."

"Okay, that's all for now, but I might need to speak to you again."

"Am I going to get into trouble for being in here today?"

"I don't see any reason to take it any further, but you mustn't come back again."

"I won't. You have my word."

I waited until he'd left before carrying out a thorough search of the apartment. I was hoping that I might find something—anything—that would give me a clue as to who might have wanted Marcy dead, but I drew a blank.

I didn't trust Leonard as far as I could throw him, so I changed my appearance, posed as a policewoman, and paid a visit to his dentist, in order to verify his alibi. The young woman on reception, whose name was Sarah, was quickly able to confirm that he had indeed been undergoing root canal treatment at the time that Marcy plunged to her death.

Call it instinct, but I still didn't like the little scrote, so I gave Edna a call.

"Edna speaking."

"It's Jill Maxwell."

"Long time, no hear. I thought you must have retired. Or died."

"*Died*?"

"You must be getting on a bit now."

The barefaced cheek.

"I'll ignore that remark. I need somebody followed. Are you free at the moment?"

"I might be. That all depends on what it's worth."

"How about you do it in return for the custard creams you stole from my desk?"

"I took those as a favour to you, so you wouldn't break your diet."

"Yeah, right. Are you going to help me or not?"

"I'll do it for half my usual fee. Call it a goodwill gesture for the misunderstanding over the custard creams I took from your desk."

"Deal. I need you to follow this guy." I gave her Leonard's details and photograph.

"What's he done?"

"I don't know. Maybe nothing. Or maybe he had something to do with his ex-wife's death."

"What do you want me to do exactly? What am I looking out for?"

"I wish I knew. For now, just take a photo of everyone he comes into contact with."

Chapter 15

I had an appointment with Honey at Ease Stables at two o'clock. Or at least, one of my many alter egos, in the form of Camilla Horton-Williams, had the appointment. I couldn't turn up in my own car because that would give the game away. As there wasn't enough time to hire one, I pulled into the first layby after I had left Middle Tweaking, and consulted my ever-reliable spell book app. A quick search turned up a number of car-related spells, but one stood out: Transform car. This seemingly simple spell would allow me to change my car into any model I required. Ideal. The only question was what model of car should I choose? As I would be posing as the rather posh Camilla Horton-Williams, I needed something expensive, but not too flashy, so I opted for a Porsche SUV.

I had a little time to spare before my appointment, and I was absolutely starving because the only thing I'd had to eat so far was a banana for breakfast. Obviously, in order to stick to my diet, I would need to find somewhere that I'd be able to buy healthy, natural food.

It was the smell of burgers, bacon and onions that drew me to the fast-food truck parked in a layby. The name on the sign was Greasy Joe's, and unless I had completely missed my guess, the gentleman behind the counter was none other than Joe himself.

"Hello, young lady. Nice motor."

"Thanks."

"What can I get for you today?"

"Per chance, do you happen to sell salads?"

"*Salads*? Does it look like I sell *salads*?"

It definitely didn't, but at least no one could say I hadn't tried my best to stay on the diet.

"What do you recommend, then?"

"How hungry are you?"

"Extremely. I've only had a banana so far today."

"A *banana*? That won't do. I think you're going to need Joe's Body Slammer."

"Okay, that's what I'll have then."

There were a number of plastic tables and chairs in the layby, and it took all my strength just to carry the Body Slammer to the nearest one.

"Wow, lady, not many people manage to eat all of the slammer," he said when I returned my empty plate.

"That was amazing, thanks."

"Don't forget to tell all your friends."

"I'll be sure to do that."

Once again, it was Honey Ease who answered the intercom and buzzed me through the gate. I wasn't worried that she would recognise me because I'd made myself look like Kathy and, thanks to the 'designer clothes' spell, I looked fabulous.

Honey was waiting for me outside the house.

"Did you find us okay?" she asked as I got out of the car.

"Yes, no problem at all. Thank you for agreeing to see me at such short notice."

"My pleasure. I'm excited to hear the sheik's plans."

"You realise this is just a preliminary look-see, I hope?"

"Of course."

"As I explained on the phone, the sheik has tasked me with researching a number of stables, to see which will be the best fit for him."

"I'm confident that you'll be happy with what you see

today, and if you have any questions, please feel free to ask."

"Thank you."

"Would you care to come inside for something to eat before we start?"

"I've just eaten, actually. I'm keen to get started, so perhaps we could begin with a tour of the stables?"

"Absolutely. This way, please."

She led the way past the house and across the extensive rear gardens to the large stable complex.

"Thomas!" She shouted to a man who had just emerged from one of the stalls. "Come and meet Mrs Horton-Williams. Remember I told you that she'd be visiting today."

"A pleasure to meet you, Mrs Horton-Williams." He made a small bowing gesture.

"Thomas is our stable manager," Honey said.

"How long have you worked here, Thomas?" I asked.

"Fourteen years."

"Rather than take up any more of Honey's time, maybe you could show me around the stables?"

"Sure." He turned to Honey. "If that's okay?"

My suggestion had clearly caught Honey off-guard, but she quickly recovered, and said, "Absolutely. Thomas, give me a call when you're done, and I'll pop back to collect Mrs Horton-Williams."

"What exactly would you like to see, Mrs Horton-Williams?" He asked once Honey had left us alone.

"Please call me Camilla. Why don't you give me the tour and point out anything that you think would help me sell your stables to the sheik. Is that okay with you?"

"Absolutely."

Thomas was in his element, as he showed me around. He clearly loved his job and was proud of the winners that the stables had produced.

"Do you ride, Camilla?" he suddenly asked.

I (Jill Maxwell, that is) had told Sonny that I'd been brought up around horses, and that I was an experienced horse rider, but I'd only done that because I thought it might help me to secure the case. Fortunately, it had worked, and I hadn't been called upon to ride a horse. In my guise as Camilla Horton-Williams, I wasn't about to tempt fate by telling the same lie to Thomas.

"Me?" I laughed. "Why no. Those beasts scare me to death."

"Oh, I just thought that—"

"You're probably wondering why the sheik would place his faith in me, to decide which stables he should entrust his horses to, when I can't even ride."

"No, I—err—it's none of my business."

"I'm no rider, but you could say that horse racing has been a part of my life since I was a young girl."

"That makes sense. Anyway, we've more or less seen all there is to see here. Would you like to go over to the gallops?"

"No, thanks, I think I've seen all I need to. You've been most helpful." Having gained Thomas' trust, it was time to probe deeper. "There is just one thing. The stables are a little quieter than I expected. How is business at the moment?"

The question had clearly caught him off-guard because he stumbled over his answer.

"I—err—well, I suppose it is a little quiet since McConnel withdrew his horses, but I'm sure things will pick up soon. They usually do."

"Oh yes, I read about McConnel," I lied. "What happened there?"

"It—err—" By now, Thomas had clearly realised he'd said too much. "It wasn't anything to do with the stables. I believe he'd decided to get out of the business. Yes, that was it. Shall I give Honey a call, and tell her you're done here?"

"Yes, please."

Honey must have been waiting on tenterhooks for the call because she answered immediately, and a few minutes later she rejoined us.

"How did it go?" she asked, somewhat apprehensively.

"Excellently," I said. "Thomas is a credit to your business."

"He certainly is." She seemed to breathe a sigh of relief. "Do you need him for anything else, Mrs Horton-Williams?"

"No, we'll let him get back to his work."

"What do you think?" Honey said.

"I'm very impressed, but that's no more than I expected. If your stables didn't have a first-class reputation, they wouldn't be on the sheik's shortlist."

"That's very kind of you. Why don't we go to the house, so you can meet my father. He's very keen to talk to you about the sheik's plans."

"I'd love to, but I'm on a very tight schedule."

"Do you have everything you need from us to allow the sheik to reach a decision?"

"Yes, I think so. Oh wait, there is just one more thing."

"What's that?"

"While I'm here, I was hoping to see Majestic Tears.

Such an incredible horse. I didn't see him during my tour with Thomas. Would it be possible to do that now?"

Although she did her best to disguise it, she was unable to fully hide the look of horror on her face.

"Majestic?" she eventually managed to splutter.

"Yes, please. Where are you hiding him?"

"I'm afraid he isn't here."

"Oh?"

"He picked up a slight strain yesterday on the gallops. Nothing serious, but Dad didn't want to take any chances, so Majestic is spending a couple of days with the vet."

Credit where it was due: that wasn't a bad recovery.

"How disappointing. Still, his health is the most important thing. Right, I'd better be going."

"Do you have any idea when the sheik will reach a decision?"

"I can't say for sure because I still have several other stables to visit. Then, I'll compile my report and recommendations and submit them to him. Realistically, it's unlikely to be less than a couple of months."

"I see. Well, if you think of anything else you need to know, just give me a call. And if you'd like to visit again, you have only to ask."

"Thank you. I don't think that will be necessary. Although, it would be nice to see Majestic. We'll see."

Honey showed me to my car.

Except that it wasn't my car. Well, it *was* my car, but it was no longer the Porsche. That would teach me not to read the fine print on the spell instructions. It must have been one of those time-limited spells, which only lasted a few hours. I hated those stupid spells with a passion.

I'm not sure who was most shocked: Me or Honey.

"Someone has stolen your Porsche." She looked mortified. "They must have driven off in it and left this old banger behind."

Old banger? My car had definitely seen better days but that was a little harsh.

I cast the 'forget' spell and then quickly recast the spell to change my car back into the Porsche.

"Are you okay, Honey? You're a little pale."

"I—err—yes, I'm fine. I just went a little lightheaded."

"Would you like me to help you back into the house?"

"No, I'm okay now, thanks."

"Right, well, thanks again for your time."

Thomas' admission that the stables were quieter than normal explained why Honey was so keen to land the sheik's business. He'd also let slip that someone called McConnel had withdrawn his horses from Ease Stables. I would need to find out what had prompted that decision because I wasn't buying Thomas' explanation. Could the real reason be in any way connected to Majestic Tears' disappearance?

***

"There's a new crime series starting on TV tonight," Jack said, as we ate the dinner he'd prepared.

"What time?"

"Eight o'clock."

"That's no good for me. I'm going to F-O-F, remember?"

"The ferret thing?"

"None other."

"Does that mean we're going to see the back of what's-his-face in there?" He gestured towards the lounge.

"His name is Sandy, and he'll be with us for one more night."

"Why?"

"Because after the F-O-F meeting ends tonight, it will be too late to take him back to the sanctuary. I'll have to take him in the morning."

"Fair enough. How did your visit to the stables go?"

"Okay, they're clearly not doing as well as they have in the past, but I'm not sure that has anything to do with Majestic Tears' disappearance."

"You managed to pull off the posh bird look, then?"

"Yeah, it was another Oscar-worthy performance, even if I do say so myself."

"It was your modesty that first attracted me to you."

"I had another meeting with Aunt Lucy and the twins this morning about Grandma's birthday party."

"How did that go?"

"Aunt Lucy has made the cake already—it's amazing. And the twins have organised the rest of the catering. I've just got to come up with some way to get her to the party on time."

"How are you going to do that?"

"I don't have a clue."

"I can't go yet," Sandy protested as I tried to get him into the basket. "I'm watching this." He pointed at the TV.

"What is it?"

"Rosedale Heights."

"Never heard of it."

"What? How can you not know about Rosedale Heights? It's the second-best soap on TV at the moment."

"I'm sorry, but we have to get going. I don't want to be late for the meeting."

"What will I have to do at this meeting?" Sandy asked.

"Nothing. Just act ferret-like."

"I *am* a ferret."

"Yeah, right. That's what I meant. Just be yourself."

"Will there be many other ferrets there?"

"I imagine so."

"Any hot ladies?"

"I don't know, and if there are, don't go getting any ideas. This is strictly work. Okay?"

"You're no fun."

I eventually managed to drag him away from the TV and placed him in the basket.

"We're off," I shouted to Jack.

"Have fun with your ferret buddies."

He was enjoying this way too much.

Chapter 16

I managed to park on Tontine Road, just a few yards from Tontine Chapel, which from the outside, at least, looked like it should have been condemned and demolished years ago. I was beginning to wonder if this was the right place, or if there was another chapel on that road, when I spotted a noticeboard on which was pinned a flyer for F-O-F.

"This place is a dump," Sandy observed from inside the basket.

He wasn't wrong.

"It's probably better inside."

It wasn't.

To my amazement, the place was already full of people. Is there a collective noun for a bunch of ferret lovers? Saddos, maybe? As far as I could make out, I was the only woman in the room, which might explain why everyone seemed to be staring at me.

"Where are the other ferrets?" Sandy said.

It was only then I realised that no one else had a ferret with them.

"I've no idea," I whispered. "It seems I may have committed some kind of ferret faux pas."

I hadn't moved an inch since I'd first stepped into the room. I was just wondering what my next move should be when a man dressed in a velvet jacket approached me.

"Good evening, young lady. I take it this is your first visit to F-O-F?"

"Err, yeah, it is."

"I thought as much." He gestured towards the basket containing Sandy. "Do you know what the first rule of F-

O-F club is?"

"Don't talk about F-O-F club?"

"No, it's no ferrets are allowed at F-O-F meetings. Don't worry. A lot of new members are caught out by that one. In the early years, we used to allow ferrets in the meetings, but members were so engrossed in looking at the little creatures that we never got any work done."

"What exactly do you do here, then?"

"The focus of F-O-F is the welfare and wellbeing of these lovely creatures. My name is Bernt. I'm the vice chairman of F-O-F."

Before I could introduce myself, another man, wearing tartan trousers, joined us.

"Who do we have here Mr Toste?"

Bernt Toste seemed annoyed to have been joined by the second guy. "I don't know yet, Gordon. I've only just met the young lady."

"I'm Jill Maxwell." I saw no reason not to use my own name on this occasion. "Bernt was just explaining that it's not the done thing to bring ferrets to these meetings."

"I'm Gordon Sandwich, the current chair of F-O-F."

"I'm pleased to meet you both, and I'm sorry about bringing Sandy."

"*Sandy*?"

"That's my ferret."

"Ah, yes. Not to worry." Gordon grinned a scary grin. "We won't hold it against you, will we, Bernt?"

"Certainly not. Tell me, Jill, how did you come to hear about F-O-F?"

"Rick Hits at the Ferret Sanctuary told me about it."

"Such a wonderful man. We've raised quite a bit of cash for his sanctuary over the years."

"Is it okay for me to stay or would you rather I took Sandy home?"

"You can stay," Gordon said. "But it might be better to leave Sandy over in the corner, so as not to distract the others."

"Okay, great. Thanks."

"Can't we get out of here?" Sandy said, as I deposited his basket in the corner of the room. "This bunch are giving me the creeps."

"No, we can't. I have to circulate, to see what I can find out about the stolen money."

"Be quick, then. I don't want to miss tonight's episode of Hunter's Legacy."

I wasn't good at making small talk at the best of times, but trying to do it with a bunch of ferret-loving losers proved to be nigh on impossible.

"Hi, I'm Jill." I introduced myself to the most normal looking man I could find in the room.

"How often do you clip his nails?" he said in response.

"Sorry?"

"The little guy over there." He nodded towards Sandy. "How often do you clip his nails?"

"I—err—" Having no idea how to answer, I decided to turn the question back on him. "How often would you recommend?"

"Well, there lies a whole can of worms. There's a school of thought that says they should be done every four weeks, but I don't subscribe to that idea."

"No?"

"In my opinion, that idea is outdated. I firmly believe that every thirty days is the optimum interval."

"Right. An interesting thought."

"It's rather more than a *thought*. That figure is based upon extensive research and experience."

This conversation was getting me nowhere, so I decided to grasp the nettle and get straight to the matter-in-hand.

"Do you know Kevin Wright?"

"*Kevin*? I—err—why do you ask?"

"I met him a while ago. When I was buying Sandy, actually. He was the one who first mentioned F-O-F. I thought I might see him here today, but he doesn't appear to be here."

"Kevin is no longer a member of F-O-F."

"Really? He seemed so enthusiastic about the organisation when we spoke. Why did he leave?"

"I—err—" He glanced around nervously. "Sorry, I've just seen someone I need to speak to. Bye."

And off he shot across the room.

I was just wondering who I should talk to next when someone tapped me on the shoulder from behind. I spun around to come face to face with a man's chest. His head was two feet above mine.

"Hello, up there," I said.

"Hi. I'm Callum Long."

"Jill."

"We don't get many ladies in here. In fact, I think you're the first one to stay for more than five minutes."

"Why's that? Aren't women interested in ferrets?"

"I'm sure a few are, but one look at this crowd and they turn tail and run a mile." He smiled. "How long have you kept ferrets, Jill?"

"To be honest, Sandy is my first, and I've only had him for a few months, but I'm well and truly smitten. They're such delightful creatures."

"I have ten of them at home."

"That's a lot."

"Too many, according to my wife. Now ex-wife. She divorced me a year ago."

"Sorry to hear that."

"Don't be. I should have known better than to get together with someone who didn't share my love for these beautiful creatures. What about you? How does your other half feel about Sandy?"

His line of questioning led me to believe he'd mistaken this for a speed-dating meeting, so I decided to employ my world class flirting skills, in order to get him to open up.

"I'm separated from my husband. To tell you the truth, that's why I got Sandy."

"Sorry, I don't understand."

"Jack, that's my husband, doesn't like animals of any kind. He wouldn't allow me to have a pet in the house."

"No wonder you left him. I don't know what I'd do without my ferrets. Do you plan on coming here every week, Jill?"

"I'm not sure. I'll have to see how it goes tonight, but things have certainly picked up since you came over to talk to me."

See! What did I tell you? World class flirting at its best.

"Would you like me to tell you about my ferrets, Jill?"

"That would be great."

How I got through the next thirty minutes without falling into a coma, I'll never know. According to Callum, every ferret has its own individual personality, and he proved the point by describing each of his in mind-numbing detail.

I suddenly realised he'd stopped talking and was looking to me for a reaction.

"They all sound amazing."

"They are. Maybe you'd like to come and meet them some time."

"I'd love to." By now, I felt like I had him eating out of the palm of my hand, so it was time to employ my well-crafted interrogation technique (also, for the record, world class). "Can I ask you a question, Callum?"

"Of course. Anything."

"I heard a rumour that there had been some kind of scandal surrounding F-O-F. What do you know about it?"

"*Scandal*?" He took a step back. "What kind of scandal?"

"I heard that the treasurer ran off with F-O-F's money. Is that true?"

"Err, sorry, I just remembered that I promised to talk to—err—Henry."

And with that, he rushed over to the opposite side of the room. So much for my world class flirting and interrogation techniques.

That pretty much set the pattern for the rest of the evening. No matter what approach I took, as soon as I raised the subject of the missing money, the person I was talking to would clam up and, shortly afterwards, take their leave.

After two hours, I knew more than I cared to about ferrets, but I'd learned pretty much nothing about the missing funds. It was clear that no one intended to discuss the subject with me, so I decided to save my sanity and leave.

"Hey, what about me?"

I was almost through the door when I heard Sandy

calling after me.

"I hadn't forgotten about you," I lied.

"It didn't look like it."

Back at the car, I placed the basket on the passenger seat beside me.

"I hope you realise that I've missed my soap," Sandy moaned.

"Sorry."

"Was it worthwhile?"

"No, it was a total bust. As soon as I tried to raise the subject of the missing money, everyone clammed up. I may as well have stayed at home."

"Maybe it wasn't."

"Maybe what wasn't what?"

"Maybe the evening wasn't a bust. These losers may not have wanted to talk to you, but some of them thought nothing of talking in front of me. After all, I'm just a stupid ferret."

"What are you saying?"

"It probably isn't important. Although, they were talking in hushed voices, as though they didn't want anyone to hear."

"Tell me."

"What's it worth?"

"You can have some custard creams when we get back."

"*Custard creams*?" He scoffed. "The information I have is worth far more than a few biscuits."

"So you say, but how do I know that's true?"

"They were talking about someone called Kevin, and they mentioned a safe. Does that sound interesting?"

"Okay, yes. What do you want?"

"It's not so much what I want as what I *don't* want."

"You're talking in riddles now."

"I don't want to go back to the sanctuary."

"Why not? It seems like a perfectly nice place, and Rick is a great guy."

"He's okay. Better than most, but I'd still rather be somewhere else."

"Where?" I asked, but I had an awful feeling that I already knew the answer.

"The Old Watermill is very nice. I'm sure I could be happy there."

"No way!"

"In that case, you'll never know what I overheard tonight."

"Come on, Sandy. The conversation you overheard may help to prove a man is innocent of stealing."

"You know what my terms are."

"Jack will never stand for it."

"I'm sure you'll be able to talk him around."

Blast this ferret. He had me over a barrel and he knew it.

"I might be able to persuade Jack to allow you to stay at the Old Watermill—"

"Yay!"

"But he's never going to go for you living in the house with us. I might be able to convince him to let you live in the hutch in the garden."

"That's no good."

"It's the best I can do. If you can't accept that, I guess I'll just have to continue my investigation without the information you have."

He considered it for a minute, then said, "What about my soaps? I can put up with living in the garden, but I can't do without my soaps."

"But they're all rubbish."

"That's my final offer. Either I get my soaps or there's no deal."

"Okay. I'll find some way for you to watch your soaps in the hutch."

"Do you give me your word?"

"Yes, I promise. Now, what did you hear?"

"I'd been watching you flit from one guy to another, seemingly with little or no success, when two of them came and stood close to my basket."

"Who were they? Do you know?"

"The first guy's name was something like *burn*."

"That's Bernt Toste, the vice chairman."

"I didn't hear the other guy's name, but he was tall. Really tall."

"That was probably Callum Long. What did they say?"

"The tall guy told Toasty that you'd asked about the treasurer. Toasty looked really worried, and he asked what he'd said to you. The tall guy said he hadn't told you anything because he didn't know anything. After the tall guy had walked away, Toasty called another man over."

"Who?"

"How should I know? I'm a ferret not a clairvoyant. He was wearing some awful trousers, though."

"Tartan ones?"

"Yeah. They should be illegal."

"Never mind the critique of his sartorial choices. What did they say to one another?"

"Bernt asked if they should let Dugger know that you'd been sniffing around, asking questions."

"*Dugger*? Are you sure that's what he said?"

"I think so, but they were talking really quietly at this

point."

"What did the other guy say in response?"

"That they should leave well alone."

"That's it?"

"Yeah."

Interesting. Perhaps this evening hadn't been a complete waste of time after all.

Chapter 17

The next morning, I couldn't bear the thought of yet another bowl of fruit for breakfast, but if Jack saw me eating my cereal, he'd give me a hard time for breaking the stupid diet. All was not lost, though, because I had a cunning plan.

I know what you're thinking: how can one person come up with so many cunning plans? What can I say? It's a gift.

First, I made sure I got down to the kitchen before Jack, then poured myself a bowl of Chococandy pops. And here's the cunning part: I cast a spell to make my cereal look like a bowl of muesli. Brilliant or what?

"I never thought I'd see the day." Jack stared in disbelief at what he thought was a bowl of muesli. "Are you feeling okay, Jill?"

"I feel fine. Why?"

"You're eating muesli."

"Oh, this? I thought I'd give it a try." I put a spoonful in my mouth. "It's actually quite tasty."

"I've been telling you that for years."

"What are you having?" I said.

"To be honest, I'm not all that hungry this morning. I'll just have a spoonful of yours."

Before I could stop him, he'd picked up a spoon, scooped up some of the cereal/muesli and popped it into his mouth.

Oh bum!

"What the—?" His face was a picture. "This isn't muesli."

"Of course it is. Look."

"I'm not stupid, Jill. This is that chocolate rubbish of yours. You've made it look like muesli, haven't you?"

Busted.

"I needed sugar."

"Why couldn't you just be honest about it?"

"Because I knew you'd be disappointed in me."

"It's got nothing to do with me. You're the one who should be disappointed in yourself."

"Fine. I won't eat it, but you're to blame if I collapse later."

"Eat it. I don't care."

"It's too late now. You've spoiled it for me."

We sat in silence for a couple of minutes, then he said, "I'll be glad to see the back of that ferret and his awful soap operas."

"Hmm, we need to talk about that."

"Jill! What have you done?"

"Sandy won't be going back today."

"When will he be going back, then?"

"I kind of told him he could stay here permanently."

"You did what? Why?"

"He overheard some important information at the F-O-F meeting yesterday, and he refused to tell me unless I agreed he could stay."

"Are you insane? I'm not sharing the lounge with that ferret for another minute."

"You don't have to."

"But you just said you'd told him that he could stay."

"I did, but not in the house. We reached a compromise."

"What kind of compromise?"

"I said he could stay but he would have to live in the hutch in the garden."

"That's not quite so bad, I suppose."

"There's a little more to it, though."

"What?"

"I also agreed he'd be able to watch his soaps in his hutch."

"Out in the garden? How are you going to do that?"

"I don't know. Buy a small TV, I guess."

"There's no electricity out there."

"I'll figure it out."

"I hope the information he gave you was worth it."

So did I.

I bumped into Goldie Barr on my way out to the car.

"Hey, Jill. Off to work?"

"Yeah. You look better than the last time I saw you. Have there been any more strange goings on at your house?"

"No, thank goodness. I'm beginning to think it was probably all in my mind. I'm sorry for freaking out on you before."

"Don't worry about it."

"Have you heard about the hotel?" she said.

"That it's been sold? Yeah."

"But did you hear who's bought it?"

I decided to play dumb. "No."

"Some company that holds cosplay conventions."

"What's that?"

"It's where people get dressed up in costumes. Superheroes and that kind of thing."

"How weird."

"I don't know what to think about it, Jill. I'm worried that we might get all kinds of weirdos wandering around the village. I'm not the only one who is concerned; there's a meeting in the village hall to discuss it, apparently."

"I haven't heard about that."

"The vicar was supposed to be delivering flyers to all the residents."

"Right. Well, thanks for letting me know."

***

For a brief moment, when I walked into the outer office where there were three huge woollen scarves on Jules' desk.

"Been knitting, Jules?" I said.

"I didn't make them. Mrs V dropped by earlier. She said that there was one for me, and one each for you and Jack."

"Right. Did she want to see me?"

"I don't think so. She was just delivering these. Which ones do you want?"

"You can choose first."

"Okay, I'll have the orange one."

"Fine. I'll have the green and white one. Jack can have that horrible brown one." I grinned. "Jules, I need you to do something for me."

"Sure." She picked up a pen to take notes.

"Can you see what you can find out about a guy called McConnel."

"First name?"

"No idea, but he's a racehorse owner."

"Okay." She looked up, expecting more.

"The only other thing I know is that he used to keep his horses at Ease Stables, but he pulled them out of there."

"I'll get straight onto it."

Winky was sitting on my desk.

"How many times do I have to tell you? Don't sit on my desk."

He mouthed something and touched his throat.

"What did you say?"

He grabbed a pen and scribbled a note: **Can't talk. I need to rest my throat for the competition.**

"Fine by me." A few days of Winky's silence was always welcome.

He scribbled another note: **I need a favour.**

"No."

More scribbling: **You don't even know what it is yet.**

"It doesn't matter. The answer is no."

Another note: **Please, this is really important.**

"What?"

A quick scribble produced: **I need you to take me to the barbers' shop choir competition.**

"In Ghost Town? Why do you need me to take you?"

His writing was getting worse: **I've never really spent any time over there. I'm worried I might get lost trying to find Spirits' Central Hall.**

"I've not spent much time over there either."

More desperate scribbling: **Pretty please.**

"With sugar on top?"

He nodded.

"Write it down."

He wrote: **Pretty please with sugar on top. Will you take me to the competition?**

"I'll think about it."

He shot me such a look.

"Okay, okay, I'll take you."

The final grovelling note read: **You're the best. Haven't I always said so?**

***

I knew nothing about Jade Holdings, so I searched online to see what I could find out about them. I wasn't much wiser after I'd finished. Something to do with computers and clouds, as far as I could see. I would just have to wing it (for a change). They were located only a fifteen-minute walk from my office.

"Jules, I'm going to pay a visit to Jade Holdings, then afterwards I'm going to see Kevin Wright. I'm not sure if or when I'll be back."

"Okay, Jill. Have you got your scarves?"

"Yeah, they're in my bag. Call me if anything urgent crops up."

"Will do."

As I walked down the high street, I noticed a new shop, on the other side of the road, called And All Things Nice. Curiosity got the better of me, so I nipped over to take a closer look.

Big mistake!

The display in the window was full of the most amazing cakes that I'd ever seen—they looked even better than Aunt Lucy's, and that was saying something. If it hadn't been for my diet, I would have been tempted to go inside.

"Hi," the young woman behind the counter greeted me with a smile.

What? I only went inside to get a better look. Sheesh, do you think I have no willpower whatsoever?

"Hi. I haven't noticed this shop before."

"We only opened a couple of days ago. That's why

we're running this offer." She pointed to a large notice on the wall behind her.

"Eighty percent off all cakes? That's really generous."

"Yes, but the offer ends today, so if you see anything you fancy, now is the time."

See anything I fancy? I didn't see anything I *didn't* fancy. But a diet is a diet, and my iron willpower wasn't going to be swayed by discounts no matter how generous.

"Would you like me to put that in a box for you?"

"No, it's okay, I'll eat it now. Thanks."

What? If it had been seventy percent or less, I would have been able to ignore it, obviously. But, come on, who can turn their back on an eighty percent discount? They were practically giving them away. And, just for the record, the cake tasted every bit as good as it looked. Yummy!

Before going into the building that housed Jade Holdings, I checked my reflection in the window to make sure I'd brushed off all the crumbs. Inside, a man and woman, dressed in identical navy-blue suits, were seated behind the reception desk. The woman was on the phone, so it was the man who greeted me.

"Good morning, madam, and welcome to Jade Holdings."

"Good morning. I'd like to see Rhonda Elpme, please."

"I'm afraid that Rhonda is no longer employed by Jade Holdings. May I ask what it's in connection with?"

"I met Rhonda at a conference some time ago, and I happened to mention that my company might be revisiting its cloud computing strategy. She suggested I get in touch when we were ready to do that. It's my fault,

I should have called first. It's just that I happened to be in the area and—"

"I'm sure someone else will be able to help you. What's your name, please?"

"Ruby Stone."

"And your company name?"

"Stone and Associates."

"If you'd care to take a seat for a couple of minutes, I'll make a quick call."

"Okay, thanks."

I'd only just sat down when another guy appeared and came over to talk to me.

"Ruby? Hi, I'm Justin. Harvey tells me that you wanted to talk about your company's cloud computing strategy."

"That's right. I was hoping to talk to Rhonda, but I understand she no longer works with you."

"Rhonda left quite recently, but she wouldn't have been the one you needed to speak to anyway. Rhonda was in marketing. You need to talk to technical, and that's me. Shall we go up to my office?"

"Sure."

We took the lift to the second floor, then walked down a corridor until he came to a door with **J. Truman** printed on the glass.

"Have a seat, Ruby. Can I get you a drink?"

"No, thanks. I'm fine."

"Why don't you tell me about your current cloud infrastructure?"

"It's—err—pretty much standard."

"*Standard*?"

"Yeah, but I feel we've outgrown it."

"Perhaps you could give me a little more detail?"

"Actually, I'm the CEO, so I don't get too involved with the detail, but I did hand Rhonda a full specification of our set up. I was hoping that we'd be able to use that as a starting point to our discussion today."

"Oh? Unfortunately, as I mentioned, Rhonda no longer works here."

"That's disappointing. I don't suppose she could have left the spec behind when she left, could she?"

"I've no idea."

"Could you take a look?"

"Err, sure. I suppose I could pop upstairs and see if I can find anything amongst Rhonda's stuff."

"Would you mind?"

"Not at all. It might take a few minutes, though. Are you sure you're okay to wait?"

"Absolutely."

As soon as Justin was out of the door, I cast the 'invisible' spell, and followed him up the stairs to the next floor. At an unmarked door, he entered a code into the lock and then walked into an open-plan office. Fortunately, the door closed very slowly, allowing me adequate time to slide in behind him. The large office was divided by screens into small cubicles. Justin walked to the far side of the room where he took a seat in a cubicle, which was occupied by a man with a bald head and ginger beard. I followed him, so I could listen to their conversation.

"Hey, Brian, did Rhonda mention anything about a company called Stone and Associates before she jumped ship?"

"Not that I remember. Why?"

"There's a woman in my office from Stone and

Associates. She reckons that she met Rhonda at a conference. According to her, Rhonda invited her to come in to discuss her company's cloud infrastructure."

"Which conference?"

"She didn't say."

"That doesn't make sense. Rhonda would only be there to hand out flyers and find hot leads. If anyone had asked her anything technical, she would have passed them onto one of the techies."

"That's what I thought. There's something weird about the woman downstairs."

"Weird how?"

"I asked her what kind of cloud setup her company had, and she said *standard*."

"What does that mean?"

"It means she has no idea what she's talking about. She reckons she handed a spec to Rhonda. That's why I'm up here. I'm supposed to be trying to find it."

"I suppose it's just possible she did give it to Rhonda."

"If she had, Rhonda would have passed it on to you, wouldn't she?"

"Normally, yeah, but she didn't give me anything from Stone and Associates. I've never heard of them."

"What shall I tell Ruby?"

"Who's Ruby?"

"The woman in my office."

"There's not much you can tell her. If she's for real, then she'll need to resubmit the spec."

"Okay, Brian. Thanks."

I followed Justin out, but I didn't bother returning to his office. Instead, I waited until I was back on the street before reversing the 'invisible' spell. I had little or nothing to show for my visit to Jade Holdings, so I would need to speak to Rhonda Elpme.

Chapter 18

Sandy wouldn't allow me to move his hutch outside until he had something to watch his soaps on out there. And Jack would have a hissy fit if he had to spend another night with that ferret in the lounge, so I had to find a suitable TV.

After leaving Jade Holdings, I made my way to the high street, and called in at a shop called Screens, which if the window display was anything to go by, sold TVs of all shapes and sizes.

Business must have been slow because I'd no sooner walked through the door than two men made a beeline for me. The taller one came from my lefthand side, the other came from my right. It was clear that they were in a race to reach me first. It was the shorter one who won the race, leaving his colleague visibly annoyed.

"Welcome to Screens!" The triumphant man enthused. "My name is Ben. How can I help you today?"

"I need a TV."

"We have plenty of those. Did you have anything in mind? 4K? QLED?"

I didn't have the first idea what either of those was, but I didn't say so. Instead, I said, "Nothing fancy. I just need something small."

"How small?"

I held my hands about a foot apart.

"That's really small. Are you sure?"

"Positive. And it will need to work out in the garden."

"Like in a summer house?"

"Sort of, but much smaller."

"I see." I could tell by his expression that he was

beginning to regret winning the race to serve me. "Our smaller TVs are over the other side of the store."

I followed him over there.

"There's quite a few to choose from." He pointed to a shelf that contained a number of TVs.

"Don't you have anything smaller?"

"I'm afraid not. Is there any reason it needs to be so small?"

"It's a small summer house. Very small." I looked again at the TVs on offer. "That one at the end might be okay."

"Great." His smile returned as he sensed a sale.

"Will it work out in the garden?"

"Do you have Wi-Fi in the house?"

"We do."

"Then there shouldn't be a problem."

"What about power?"

"Don't you have a power supply in the summerhouse?"

"No."

His smile evaporated.

"The TV will need power to work. Maybe you could run an extension cord from the house?"

"I'd rather not."

"In that case, you're going to need a TV that takes rechargeable batteries, but I'm afraid we don't stock those. There isn't much call for them."

"Do you have any idea where I might get one?"

"Sorry, no idea."

It was obvious he'd lost all interest in me and was already eyeing a couple of other customers who had just walked into the store.

"Okay, I guess I'll leave it."

How could buying a TV for a ferret be so difficult?

***

Back at the office, Jules had some good news.

"I think I've found that McConnel guy."

"Great stuff. What did you find out?"

"Like you said, he's a racehorse owner. Very successful, by the look of it." She handed me a few sheets of paper. "I printed these recent news articles about him."

"Thanks, Jules. Good job."

When I walked into my office, Winky was on the desk. He mouthed something, then pointed to the writing pad: **We're out of full cream milk.**

"You'll have to wait until I can get you some in the morning."

Clearly unhappy with my response, he scribbled: **I need milk to keep my throat lubricated for the competition.**

"Okay, I'll ask Jules to go and get some." Without thinking it through, I went out to Jules and said, "Do you think you could pop out and buy some full cream milk?"

"Sorry?"

"Full cream—" Oh bum! What was I doing?

"I knew it, Jill. You're still not over that cat, are you?"

"No, it's—err—"

"It's okay, I get it. When I was a kid and BoBo died, I was devastated for weeks."

"*BoBo*?"

"My hamster."

"Right. No, honestly, it's not like that. I just have a craving for some whole milk. Would you mind?"

"Sure, but if you ever feel like you need to speak to someone about the grief you're still feeling, I know a good therapist."

"I'm fine. Just go and get the milk, would you?"

"See what you've done," I said to Winky. "Jules thinks I'm losing my marbles."

He scribbled another note: **Losing? You lost those a long time ago.**

While Jules was out, I read the various articles that she'd printed out for me. The majority were related to the achievements of his horses, but one cutting, in particular, caught my eye. Headed: **All Change For McConnel**, it broke the news that McConnel had moved all of his horses from Ease Stables to Westlington Stables. The journalist who had covered the story had contacted Archie McConnel and Dez Ease, but both had refused to comment.

Interesting. Very interesting.

"Sorry it took me so long." Jules handed me the bottle of milk. "The two nearest convenience stores were all out of whole milk, so I had to go across to Market Street."

"Thanks, Jules."

"Would you like a glass for the milk?"

"No, it's okay. I'll drink it from the bottle. Will you see if you can set up an interview with McConnel for me?"

"Who shall I pretend you are?"

"Tell him the truth, that I'm a private investigator."

"What shall I say if he asks what it's about?"

"Tell him that you're not able to discuss it on the phone, but that it concerns an international ring of horse thieves."

"Is that true?"

"It could be. Someone must have taken Majestic Tears."

"What if he says no?"

"Then I'll just have to think of something else. Give it

your best shot."

"Will do."

"Here you go." I poured the milk into Winky's bowl—the one I had to keep hidden from Jules.

Before drinking it, he scribbled a quick note. I assumed it was to thank me, but it actually read: **About time**.

If that cat wasn't dead already, I would have gleefully murdered him.

***

As I left the office, Jules confirmed that McConnel would see me the following day. He'd tried to press her to tell him more about the international ring of horse thieves, but she'd insisted she couldn't say more over the phone.

When I got home, Jack had left me a note on the kitchen table, to say that he would bring fish and chips for our dinner.

That was the best news I'd had all day. The nearest fish and chip shop was in the next village, so we didn't have them as often as I would have liked. I still lived in hope that someone would open one in Middle Tweaking one day.

Jack turned up at six-thirty, fish and chips in hand.

"They smell delicious." I took them from him. "What did you get for me?"

"I knew you were on a diet, so I just got you a small portion of chips."

"And?"

"That's it."

"What? I'm starving."

"Your face." He laughed. "I've got you fish, chips and mushy peas."

"You're a star."

Twenty minutes later, we'd both cleared our plates.

"They were delicious," I said. "Why don't you turn the store into a fish and chip shop, so we could have these all the time?"

"You don't think that might be a drastic step?"

"Not if it means I get fish and chips every day."

"Have you moved that ferret into the garden?"

"Not exactly."

"What does that mean?"

"I've not been able to get him a TV yet. Apparently, I need one with rechargeable batteries, but they didn't sell them in the shop I tried."

"Couldn't he manage just one night without a TV?"

"I suggested that, but he's holding me to my word: no moving out into the garden until he has a TV."

"Great."

"Don't sulk. It's only for one more night."

"I'm not sulking. I just don't appreciate playing second fiddle to a ferret."

"I know something that will cheer you up."

"Now, you're talking." He grinned. "Race you upstairs."

"Not that. Jeez, you have a one-track mind. I've got something for you from Mrs V." I went out into the hall to get the scarf. "Isn't that great? She knitted three of them: one for Jules, one for you, and one for me."

"It's a horrible colour."

"Don't be so ungrateful. I think it's nice."

"Where's yours?"

"In my bag."

"Can I see it?"

"Sure." I quickly grabbed mine from out in the hallway.

"Let's swap," Jack said.

"No."

"Why not? You said you thought this one was nice."

"It is, but Mrs V specifically said that I should have the green and white one."

"I think you should let me have it. It's the least you can do to compensate me for having to put up with that awful ferret."

"Fine." I handed over the scarf.

"This really suits me." He gloated. "I think I'll wear it tonight at the meeting."

"What meeting?"

"Don't tell me you've forgotten already. It's the meeting at the church hall, about the hotel's new owners."

"How could I have forgotten about it? I never knew about it in the first place."

"The vicar dropped a leaflet through the letterbox yesterday morning."

"And you did what with it?"

"I thought I left it on the table for you to see."

"Nope. Never happened."

"But I was sure that—" He hesitated.

"Yes?"

"Come to think of it, I put it in my pocket because I was on my way out. Didn't I tell you about it last night?"

"That would be another *nope*. Anyway, it doesn't matter because we aren't going, are we?"

"We have to."

"Why?"

"We've had this discussion before, and we agreed it was important that we play a full part in village life."

"But I've had a long, hard day."

"It'll only last an hour and it's the least you can do considering that you've lumbered me with that ferret."

"I already sacrificed my scarf for that."

"Come on, Jill. Please."

"Okay, but it had better not run on and on like the last one we went to."

"That was your fault."

"How was it my fault?" I protested. "That was all down to Flat Head."

"You've got to stop calling him that."

"He does have a flat head. You've seen it."

"If you hadn't got into an argument with him, we would have been out of there half an hour earlier."

"The man's an idiot. You heard what he said. He wanted everyone in the village to trim their hedges to the same height. What business is it of his what height our hedge is?"

"We don't have a hedge."

"That's not the point. It's the principle that matters."

"You just like arguing."

"No, I don't."

"You're doing it now. Do you promise not to get into it with Flat—err—Mr Flatley?"

"I'll try my best. I don't see why there needs to be a meeting, anyway."

"People are worried about what might happen at the hotel."

"They've had vampires, werewolves and all manner of sups living there for the last few years, and no one complained."

"No one knew. Come on, we'd better get a move on, or we'll be late."

As we approached the church hall, I grabbed Jack's arm.

"Look, Flat Head is over there."

"Stop calling him that. He might hear you."

"But his head is—"

"You promised me that you'd behave."

"Sorry."

Flat Head was leaning against the wall next to the entrance, and as we approached, he flashed that creepy smile of his.

"Hello, Mr Maxwell. Mrs Maxwell."

"Hello, Mr Flatley," Jack replied.

I just gave him a nod as we walked by.

"It's a good turn out," Jack remarked as we found a couple of free seats.

"It's a pity they don't have anything more exciting to do—like watching paint dry."

"Shush! Someone might hear you."

A few minutes later, Flat Head took a seat at the opposite side of the room, and the vicar stepped onto the stage.

"Good evening, everyone. Thank you all for coming."

"Aren't there any drinks?" Mrs Richardson said.

"Sorry, Mrs Richardson. It was too short notice for me to arrange anything for tonight."

"In that case, I can't stay. If I don't get my cup of tea by eight, I won't sleep tonight." And with that, she stood up and made her exit.

"Okay," the vicar carried on undaunted. "You all know

the purpose of this meeting. We're here to discuss the hotel. I'm sure that, like me, you were all disappointed when Mirabel Millbright decided to sell the hotel."

Almost everyone in the room nodded in agreement.

"Hear, hear!" Flat Head piped up.

"Anyway," the vicar continued. "What's done is done. The hotel has now been sold to a company called CCI, which apparently stands for Cosplay Conventions International."

"What is that?" Old Mrs Johnson asked.

"I believe it's something to do with dressing up, but I was hoping that maybe someone here would know more about it."

Before I could stop him, Jack had raised his hand.

"Yes, Jack," the vicar said.

"Jill and I know a little about Cosplaying."

Why did he have to drag me into it?

"Maybe you'd care to fill the rest of us in."

"Sure." Jack was centre of attention and loving it. "It's basically dressing up as someone or something. Usually a fictional character."

"Why would anyone want to do that?" Flat Head scoffed.

"It's fun," Jack said.

"Have you and Jill—err—cosplayed?" the vicar asked.

"Say *no*," I whispered.

"Yes, we have. We dressed up as vampires."

Everyone in the hall stared at us, as though we'd lost our minds. I'd warned Jack this would happen, but as usual he'd taken no notice.

"Why would you dress up as vampires?" Flat Head, who else, asked.

"It was SupCon," Jack said.

"*Soup*? What does that have to do with vampires?"

I jumped in before Jack could do any more harm. "It's not soup. It's *Sup*!"

"What's a sup?"

"It stands for supernatural," Jack answered.

"We don't want people dressed as those horrible creatures walking around our village," Flat Head said.

Little did he realise that real vampires had been visiting the hotel for several years. To give Grandma her due, she'd kept the residents of the hotel on a very short leash with the result that there had been very few incidents during the time the hotel was in business.

"The point is that cosplaying is harmless fun," I said. "It might seem a little silly to outsiders, but the people who take part aren't doing anyone any harm."

"But people might be scared if they meet a vampire in the street," Mrs Kresson said.

"They won't always be dressed as supernatural creatures," I said. "That was just an example. It could be anything: cowboys, pandas, toothbrushes."

"*Toothbrushes*? Why toothbrushes?"

"It all depends upon the theme of the con."

"We don't want con men in the village," Mrs Mandaville said.

"Con doesn't stand for con man. It stands for convention. The hotel will hold conventions with various themes. There really isn't anything to worry about."

Thankfully, the vicar came to my rescue. "I for one am reassured by what Jack and Jill have told us. In fact, it sounds like it could be quite fun."

"Having weirdos walking around the village?" said Flat

Head, who was the biggest weirdo in the village.

"And just think about the money it will inject into the businesses in Middle Tweaking," Jack said.

"You would say that, wouldn't you?" Flat Head snapped. "Your store will be the major beneficiary of all this nonsense."

"Can I turn him into a rat?" I whispered to Jack.

Chapter 19

The next morning, I was back to eating fruit for breakfast. Yummy.

"You should have let me do it to him," I said to Jack.

"Don't you think someone might have noticed if you'd turned Flatley into a rat?"

"Why would they? He already is one."

"You shouldn't let him wind you up so much."

"I can't help it. It makes my flesh crawl just to look at him, and he's deliberately argumentative. If I'd said I thought cosplay would be bad for the village, he would have said it's the best thing since sliced bread."

"Maybe, but I reckon that the majority of people went away from the meeting feeling much happier about the new owners of the hotel. And that was thanks to you and me."

"Thanks to *me*, you mean. No one was impressed by you gloating that the store stands to benefit from all the people attending the cons."

"Let's change the subject. What are you up to today?"

"I'm interviewing my prospective new accountant this morning."

"I assumed you'd already found one. It's ages since old Mr Bacus retired. What have you been doing since then?"

"I've been doing them myself."

"Oh boy."

"What does that mean?"

"Nothing. But maths isn't exactly your strong suit, is it?"

"There's nothing to it. I'm not sure why these accountants make such a big fuss about it. In fact, I'm fully expecting the people I interview to tell me that I don't need their services when they see what a good job I've being doing."

***

After spending fifteen minutes looking through my accounts, Sylvia Silver looked up.

"Would you like me to be honest with you, Jill?"

"Of course."

This was the point where she told me that I would be wasting my money by employing her services.

"In all the years I've been doing this job, I've never seen a set of accounts in such an awful mess. Who was your previous accountant?"

"He—err—"

"It doesn't matter. Whoever it was should be thrown out of the profession. It's a good job you called me when you did."

"Surely, they can't be all that bad, can they?"

"Your invoices have been posted to the wrong side of the ledger, and that's not even the worst of it."

I almost asked what a ledger was, but I thought better of it.

"It can all be put right, though. Right?"

"Yes, but it's going to take a lot of work."

I picked up the list of fees she'd handed to me at the beginning of our meeting.

"Your monthly fees are quite a bit higher than my last accountant."

"If this is the standard of his work, are you really surprised? And, I should add, that having seen this—err—

mess—there would be a separate one-off fee, just to get the books in order."

"How much would that be?"

"Eight-hundred pounds."

"*Eight* hundred?"

"And you'd be getting a bargain."

I was beginning to think this woman was trying to rip me off: monthly fees that were half as much again as Mr Bacus, and she wanted a lump sum of eight hundred pounds. I was sure I could do better.

"I'll need to think about it."

"As you wish, but as my assistant told your PA, I only have a couple of free slots at the moment. Once they've been taken, I won't be able to accept any more clients."

"I understand. Thank you for coming in."

After she'd left, Winky passed me a note. I assumed he was asking for salmon or milk, but the note actually read: **I told you that you should let me do your accounts. My fees are quite reasonable compared to hers.**

"No chance."

Jules popped her head around the door. "How did that go, Jill?"

"The chemistry wasn't right. Who's the next accountant on your list?"

"Phillip Philmore."

"Will you set up a meeting with him, please? As soon as possible."

"Will do."

***

I'd had to agree to let Sandy live with us, but I felt it

was a small price to pay for the information he'd been able to provide on the F-O-F case. He'd witnessed the reaction of Gordon Sandwich and Bernt Toste when they'd learned I'd been asking about the scandal surrounding Kevin Wright. Sandy had overheard them mention someone he believed was called Dugger. I needed to find out who Dugger was and what he knew about the stolen money, so I gave Kevin Wright a call.

"Kevin, it's Jill Maxwell."

"Do you have news for me?"

"Nothing solid yet, but I do need to ask you something."

"Okay?"

"Do you know someone who goes by the name of Dugger?"

"*Dugger*? No, I've never heard of them."

"Are you sure? Think very hard. It could be a nickname."

He fell silent for a moment, but then said, "Sorry, Jill, that name doesn't mean anything to me. Why? Who is it?"

"I don't know. Maybe no one. It doesn't matter."

"Did you go to the F-O-F meeting?"

"I did, yes."

"And?"

"I'm still working on a few ideas. Where does Gordon Sandwich work?"

"Gordon? Do you think he had something to do with stealing the money?"

"I have no proof of that, but I would like to speak to him again. Do you know where he works?"

"He's the assistant manager at Kingsford Furniture Emporium. Do you know it?"

I did. It was the most expensive furniture store in Washbridge. I had no idea how anyone could afford their prices.

"Yeah, I know it. Thanks."

"Is that it?"

"For now. I'll call you again when I have more to tell you."

I'd just finished on the call when Jules came through to my office.

"I managed to get hold of Mr Philmore, Jill. He already has a meeting in this area late this morning. He wondered if he might drop in and see you then."

"Is he still on the phone?"

"No, I said I'd check with you and call him back."

"Okay. Tell him if he can get here before eleven, then he can come, otherwise it'll have to be another day."

"Will do."

Jules had no sooner gone back through to her office than my phone rang; it was Aunt Lucy.

"I'm sorry to call you while you're working, Jill."

"That's alright. What's up?"

"I was just checking that you're still okay to partner me on Magic Or Not."

Oh bum! I'd forgotten all about the stupid gameshow.

"It's not this weekend, is it?"

"No, it's the weekend after. The day before your grandmother's birthday party. You're still on for it, aren't you? I hope so, because I don't know who else to ask if you back out."

I would have liked nothing better than to back out, but after all the things Aunt Lucy had done for me, there was no way I could let her down.

"Of course I'm still on for it. I'm looking forward to it."

"That's great. In that case, we really should get together before then, to practise. Will you have time this weekend?"

"I guess so."

"Great. How about Saturday morning? Is nine o'clock too early?"

"No, that'll be fine."

"Okay, I'll see you then. This is going to be so much fun."

I seriously doubted that.

"Sorry, Jill," Jules was standing in the doorway. "I didn't know you were on the phone."

"That's okay. I've done. What did he say?"

"He said he'll be here at eleven."

"Great. Let's hope this guy knows what he's talking about, unlike Sylvia Silver."

"Is this a joke?" Philip Philmore gave me a puzzled look.

When he'd walked into my office, he'd cut a striking figure in his designer suit and slick hairstyle. His handshake had been firm, which was always a good sign, and he'd sounded enthusiastic about winning my business. It was only when I showed him my books that I began to have my doubts.

"Sorry?" I said. "What do you mean?"

"Are these really your books?"

"Yes."

"I assume you fired your last accountant?"

"Actually, no, he retired."

"Judging by this mess, he should have retired some time ago."

"I thought they were pretty much up to date."

"Up to date they may be, but they're a complete mess. The figures for the last six months in particular make no sense. It's like they were done by a five-year old."

"But you can sort them out?"

"Yes, but it will take some time, just to get them squared off."

"Would that be covered by your monthly fees?"

"No. There would be a one-off charge to sort out this mess."

"How much?"

"It would depend on how long it takes, but it won't be less than twelve-fifty."

"One thousand, two-hundred and fifty pounds?"

"At least that."

"I see."

"If you can give me the go ahead now, I can make a start next Monday."

"Err, actually, I have one more accountant to see before I make a decision."

"Okay, I'll leave you my card. I hope to hear from you soon."

"How did that go?" Jules asked after Philmore had left. "Was he any better?"

"Not really. Who was the other person on the list?"

"Laurence Enger."

"Give him a call and see if you can get him to come in, please."

"Today?"

"No. Two accountants in one day is too many. See if

you can set up something for tomorrow or next week."

"Will do."

Winky was giving me a weird look and shaking his head.

"What?"

He shrugged.

"Come on. You clearly have something on your mind."

He scribbled a note: **Search for a new accountant isn't going very well, is it?**

"It's going just fine, thank you. These things can't be rushed."

I had a meeting with McConnel in the afternoon, but first I had to locate a TV that ran on rechargeable batteries. With little or no expectation, I searched online, and to my amazement and delight, it threw up a shop called **Rechargeable Battery TVs**, right here in Washbridge.

"Jules, I have some shopping to do and then I'm going to see Mr McConnel. I should be back some time this afternoon."

"Okay, Jill. I managed to get hold of Mr Enger. He's coming to see you first thing in the morning. I hope that's okay?"

"That's fine. Hopefully, I'll be able to put this accounts thing to bed once and for all. While I'm out, there are a couple of things you can do for me."

"Okay."

"Do you know Scotty who works in this building?"

"The security guy, you mean?"

"That's him. See if you can get hold of him. Tell him I'd like a few minutes of his time if possible. Ideally, this afternoon when I get back."

"Will do. What else?"

"This is going to be more difficult. A young woman called Maxine Westlake works as a stable hand at Ease Stables. I'd like you to try and find an address for her."

"Okay, I'll do my best."

I thought the address for Rechargeable Battery TVs was familiar. It turned out to be the shop that had housed Vinyl Alley until Mad and Brad had moved to their current premises.

The man behind the counter was a wizard, and before I could greet him, he said, "You're Jill Maxwell, aren't you?"

"That's right."

"This is such an honour. Just wait until I tell my Mum. She's such a big fan of yours. We're always watching reruns of your best bits from the tournaments. You were amazing. I don't know why you gave it up."

"I'm too old for all that stuff."

"Rubbish. Your grandmother was competing when she was much older than you are now."

"Still, I'd had enough of them."

"I don't suppose I could get a selfie with you, could I?"

I hated having my photo taken, but it seemed churlish to refuse.

"Sure."

He snapped a couple of photos of the two of us together.

"Thanks. Mum will be thrilled. Now, I'm guessing you're after a Rechargeable Battery TV?"

"You guessed right."

"Rat?"

"Sorry?"
"A chinchilla?"
"You've lost me."
"The TV. I assume it's not for you."
"It's actually for a ferret, but how did you know?"
"Ninety per cent of the TVs I sell are for little creatures like that ferret of yours."
"Really?"
"It's the reason I set up this business. I spotted a gap in the market and here I am. Lots of sups, living here in the human world, own small pets, and they all have one thing in common."
"What's that?"
"They all love soaps. I'm guessing your little guy is no different."
"You're right." I glanced around the shop. "Which model would you recommend?"
"A ferret, you say. Does he watch a lot of TV?"
"He never turned it off while he was in the house with us."
"In that case, I'd recommend the RB667766. It's ideal for outdoor use and has just the right size screen for a ferret. It's over here. Come, take a look."
"It looks okay, I guess."
"A two-hour charge will give you between eight and ten hours viewing."
"I'm not sure that's long enough."
"In that case, you should take a spare set of batteries, so that while one set is on charge, you can use the other set."
"That would work, I guess. How much would all that cost?"
"Including the spare set of batteries, that's going to set

you back two-hundred and ninety-four pounds."

"That much?"

"Seeing as it's you, I can give you a ten percent discount."

"Okay, then, thanks. I'll take it."

Chapter 20

It was over a hundred miles to McConnel's stables, and when I checked the planner, it showed a major delay on the route there. Worried that the delay might make me late for my appointment, and also because I just didn't fancy such a long drive, I resorted to magicking myself there.

The security at McConnel's stables was next level. The whole area was surrounded by a high wall with what looked like razor-wire on the top. The only entrance appeared to be through a gate controlled by a guard in a small cabin.

"Hi." I knocked on the glass.

The man inside was wearing a grey uniform with an embroidered badge on the breast pocket. The badge was an image of a horse in gallop, and below that was the word: McConnel. He glanced up, saw me, and made his way out of the booth.

"Yes?"

"I'm here to see Archie McConnel."

"Do you have an appointment?"

"I do, but I'm a little early. My name is Jill Maxwell."

"Wait there." He went back into the cabin, picked up the telephone and spoke to someone. Moments later, he came back out. "Mr McConnel is sending someone to collect you."

"It's okay. I can walk."

"I don't think so." He grinned, as he let me through the gate.

A few minutes later, a small vehicle, which resembled a golfcart, came trundling down the driveway.

"Jill?" The woman behind the wheel had her blonde hair in a messy bun. "Jump in."

I had barely taken a seat when she did a U-turn, and started back up the driveway. It soon became obvious why the guard had found my suggestion that I walk up the drive so amusing because, after a couple of minutes, there was still no sign of the building.

"I didn't catch your name," I said.

"I'm Gina. I'm Mr McConnel's PA."

"Is it much further?"

"Once we get around that copse, you'll see the stables."

A few minutes later, we skidded to a halt in front of an impressive, Mediterranean style building. Gina jumped down from the cart and beckoned me to follow her inside.

"Mr McConnel is in the Blinkers Room. Can I get you something to drink?"

"No, thanks, I'm fine."

I knew from my research that Archie McConnel had started his career as a jockey, but he was even shorter than I'd expected. What he lacked in height, he more than made up for in girth; he was clearly a man who enjoyed his food.

"Nice to meet you, Mrs Maxwell." He shook my hand.

"Please call me Jill. May I call you Archie?"

"Of course. Why don't we sit out on the patio?"

From there, we had a clear view of the gallops where several horses were being put through their paces.

"Your assistant said you were a private investigator."

"That's correct."

"Who are you working for?"

"Unfortunately, I'm unable to disclose that. Client confidentiality and all that. I'm hoping that won't prevent you from talking to me, though."

"I don't see why it should. After all, I'm quite intrigued by the talk of an international ring of horse thieves. Can you at least tell me more about that?"

"I'm limited on what I can tell you, but what I can say is that there have been a number of high-profile thefts over the last few months."

"I find that almost impossible to believe. I would have heard about it."

"Apparently not." I made a point of maintaining eye-contact with him.

"And I don't suppose you can tell me which horses have been taken?"

"All I can say is that they are names that you'd recognise."

"Okay, but how can I help?"

"Our intel suggests that the people responsible for these thefts carried out extensive surveillance on the stables before making their move. We believe they may have studied several other stables, and I was wondering if there have been any incidents of concern here?"

"No, definitely not."

"You seem very sure. The people we're dealing with aren't amateurs."

"Our security is state of the art. We spent almost a million pounds upgrading it only last year."

"That's impressive. Is that why you decided to pull your horses from the Ease Stables?"

"Is everything I tell you confidential?"

"Of course. You have my word."

"I have the greatest respect for Dez Ease. He's one of the best trainers this country has ever known. That's why I placed several of my horses with his stables."

"And yet, you withdrew them?"

"Reluctantly, yes."

"Why?"

"Dez is a great trainer, but he's stuck in his ways. Times have moved on, but he hasn't moved with them. And that's particularly true when it comes to security. I tried on several occasions to convince him to upgrade his security, along the lines of what we've done here, but my pleas fell on deaf ears. His kids understand the need to do something, but while Dez is in charge, I can't see things changing."

"So you pulled your horses out?"

"Yes. Was Ease Stables one of the those hit?"

"I'm sorry. I can't comment on that."

"I heard that Majestic Tears has pulled out of next month's Greenacre Cup. Please tell me he wasn't one of the horses stolen."

I stood up. "I'm very grateful for your time, Archie."

"My pleasure. I wish you well with your investigations. This is all most disconcerting."

"I trust you won't mention anything I've told you to anyone else."

"You have my word, but then, you haven't really told me much, have you? Wait there, and I'll get Gina to give you a lift back to the gate."

My visit to McConnel's stables had confirmed my own observations: that the security at Ease Stables was far from optimum. Had the horse thieves chosen Ease because they'd identified it as an easy target? Even if that was the case, it didn't explain why no ransom note had been received. Hopefully, Jules would have come up with an address for Maxine Westlake. By all accounts, she was the person closest to Majestic Tears.

***

I'd just magicked myself back to a quiet alley in Washbridge when my phone rang.

"Jill, it's Jules. Are you okay to talk?"

"Yeah, what is it?"

"I managed to catch Scotty. He said he can spare you some time at three o'clock, but I wasn't sure if you'd be back by then."

It was two-forty-five, and I was only five minutes away, so I told her to tell Scotty I'd be there.

"Did he say where?"

"In his office."

"Okay, I'm on my way."

Scotty's office was on the ground floor at the rear of the building. The sign on the door read: Head of Security. As soon as I knocked, he opened the door.

"Jill. Welcome to my humble abode." He beckoned me inside. "I've just made a brew. Would you like a cup?"

"That would be great, thanks."

He poured my tea into a mug that bore the words: **World's Best Dad**.

"Thanks, I'm ready for this."

Since moving into my new office, I'd had a number of brief conversations with Scotty. Ex-military, he'd spent much of his career, since leaving the forces, working in security in one form or another. Although he must have been approaching sixty years of age, he still cut an imposing figure.

"That beautiful young assistant of yours said you had something you wanted to talk to me about?"

"Did you know Marcy Bowkoo, Scotty?"

"Isn't she the woman who—" He hesitated.

"Yeah."

"That was so terrible. I can't say I actually knew her, but we exchanged hellos occasionally."

"She was a good friend of mine."

"I'm sorry, Jill. That must have been very painful for you."

"It was. It still is."

"Did you know she was having problems?"

"That's just it, Scotty. I don't believe she was."

"It's not always possible to tell, though, is it? Some people keep—"

"She and I were having a cup of tea and a chat just like you and I are doing now. When she left my office, Marcy was fine. There's no way she went straight up to the roof and threw herself off."

"You seem to be saying that you don't think it was suicide."

"That's exactly what I'm saying. And that's why I wanted to talk to you."

"You realise the police have declared her death a suicide, I assume?"

"Yes, I'm aware. Talking of the police, did they interview you?"

"They did, but I wasn't able to tell them anything."

"What about CCTV? Did they check that?"

"There are no cameras on the roof, but they did ask to see the footage taken from inside the lift."

"And?"

"And nothing. The tape shows Marcy alone in the lift, travelling from your floor to the roof where she gets out."

"You've seen it?

"Of course."

"Could I see it?"

"I'm not supposed to let anyone see our CCTV footage."

"I won't tell anyone if you don't. Please."

He thought about it for the longest moment.

"I simply can't. Sorry." He clicked on the mouse and brought up the CCTV program on his computer. "But I do have to check on something, and I'll be gone for about fifteen minutes." He gave me a knowing wink on his way out of the door.

As soon as I was alone, I grabbed the mouse and worked my way through the on-screen menu. After first bringing up the footage from the lift, I focussed in on the date and time when Marcy had fallen from the rooftop. Moments later, I was looking at footage of Marcy entering the lift. After pressing the button, she leaned against the wall, and adjusted her hair while looking at the full-length mirror on the opposite side of the lift. The rest of the footage lasted no more than half a minute. When the doors opened again, Marcy hesitated for a moment and then stepped out.

Having viewed the footage, I was none the wiser. No one had been in the lift with Marcy, so there was no question of someone forcing her to go up onto the roof. The thing that bothered me most was seeing her adjust her hair. If she'd decided to end her life by throwing herself off the roof, why would she care what her hair looked like? It didn't make any sense.

***

"How much?" Jack was clearly horrified at the price of the mini TV.

"You were the one who insisted we put Sandy outside. I was quite happy for him to stay in the lounge. He wouldn't have needed his own TV then."

"And I would never have got to watch my programmes again."

"There you are, then. Money well spent."

"That ferret had better appreciate this."

"I'm sure he does. Just like I appreciate you, my darling." I gave him a kiss.

"What do you want this time, Jill?"

"What do you mean? Can't I kiss you without having an ulterior motive?"

"You could, but I doubt you did. What do you want?"

"I'm all out of custard creams."

"What does that matter? You're on a diet."

"No, I'm not. That's finished now. Daisy says I have made remarkable progress."

"Hmm."

"So, will you nip back to the store and get me some custard creams?"

"Sure." He held out his hand.

"What's that for?"

"Money."

"You're not going to make me pay for them, are you?"

"We've had this discussion a thousand times. The food in the store isn't ours. We have to pay for it like everyone else."

"That doesn't seem right."
"Do you want the custard creams or not?"
"Do I at least get a discount?"

Chapter 21

The next morning, when I came downstairs, Jack was already seated at the table. In front of him, was a half-empty packet of custard creams. I could have sworn that I'd put those in the cupboard before I went to bed the previous evening.

"Aren't you having any breakfast?" I said.

"I've already eaten it." He tapped the packet of biscuits. Any comment?"

"Sorry, I thought I'd put those away last night."

"You did."

"Then, what are—?"

"You ate half a packet of these after I'd gone to bed. *Half a packet*!"

"No, I didn't." I looked at the evidence in front of him. "I only ate two or three. Four at the most."

"Then how come there's only half a packet left?"

"I—err—oh yes, I remember. I took some out to Sandy. You know how much he likes them."

"Do you really expect me to believe that?"

"Go and ask him if you don't believe me."

"I really wish I could."

"Seeing as how the biscuits are out, I might as well have a couple with a cup of tea."

"For breakfast?"

"Why not? It doesn't get any healthier than custard creams."

"You're hopeless. I forgot to ask yesterday: did you manage to sort yourself out a new accountant?"

"Not yet. The second one I interviewed was even worse than the first."

"What was wrong with this one?"

"He tried to make out my books are in a real mess, so that he could charge me a small fortune to put them right."

"Haven't you been looking after them since Bacus retired?"

"Yeah."

"Hmm."

"What does that mean?"

"Nothing. What are you going to do?"

"I've got another guy coming in today, and I have good vibes about this one."

***

"What's so funny?" I demanded.

"Sorry." Laurence Enger had tears running down his cheeks, and he was doubled up with laughter. Eventually, he managed to compose himself enough to say, "I do apologise."

"Look, Mr Enger, I—"

"Call me Loz, please."

"Okay, Loz. What are you laughing at?"

"I assume this is a wind-up. Who put you up to it? Was it Bertie? Just wait until I see him again."

"I don't know anyone called Bertie, and I still don't know what's so funny."

"These books. I've never seen anything quite so hilarious. They aren't really your accounts, are they?"

"Yes, but as I explained, my previous accountant retired about six months ago."

"So I see. Up to that point, the figures look fine. Who

has been taking care of them since then?"

"I—err—used a temp agency."

"Oh dear. I would seriously think about suing them if I were you."

"Surely, they can't be that bad, can they?"

"They really are. I'd need to scrap the figures for the last six months and start again."

"Would that be covered in your monthly fees?"

"To sort this lot out? I'm afraid not. I'd require a one-off payment before the monthly fees begin."

"How much?"

"Two thousand should do it."

"Two grand?"

"It really should be more. When would you like me to make a start?"

"Actually, I have a couple of other people to see before I make a decision."

"No problem." He dropped his card onto my desk. "You know where to find me." He was about to walk through the door when he hesitated. "And thanks for the laugh. That's cheered me up no end."

"Any good?" Jules asked after he'd left.

"No. Horrible little man."

"Shall I find some more accountants for you to interview?"

"No, I don't think I could stand it. Call Sylvia Silver and ask her to pop in again, will you?"

"I didn't think you rated her?"

"I don't, but she's the best of a bad bunch, and I can't allow this to drift on any longer."

"Will do."

Winky didn't speak; he didn't even scribble a note; he

just sat there with a grin on his face.

***

According to Kevin Wright, Gordon Sandwich was the assistant manager of Kingsford Furniture Emporium. Although I'd walked past the upmarket furniture store numerous times, I'd never actually stepped inside the shop. It wasn't that they didn't sell anything that caught my eye; the furniture displayed in their windows was always amazing, but the prices were well above my pay grade.

Before entering the store, I used the 'doppelganger' spell to make myself look like Bernt Toste. Inside, the space had been divided into separate sections for different rooms of a house. The first section I came to was dedicated to the lounge, and was full of sofas of all shapes, sizes and colours. I spotted a gorgeous small two-seater sofa and matching chair, which would have looked amazing in the Old Watermill, and stupidly took a look at the price tag.

How much? Did people really pay that kind of money for a sofa and chair?

"That's the Montrose, sir."

I looked up to find a man, who looked like a cross between a mad professor and a Latin-American dance instructor, standing next to me.

"It's very nice," I said.

"Feel the quality." He rubbed his hand along one of the sofa's arms.

I did the same. "It's very soft."

"Take a seat. You won't believe how comfortable it is."

I practically sank into the seat. "It's lovely."

"What colour was sir thinking?"

"Actually, I'm only here to see Mr Sandwich."

"Gordon?" The young man couldn't hide his disappointment. "Is he expecting you?"

"No, but I'm a friend of his. My name is Bernt Toste."

"Burnt toast?"

"That's right. It's spelled: B-E-R-N-T and then T-O-S-T-E."

"I'm not sure if he'll be able to see you. Mr Sandwich is a very busy man."

"Please try. Tell him it's regarding F-O-F."

"S-O-S?"

"No. F for Funky."

"That should be foxtrot," he corrected me.

"What should?"

"In the phonetic alphabet, Foxtrot is used for F."

"Okay, then: Foxtrot-Ostrich-Foxtrot."

"Foxtrot-Oscar-Foxtrot, actually."

This guy was really starting to get on my nerves.

"So, will you tell Gordon I'm here?"

"Okay, but as I said, he is a very busy man."

Mr Smarty-pants went upstairs, leaving me to contemplate the stupidity of the phonetic alphabet, and wondering if foxes did actually trot. Clearly, Gordon Sandwich was not all that busy because less than a minute later, he came hurrying down the stairs.

"Bernt? What are you doing here? You know I don't like to be contacted while I'm at work. Duncan said it was about F-O-F. Has something happened?"

"I'm worried, Gordon."

"Keep your voice down. Worried about what?"

"That woman who came to the meeting the other night."

"Why are you worried about her?"

"You heard what Callum said. She knew that the money had gone missing."

"So what if she did? That's all she knows."

"You can't be sure of that."

"If you think I'm going to say anything to Hurst, you're insane."

Hurst? Who was that, I wondered.

"Why not?"

"Because the man is an animal. He might think we've told her something, and then we'll both be dead men."

"But I—"

"Forget it. We do nothing and we say nothing. Especially not to Hurst. Got it?"

"Okay, yeah. I guess you're right."

"Of course I'm right. Now get out of here. I have work to do."

Once out of the shop, I found a secluded alleyway and reversed the 'doppelganger' spell. At long last, I felt like I was getting somewhere. Or at least I did until I called Kevin Wright.

"Kevin, It's Jill Maxwell. Does the name Hurst mean anything to you?"

"No, it doesn't ring any bells."

"Are you sure? This could be crucial to the investigation. Think, please."

After a brief silence, he said, "I do know someone called Hurst."

"Good. Now, we're getting somewhere. Who is he?"

"He was my science teacher at secondary school."

"Does he have any connection to F-O-F?"

"No."

"Are you sure?"

"Positive. He moved to Canada about ten years ago, and then I heard that he'd died last year."

"Right. Do you know anyone else called Hurst?"

"Not that I can think of. Should I?"

"It doesn't matter. If you do remember anyone by that name, give me a call."

I'd felt sure that Kevin would recognise the name Hurst, but no such luck. Even so, I was convinced that this was the key to cracking this case. Whoever Hurst was, one thing was for sure: both Gordon and Bernt were terrified of him.

***

Back at the office, Jules had some much-needed good news for me.

"I've found an address for Maxine Westlake."

"Well done, Jules. How did you manage that?"

"I found her on social media, and some of her posts tied her down to a small village called Heath Green, which isn't far from McConnel's stables. It wasn't difficult to find her actual address once I knew that." She handed me a slip of paper. "I've written it on here."

"Good job. Thanks."

"I also managed to get hold of Sylvia Silver. She's in the area this afternoon, and she can drop in later if you'd like her to."

"Definitely. Call her back and ask her to pop in. I'd like to get this sorted for the weekend."

"Will do."

"Are you up for another challenge, Jules?"

"Sure."

"A woman called Rhonda Elpme has just started working for Slade Marketing."

"Isn't that where Marcy used to work?"

"That's right. In fact, she's taken over Marcy's old job. I want to talk to her, but I'm not sure she'll agree if she knows I'm a PI."

"What do you have in mind?"

"I thought she might be amenable to doing an interview with a journalist who was interested in talking to Washbridge's movers and shakers."

"Which magazine shall I say you work for?"

"We'd better not use a real one in case she tries to check with them. Why don't you say I'm with Washbridge Business First? Tell her it's a brand new publication and she would be in the main feature. Do you think you can handle that?"

"I'll give it a go."

"Probably best not to use my real name."

"What shall I say your name is?"

"You can make something up but keep it simple."

"Will do."

Winky was not alone; he was deep in conversation with Daisy.

"I thought you were conserving your voice," I said.

"We were just talking about you."

"I'm flattered."

"Daisy came in to discuss your progress."

"I'm sure you'll be very pleased with what I've

managed to achieve," I said. "I wasn't sure I'd be able to stick to the diet, but my willpower is even stronger than I thought. I'm ready to move forward with the fitness regime."

The two of them exchanged a look, and Winky said, "What did I say? I told you that she'd lie through her teeth. It's second nature to her."

"Wait a minute!" I objected. "It's the truth. It hasn't been easy, but for the most part, I've managed to keep to the diet you gave me."

"Oh dear." Daisy sighed. "I had such high hopes for you."

"And I've kept—"

"Joe's Body Slammer," she said.

How on earth did she know about that? Still, I had to hold my nerve and brazen it out.

"Okay, but that was just one little slip."

"There was nothing little about Joe's Body Slammer."

"Yes, but I—"

"Stop!" Daisy raised her paw. "Please don't embarrass yourself any further."

"I promise I—"

"Here's the thing, Jill. Winky warned me that you wouldn't have the willpower to stick to the diet."

"Traitor!" I shot him a look.

She continued, "That's why I got some of my girls to follow you around."

Oh bum!

"I didn't see anyone."

"Do you realise that angels can make themselves invisible? And that includes angel cats. They've been following you ever since I gave you the diet." She took out a sheet of paper. "This is a list of all the things that you've eaten that were not allowed under the diet: Sausage cob, two cupcakes, chocolate bar, half a packet of custard creams—would you like me to continue?"

"No, it's okay."

"So, you see, there's no point in talking about an exercise regime."

"Maybe I could try again?"

"If it had just been the odd slip, I might have agreed, but just look at this list." She waved it in front of my face. "It would be pointless. I'm afraid you're a hopeless case."

"I did warn you, Angel," Winky said.

"I know you did, Cutie, but I always try to give people the benefit of the doubt. Anyway, I'd better be going."

She gave him a kiss and then disappeared into thin air.

"You set me up, Winky," I screamed at him.

He put his paw on his throat and shook his head, to make out he couldn't talk.

"Don't give me that. You were talking okay a minute ago."

He scribbled a note and held it up: **I've got the competition to think of.**

Chapter 22

Grandma's surprise birthday party was a little over a week away, and I still hadn't come up with a plan, cunning or otherwise, for how I was going to get her to the event without raising her suspicions. On the surface, it might seem that I'd landed the easy part. Aunt Lucy had to make the cake, and the twins had to provide the venue and all the other catering, but my part in this charade was much more difficult. Anyone could bake a cake, (okay, maybe not me, but you get my drift), but it was going to take a genius to pull the wool over Grandma's eyes.

Jules came through the door and broke my train of thought.

"Sylvia Silver is here, Jill."

"Great. Send her in, please."

"Sylvia, great to see you." I shook her hand. "Please take a seat. Can I get you a drink?"

"No, thanks. I have another appointment close by in about thirty minutes, but your assistant said this was urgent."

"I just wanted to tell you that I'd like you to do my accounts from now on."

"I have to say that I'm surprised. When I was here last time, I got the impression that you weren't happy with the fee I quoted for bringing your books up to speed."

"What? Nothing could be further from the truth. Your quote of seven-hundred pounds is most acceptable."

"It was eight hundred."

"Right. That's what I meant. So, when can you make a start?"

"You're quite fortunate. I have already filled one of my

free slots, so there's only the one remaining."

"It's just as well I called you, then. Do you want to take the books away with you?"

"Actually, I'd prefer to do the initial work here in your office if that's okay."

"Oh?"

"It's just that they're in such a mess, I'm bound to have questions. It will go much quicker if I have you on hand to ask for clarification."

"I—err—"

"It would only be for that first catch-up. Once the books are up to date, I will of course carry out the day-to-day routine work from my own office."

"Okay, if that's what's needed."

"Great. The sooner I get started, the better. Would you be okay with me coming in next Monday?"

"Sure, why not."

"Great." She stood up. "And I'll require the payment of eight-hundred pounds on that day."

"Okay, I'll see you on Monday."

***

As I drove into the village, Goldie Barr flagged me down. Judging by her expression, something was amiss.

"Goldie, what's wrong?"

"It's happened again, Jill."

"Hold on. Let me drop the car at the old watermill, and I'll pop back down."

"Okay, thanks."

After I'd parked the car and walked back, Goldie was standing on the doorstep.

"Did you see them this time?" I asked.

"No."

"What happened, then?"

"Come in. I'll show you."

I realised that I hadn't been inside Goldie's house since Liam had walked out of her life, but from what I could see, very little had changed since then.

"In here, Jill." She led the way into the kitchen. "See."

I'd half expected to find the room ransacked, but it looked perfectly fine. "Sorry, Goldie, I'm not sure what—"

"Those!" She pointed to three identical blue bowls on the table.

"The bowls? What about them?"

"I nipped over to the store to get some bread. When I came back, they were there."

"Are you saying they weren't there when you left the house?"

"Yeah, they were in the cupboard."

"Are you sure you didn't leave them there? I'm always leaving—"

"I'm positive. Why would I need three bowls? There's only me here." She started to well up.

"Sit down." I put my arm around her shoulder. "Take a breath."

"You probably think I'm losing my marbles, Jill, but I know I didn't take those out of the cupboard."

"I believe you. Did you lock the door when you went to the store?"

"Definitely. I always check and double check."

"And there was no sign of forced entry?"

"No, I checked all the doors and windows."

"Who else has a key?"

"Just my mother."

"Is it possible she popped over?"

"She's on holiday in Greece."

"Are you sure Liam couldn't be doing this? I know you said he'd moved to Newcastle, but you two didn't exactly have an amicable split, did you?"

"I don't see how it could be him, but I suppose I could contact him, just to be sure."

"You still have his number?"

"Yeah. Unless he's changed it."

"I think it's worth a try. The other option is to call the police."

"And tell them what? That someone put milk in my fridge and took bowls out of the cupboard. They'd think I was crazy."

"Okay, try calling Liam and see what he has to say. If you think he's behind it, let me know, and I'll have a word with him, to make sure it doesn't happen again."

"Thanks, Jill."

"Will you be okay here alone? I could stay with you tonight if you'd like me to."

"Thanks for the offer, but I think I'm going to call my friend, Barbara, and ask her to come over tonight."

"Okay. You know where I am if you need me."

***

It was time to take my second class at CASS, and I was dreading it. The first one had been a disaster because Florence had decided to play up. I'd pretty much let it slide that time, but I couldn't allow her to get away with it again. If I did, I would rightly be accused of showing favouritism. I had hoped that talking to her would make her see sense, but she'd made it perfectly clear that she had no intention of letting up. That left me with no choice: if she misbehaved again this week, I would have to put her in detention.

I arrived at the classroom ahead of time and waited by the door in order to greet the kids when they arrived. I didn't have long to wait before I heard their voices echoing down the corridors.

"Hello, Mrs Maxwell," said Rodney Moonrake, the smallest kid in the class.

"Hi."

"What are we doing today, Miss?" Julie Hardwire asked.

"I thought we'd look at the job the rogue retrievers do."

"Brilliant! I have a poster of some of them on my bedroom wall."

Several of the kids greeted me as they filed in, but so far, there was no sign of Florence. What would I do if she didn't turn up? I was still pondering that question when she and another girl turned the corner and headed into the classroom. Neither of us spoke.

"Okay, class, in today's lesson, we're going to talk about the rogue retrievers. Who knows who they are and what they do?"

A number of hands flew up; one of which belonged to Florence. I hesitated before calling on her because I was worried about what she might have planned.

"Yes, Florence."

"The rogue retrievers are responsible for ensuring sups, who live in the human world, don't do anything which might reveal our true identity to humans."

I'd expected a smartass comment. Was this some kind of trick?

"That's right. Very good. Can you name any of the rogue retrievers, Florence?"

"I think the head rogue retriever is called Daze, but I don't know any of the others."

"Actually, Daze retired some years ago. I'm proud to say that she and I have been friends for many years."

Much to my surprise and relief, that set the tone for the lesson. Florence was on her best behaviour, and she made several meaningful contributions. When the bell sounded at the end of the lesson, the kids began to file out.

"Florence, would you stay back for a minute?"

"Sure."

I waited until we were alone, then said, "What happened?"

"What do you mean?"

"After last week, I thought you and I were going to have a problem."

"I'm sorry about last week."

"You are?"

"Yes, I was out of line."

"I'm pleased to hear you say that, but I have to confess that I'm surprised. What's changed?"

"After last week's lesson, lots of the kids were saying how cool you were and how lucky I was to have a rockstar mother."

"*Rockstar*? Is that really what they said?"

"Yeah, but I wouldn't let it go to your head. The first time you give them lines or detention, they'll soon change their minds about you."

"Still, I'll take it for now. And I'm so glad you and I are

okay again. I hated what happened last time."

"Me too."

"I assume this means you're happy for me to continue to teach here?"

"Sure, just as long as you always give me top marks." She grinned.

"No chance."

"It was worth a try. Love you, Mum."

"Love you too."

***

Not long after I'd magicked myself back from CASS, Jack came back from the store.

"You look like the cat that got the cream," he said. "Have you been at CASS?"

"Yes, I've just got back from there."

"I was expecting the worst. How come you're all smiles? What happened?"

I told him about the lesson and what Florence had said.

"I'm so pleased for you, Jill." He gave me a hug. "I know how upset you were last week."

"She told me she loved me."

"Of course she loves you. Even when she was hurling abuse at you, she still loved you."

"I know, but it was still nice to hear her say it."

"I take it that you're going to continue with the teaching now?"

"Definitely. Apparently, I'm cool. All the kids think so."

"I shouldn't get too excited about that. Kids are very fickle. This time next week, they'll probably all think you're a boring old fuddy duddy."

"Who are you calling old?"

Dinner was a joint effort. In as much as Jack did all the work, and I made encouraging noises. By the time it was ready, I was ravenous.

"This is delicious, Jack."

"Thank you, kind lady. I do my best."

"Goldie Barr flagged me down on my way home tonight."

"Is she okay?"

"I'm not sure. Apparently, she had another incident."

"Like the milk bottles?"

"Sort of. This time she took me into her kitchen to show me three bowls on the table."

"And?"

"And that's it. She swears the bowls were in the cupboard when she popped out to the store."

"This is sounding very much like the milk bottles thing."

"I know."

"What do you reckon? Is there something to it or is she cracking up?"

"I honestly don't know. When Liam walked out, it left her devastated, but that's two years ago now. I thought she was over it."

"What did you say to her?"

"There wasn't much I could say. She doesn't want to report it to the police, and I can't say I blame her. Can you imagine the reaction she'd get? I told her she knew where I was if she needed me."

That evening, the two of us settled down in the lounge

to watch TV.

"It's nice not to have to share the TV with that stupid ferret," Jack said.

"Agreed. We should celebrate with Black Forest gateau."

"I wish." He sighed.

"There's some in the fridge."

"How come?"

"I picked it up on my way home. Want a piece?"

He didn't bother to answer. Instead, he sped from the room and returned a minute later, carrying the gateau.

"This is delicious," he said.

"You've got cream on your nose."

"What happened to your diet?"

"I'm done with all that. Why should I let a cat dictate what I can and can't eat? Besides, it's the weekend."

"Not much of one for me. I'm going to have to work at the store tomorrow and Sunday."

"What about Kiki? Can't she work one day?"

"She had a weekend away booked before I set her on. She did tell me when I interviewed her, and I said I'd honour it."

"My weekend isn't going to be much better. Tomorrow, I've got to go to Aunt Lucy's to practise for that gameshow, and then I've got to take Winky to his barbershop choir competition in Ghost Town. As if that wasn't bad enough, on Sunday I have to help Grandma move her WHS stuff."

"Isn't it your grandmother's surprise birthday party this weekend too?"

"No, that's the weekend after. At least, it's supposed to be."

"Is there a problem?"

"Yes, a big one. I have to get Grandma to the party without raising her suspicions, and I haven't got a clue how I'm going to do it. If I blow it, the twins will kill me."

"You'll come up with something."

"I wish I shared your confidence. Hey, why don't you come up with a plan for me?"

"Me?"

"Yeah, you're the one with the brains in this family."

"Said you never before."

"Please, Jack, I'm really struggling with this. I did buy you gateau."

"Okay, I'll see what I can come up with."

"You're the best."

Chapter 23

The following morning, when I eventually managed to drag myself out of bed, Jack was at the table, eating muesli.

"I thought you had to go into the store?"

"I do, but Monty is covering the early shift. Want some muesli?" He held out the box.

"No, thanks. Now I'm done with that stupid diet, I'm back on real cereal." I got the box of Chococandy Pops out of the cupboard and poured some into a bowl.

"What exactly is this gameshow you're taking part in?"

"It's called Magic or Not."

"What's the format?"

"I have no idea. The only thing I know about it is its name. Hopefully, I'll know more after our practice session today. I'm really not looking forward to it." I sighed.

"I know what would cheer you up."

"More gateau?"

"Even better than that. I might have come up with a way for you to get your grandmother to her party without her realising what you're doing."

"Really? Tell me."

"Why don't you make out that the twins are holding a competition to see which of their customers can make the best cupcake?"

"How does that get her to the party?"

"Patience. If there's one thing that I know about your grandmother, it's that she has a giant ego. Tell her that the twins want her to judge the competition."

Jack was right about Grandma's ego, but I saw a problem. "She's going to wonder why they didn't ask

Aunt Lucy to be the judge."

"That's just it. You tell her that they think she's better qualified than your Aunt Lucy."

"She isn't, though."

"It doesn't matter whether she is or not. Tell her that you, the twins and your Aunt Lucy all decided that she was the best person for the job."

"I'm not sure about this."

"Do you have a better plan?"

"Not really."

"Well then. You're welcome." He stood up. "I'd better be making tracks. Good luck with the gameshow."

After he'd left for the store, I gave some more thought to his plan. For it to succeed Grandma's massive ego would need to blur her judgement, which meant it might actually work.

***

I had never been a fan of TV gameshows, and I'd certainly never harboured any desire to participate in one, but Aunt Lucy had always shown such kindness to me that I hadn't had the heart to turn her down.

Still, even now, I lived in hope that I might be able to persuade her that I wasn't the best person to partner with.

"Jill, thanks for giving up part of your weekend to do this."

"It's not like I'll lose any time in the human world by being here."

"I always forget about that. How about we start with a nice cup of tea and one of the cupcakes I made yesterday?"

One?

"That sounds like a great idea."

A few minutes later, she held out a tray full of cupcakes. "Take your pick."

"It's difficult. They all look so delicious."

"Take two, then."

"If you insist." I bit into the lemon one. "Mmm, this is amazing."

"Did you get a chance to look up the format of Magic Or Not, Jill?"

"Sorry, but I've not had a minute. Do you think it might be better if you partnered with someone who is familiar with the show? I really wouldn't mind."

"Certainly not. You'll do just fine, I'm sure. And besides, we're not allowed to change the team members once they've been submitted."

"Right."

"I think the quickest way to get you up to speed will be for us to watch an episode. Sound good?"

"Sure."

She grabbed the remote control and switched on the TV, then took hold of another control and teed up the program. To one of the cheesiest soundtracks I'd ever had the misfortune to hear, a wizard, dressed in a blue sequin suit, appeared centre-screen. To either side of him was a desk behind which were the contestants.

"Good evening, friends one and all. My name is Lucius Wonderheart, and it is my pleasure to be your compere this evening."

The man gave slimy a whole new meaning, as he smarmed up to the two teams of contestants. Just watching him made my flesh crawl. Eventually, after much small talk, and terrible jokes from the compere, the gameshow began.

We watched in silence for the first five minutes of the show until Aunt Lucy paused the recording.

"Do you get the gist of it, Jill?"

"I think so. He plays them a short clip of film, and the contestants have to say if what they saw was magic or not."

"You've got it."

"That's it?"

"Yeah, but it's a lot more difficult than it might appear."

"O—kay?"

"Watch this next one and you'll see what I mean." She pressed play on the remote.

On-screen, the compere played a short clip of a man sawing a woman in a box in half. Watching that brought back bad memories of Winky, AKA The Great Winkini, who had done that to me. Once the clip had finished, the compere turned to the contestants and asked them to say whether they thought what they had just witnessed was magic or not. Before they could give their answers, Aunt Lucy paused the recording again.

"Well?" she said. "What do you think?"

"It's definitely not magic. That's a trick that lots of human magicians perform."

"Is that your final answer?"

"Yeah, it's obvious."

"Okay." She restarted the recording.

Unsurprisingly, all four of the contestants agreed with me. This was way too easy.

The compere said, "Let's take a look to see if you're right." He pressed a button on the panel in front of him, and the screen behind him flicked between the words: **Magic** and **Not**.

After a short while, the screen stopped flicking and displayed the single word: **Magic**

The four contestants looked every bit as shocked as I was.

"Let's take another look," the compere said.

This time, the clip showed the man who we'd just seen sawing a woman in half. He spoke directly to the camera.

"Hi, all you Magic or Not fans. I'm Martin Wilberforce, and I'm a wizard. I'm going to explain how I used magic to saw a woman in half. First, though, I need to introduce you to my assistant, the lovely Raquel Heart."

The woman who had just been sawn in half came and stood by his side.

"Hi there." She waved at the camera. "I'm Raquel and I'm a witch."

The first thing that struck me about her was her height. In the box, she'd appeared to be at least six feet tall, but standing next to the wizard, it was clear she was actually quite short.

The wizard continued, "You're probably wondering which spell we used today. Over to you, Raquel."

"Thanks, Martin. To perform this particular trick, I used the 'duplicate' spell."

The words were no sooner out of her mouth than a second Raquel appeared at her side.

"I haven't heard of that spell," Aunt Lucy said.

"I have. Florence caused havoc with it some years ago. She filled her bedroom with duplicates of herself."

On screen, the two Raquels walked over to the wooden box that would be used in the trick, and both of them climbed in. One of them popped her head out of the hole at the top of the box while the other one popped her feet out of the bottom. The wizard then closed the lid of the box.

He turned to the camera again. "And now for the interesting part." He picked up a saw and slowly cut the box in half. When he'd finished, he pulled the two halves of the box apart, but was careful to angle both parts of the box in such a way so as to not reveal the head of the duplicate Raquel.

At this point, the clip ended, and the focus returned to the compere in the studio.

"No points for either team in the studio, I'm afraid. How did you guys at home do? Did you vote for Magic? If so, give yourselves a big pat on the back."

Aunt Lucy stopped the recording.

"Do you get the idea, Jill? Or would you like to see another one?"

"I don't think that's necessary. I get the gist."

"It's such a great game format," she gushed. "I can't wait until next Saturday, can you?"

"I'm already counting the days."

The whole thing looked about as much fun as a root canal.

***

I'd arranged to go to the office at four o'clock, to collect Winky and take him to the barbershop choir competition in GT. For some inexplicable reason, he seemed to have total confidence in my ability to find my way to the location of the competition. Having spent very little time in GT, I didn't share his optimism. I wasn't too worried, though, because I planned on asking Mad for help. She knew every square inch of GT and would be able to give me directions.

On my way to the office, I dropped in at Mad Hour. I couldn't see Mad anywhere, but Brad was busy behind the record counter.

"Hey, Brad, is Mad around?"

"No. Her mother was taken ill on her cruise."

"Is Deli okay?"

"I think so. They had to fly her and Nails to a hospital on the mainland. Mad is spending a couple of days with her. You might be able to get her on the phone if it's urgent."

"Nah, it's nothing important. Tell her to give Deli my best wishes when you speak to her next, would you?"

"Will do."

Poor Deli, but at least it sounded like she was going to be okay. I should have contacted Mad earlier in the week instead of leaving it until the last minute. Now, I would just have to hope I could find the venue for the barbershop choir without her help.

No pressure, then.

"I was beginning to think you weren't coming," Winky said when I walked through the door.

"There's plenty of time. The competition isn't until six o'clock, is it? That gives us well over an hour."

"Do you know where Spirits' Central Hall is?"

"Yeah, you gave me the address."

"But do you know how to get there?"

"Of course I do. Give me your paw."

"Why?"

"It will be easier if I magic us both over there together."

"Okay, but it had better not hurt."

"Don't be such a wuss. Give me your paw."

Moments later, we were both standing in the market square, which was the central point of GT. The place was bustling as always.

"Which way do we go?" Winky asked.

"I—err—" I turned slowly around.

"You don't know, do you?" he snapped. "I thought you knew your way around GT?"

"I never said that."

"Why didn't you find out where it was?"

"I was going to ask Mad for directions, but she's with her poorly mother."

"That's just great, so what do we do now?"

"Don't panic. I'll get us there."

"You better had."

"Tell me again the name of the street where the Spirits' Central Hall is located."

"Spooky."

Spooky what? Street?"

"I assume so, yeah."

"Okay, I'll ask someone for directions. Stay here."

The market square was packed with people hurrying this way and that. I managed to collar a young male ghost as he passed by.

"Excuse me. Could you tell me where Spooky Street is?"

"Sure. Take Grave Road over there, and it's about half a mile on your righthand side."

"Great, thanks." I picked up Winky. "It's down here."

"How far?"

"About half a mile, according to that guy."

"Come on, then. Hurry up or we'll be late."

"I'm going as fast as I can. You're no lightweight, you know."

By the time I turned onto Spooky Street, I was shattered, so I put Winky down.

"I don't see the hall," he said.

"It's probably further down the street. Come on, let's take a look."

"Pick me up."

"I can't carry you any further. You'll have to follow me."

I hurried down the street with Winky a few yards behind me.

"Slow down," he said. "My chest is on fire."

"You're the one who said we were going to be late. Come on, it can't be much further."

A minute later, and we'd reached the end of the street, but we still hadn't come across the Spirits' Central Hall.

"It isn't here," he said.

"It must be." I stopped an elderly woman who had just come out of a candle shop. "I'm sorry to trouble you but is this Spooky Street?"

"Yes, dear. What are you looking for?"

"The Spirits' Central Hall. I was told it was on this street."

"I can't say I've heard of it. Could it be on Spooky Avenue?"

"It's possible, I guess. Is that close by?"

"I'm afraid not. You need to take a right here, and then it's a mile up the road on the left."

"Okay, thanks. Come on, Winky."

"I can't run another step. You'll have to pick me up."

"Come here." I picked him up and started down the street.

"Go faster. I'll be late."

"I'm going as fast as I can."

By the time I turned onto Spooky Avenue, I was dead on my feet, and ready to strangle Winky, who had been giving me grief every step of the way. Spooky Avenue was much shorter than Spooky Road, and I could see already that there was no sign of a hall.

"It's not here." I sighed.

"It has to be."

"Well, it isn't. Look."

"This is all your fault."

"How is it my fault? It's your competition. Why didn't you take the time to find out where it was being held?"

"Just ask someone else where the hall is."

I stopped the first person who walked by; a man who was eating a sausage roll.

"Excuse me. I'm looking for Spirits' Central Hall. You don't happen to know where it is, do you?"

He nodded but was unable to talk because he had stuffed the whole sausage roll in his mouth. I had no choice but to wait until he'd swallowed it.

"It's on Spooky Road."

"Right, and I don't suppose for one minute that's anywhere close by."

"Actually, it is. Take a left down there and you'll be on Spooky Road. The hall is about halfway down on the righthand side."

"Great, thanks very much."

"Come on," Winky shouted. "Leg it!"

Thankfully, the man had been right, and a couple of

minutes later, we came to the hall. Standing on the steps outside, were the other three members of the GT Feline Barbershop Choir.

"Winky, where have you been?" one of them demanded. "We're due on stage in less than two minutes."

"Sorry, guys. She got us lost." He jumped out of my arms and headed inside, leaving me standing there, exhausted and fuming.

I'd originally planned to go inside to watch the competition, and even to cheer on Winky's troupe, but after the way he'd just treated me, I didn't trust myself not to boo when they came on stage. Instead, I magicked myself back home.

Chapter 24

"Are you in a better mood this morning?" Jack asked over breakfast.

"I'm sorry if I bit your head off last night, but I'd had a rough day."

"With the gameshow practice, you mean?"

"No, that was okay. The gameshow is stupid but it's simple enough. It was Winky who got me so riled up."

"I thought once he'd died, that you wouldn't have any more problems with him. It strikes me that he's even worse now he's a ghost."

"You've got that much right."

"What did he do this time?"

"You know how he asked me to take him to the barbershop choir competition in Ghost Town?"

"Yeah."

"Well, he didn't even know where it was being held."

"How could he not know?"

"He knew the name of the hall, but not the name of the street where it was located. Anyway, to cut a long story short, we ended up running all around GT, trying to find it. Or, more accurately, muggins here was doing the running while carrying that big lump."

"Did you manage to find it?"

"Yeah, just in the nick of time. Then he had the cheek to tell his buddies that it was my fault we were so late."

"Did they at least win?"

"I don't know. I was too angry to hang around to find out."

"Would he be able to find his way back by himself?"

"Hopefully not."

***

After a rotten Saturday, I wanted nothing more than a restful Sunday to make up for it, but there was no chance of that because I had to help Grandma to move WHS to its new home.

We'd been ordered to meet her at Candlefield Science Park, which was to be the new home of the Witch Heritage Society, and the twins were already waiting outside when I arrived.

"Where's Grandma?" I said.

"That's anyone's guess." Pearl shrugged. "I wish she'd hurry up, though. We've had to pay staff double-time to come in on their day off."

"She's so inconsiderate," Amber said.

"She isn't already inside, is she?" I asked.

"No." Pearl shook her head. "We've already checked. There's no sign of her. The major exhibits are already in place, though."

"When did they bring those over?"

"No idea. Yesterday, I guess."

"Have you come up with a plan to get Grandma to her birthday party yet, Jill?"

"Don't worry. It's all in hand." I considered telling them about Jack's plan, but knowing those two, they would have let it slip, so I decided to say nothing.

"This must be her." Amber pointed to a white van coming down the road.

The van parked in front of the steps to the building, and sure enough, Grandma was behind the wheel.

"Wonders will never cease," she said, as she climbed

out of the cab. "I would have put money on at least one of you lot calling in sick."

"We would never let you down, Grandma," Pearl said. "Would we, Amber?"

"Never. You can always rely on us."

Those two were such two-faced sycophants.

"Let's get started," I said. "The sooner we begin, the sooner I can get back."

"Not until I explain how this is going to work." Grandma took a sheet of paper out of her inside pocket and opened it up on the steps. "This is a plan of our new home. You'll see the space is divided into three distinct areas." She pointed to the plan, which showed an area made up of three rooms. The central room was circular in shape and had one square shaped room on either side. "You'll see that I have designated these rooms A, B and C."

The three of us studied the plan, and then I asked, "What are all these numbers?"

"Those are the markers for where the exhibits are to be placed. So for example, if an object is marked A12, it should be placed in the central room, in the position marked number 12. Understand?"

It was obvious that Grandma had put a lot of thought into this move, and she'd planned it meticulously.

"That seems straightforward enough," I said.

"Because I knew you three would be doing this, I made it idiot-proof. Come on, let's get you started." She led the way around the back of the van and unlocked the doors.

"It'll take the four of us ages." I stared at the pile of crates that filled the back of the van.

"The three of you," Grandma corrected me. "I have

other things I need to attend to today."

"You're not leaving us to do this by ourselves, are you?" Amber said. "What if we get it wrong?"

"You won't. Not if you follow the plan. I'll be back in about three hours, which should be more than enough time to get it all done."

"But—"

It was too late; she'd already disappeared.

"That's just typical of her," Pearl said.

"Yeah, it's not right." Amber frowned.

"You two have changed your tune. Five minutes ago, you were sucking up to her."

"Rubbish," Pearl said. "Amber, grab that plan. The sooner we get started, the sooner we'll be finished."

It took us a while, but pretty soon we'd found our rhythm. Two of us would lift a crate out of the van and carry it inside. If it was marked with an A, it was for the central room. If it was marked with either a B or C, it was for one of the side rooms. Once we'd placed the crate in the room, we jemmied it open, and carefully removed the exhibits, each one of which was marked with a number. We then placed the exhibit in the location indicated by the corresponding number on the plan.

It was tiring work, but the three of us got stuck in, and after two and a half hours, there was only one crate left inside the van. Pearl and I grabbed it, but it was way heavier than all the other crates we had already taken inside.

"Hey, Amber," I shouted. "You're going to have to give us a hand with this one."

Between the three of us, we managed to get it inside. Thankfully, it was marked with an A, so we didn't have too far to carry it.

"Whatever is in this one?" Pearl said, as she waited for me to open it.

"Looks like more of the same stuff," Amber said, once it was open.

The three of us set about emptying the last crate and placing everything in its designated place.

"Look at this," Amber said. "No wonder it was so heavy."

"What is it?" Pearl peered into the crate.

"It looks like a cannonball."

"Don't be ridiculous," I sneered.

"See for yourself."

I glanced inside the crate and, sure enough, there at the bottom was a large metal ball. "It can't be a cannonball."

"What else could it be?"

"No idea, but you'd better get it out."

It took both of the twins to lift the ball out of the crate.

"There's no number on it," I said.

"There must be."

"There isn't."

"Where shall we put it?" Amber said.

"How should I know?" I shrugged.

"You'd better hurry up and decide," Pearl snapped. "I'm going to drop it."

"Just put it on top of that chest for now. We can ask Grandma later."

The three of us were pretty much shattered but we didn't have time to rest because Grandma came walking into the room.

"How's it going, girls?"

"All done, Grandma," Pearl said.

"You followed the plan, I hope."

"Of course," Amber confirmed. "You made it very easy to follow."

"Can we go now?" I said.

"After I've checked everything is where it should be." She walked towards the room to the right.

"What about the cannonball?" Amber said to me.

"I'll ask her about it when she's checked that room."

Grandma was only gone a matter of seconds which, at first, I took to be a good sign. That was until I saw her face.

"Unbelievable!" She hurried across the central room towards the room on our left.

"What's wrong?" Pearl asked me.

"No idea. Unless one of you two put something in the wrong place."

"Why do you automatically assume it was one of us?"

Before I could answer, Grandma returned to the central room. She was so red in the face that she looked like she might explode at any moment.

"Is everything okay, Grandma?" Amber said. "We followed your plan to the letter."

"Did you now? Where is the plan?"

Pearl retrieved it and handed it to Grandma who opened it up on the table.

"Gather around." She waited until the three of us were looking over her shoulder at the plan. "What is this?" She pointed to the centre of the three rooms—the one we were currently standing in.

"Room A," Amber said.

"And this?" She pointed to the room to the left.

"That's room B," Pearl answered.

"And this one?" She looked at me.

"Room C."

"Excellent. And what's this?" She pointed to a pair of parallel lines on one side of room A.

"It's the main door," Pearl said.

"Correct again. Now, take a look around and tell me what you notice."

The three of us looked around, and it was clear that none of us knew what she was getting at, but I was sure that whatever it was, it wasn't good.

Grandma must have seen the blank expressions on our faces because she exploded. "Where's the door?"

"It's over there," Pearl said.

"Yes, it is. And where is room B in relation to that door?"

That's when it hit me like a ton of bricks, leaving me sick to my stomach.

"We had the plan upside down," I said.

"Yes, you did. And what does that mean, Amber?"

"We've put the exhibits that should be in room B into room C?"

"Correct, and what else, Pearl?"

"We put the exhibits that should be in room C into room B?"

"Once again, you are correct. Final question for you, Jill. What are you going to do about it?"

"Swap them around?"

"Give the girl a coconut."

"Couldn't we just leave—" Amber started but then thought better of it. "We'll get straight on it."

"This is all your fault, Jill," Pearl said, as we started to swap the exhibits from one room to another. "You placed the plan upside down."

"Rubbish, you two were in charge of the plan."

"Stop gabbing and get on with it!" Grandma yelled.

***

"What a day," Jack said when he got back from the store, just after six o'clock. "I reckon everyone and their mother has popped into the store today. Still, I shouldn't complain; the takings will be up this week."

"If you think you've had it bad, you should have been in my shoes today."

I told him about the whole room plan fiasco.

"Why didn't she just let you leave them in the rooms where you'd put them?"

"Because she's Grandma."

"Whose fault was it?"

"The twins of course, but those two are blaming me."

"It sounds like we've both had a grueller. What do you fancy for dinner?"

"I've already had mine. You'll have to eat alone, I'm afraid."

"How come?"

"I'll be working on the Majestic Tears case. I'm going to try and talk to the stable girl who was responsible for Majestic."

"How long will you be?"

"There's no way of knowing. I have her address, but I don't want to just turn up on her doorstep. She's less likely to be on her guard if we just happen to bump into one another."

"How are you going to manage that?"

"I've no idea."

"Seeing as you won't be here, I can't be bothered to make dinner just for myself. I think I'll order a takeaway from Pidgeon's. Do you want me to get some for you to have later?"

"Cold pizza? No, thanks. Besides, I still don't trust them."

"You've got to get over their name, Jill. Do you honestly think they put pigeon meat on their pizzas?"

"Why else would they call it Pidgeon Pizza?"

"I've told you why. The owner's surname is Pidgeon."

"That's what he says."

Pidgeon Pizza, which was located a couple of miles from Middle Tweaking, opened about six months ago. I was quite excited when I heard that we would be getting a pizza shop, but that was before I found out about the name.

It had taken Jules a little time to settle in but, in recent months, she had come on in leaps and bounds, to the point where I was able to delegate more and more work to her. I knew, because she had mentioned it a couple of times, that she was hoping one day to become a fully-fledged PI. She wasn't ready for that just yet, but I certainly didn't rule it out in the future. After all, I hadn't been much older than she was when I'd begun to work as a PI with my father. That seemed a long time ago now.

As I'd said to Jack, I wasn't inclined to just turn up at Maxine Westlake's door. I had no reason to believe that she'd had any direct involvement in Majestic's disappearance, but there was always that possibility. Instead, I had to somehow engineer a way to casually bump into her and initiate a conversation, to see where it led. The only problem was that I had no idea when, or even if, Maxine would leave her house, so there was every chance I might have to wait around for hours, and potentially have to return on subsequent days.

For once, though, the PI gods were smiling down on me because I'd only been standing in the doorway of an abandoned shop for a matter of minutes when a young man walked down her drive and knocked on the door. Moments later, Maxine, who I recognised from a photo Jules had printed off Facebook, emerged and the two of them set off down the road, arm in arm. I'd never met Maxine, so there was no reason why she would recognise me, but I'd taken the added security of making myself look like Kathy. I followed them at a distance and, less than a mile from her house, they went inside a pub called The Killing Spoon. I gave it a few minutes and then followed them inside, where they were already being served. I hung back just long enough for them to get their drinks, and then I ordered a glass of Coke. The pub was divided into three separate areas: a dining room, the main bar and a small games room, which had a pool table and dartboard. It was obvious that Maxine had wanted to sit in the main bar, but her boyfriend led her through to the games room where he was greeted by several other young men. Maxine didn't look impressed, which I hoped might work in my favour. Within a few minutes, her boyfriend was playing pool with three of the other young men, leaving Maxine to stare at her phone. This was my chance.

"Hi," I said, as I took a seat at the table next to her.

"Hi?" She eyed me suspiciously.

"Men, eh?" I rolled my eyes.

"Tell me about it." She sighed. "He promised me he wouldn't play pool tonight."

"At least your guy turned up. My husband just rang to say he had to work late. We were meant to be having a meal here tonight."

"Typical."

I sensed she had let her guard down as she recognised a kindred spirit.

"It wouldn't have been so bad if he'd let me know before I set off, but now I've come all this way, I thought I might as well at least have a drink. Even if it is just a Coke. Are you a local?"

"Yeah, I live just around the corner."

"It must be nice to live in the countryside. I live and work in the city."

"I'd hate that."

"Do you work locally as well?"

"Yeah, I work at Ease Stables. It's only a couple of miles away, so I can walk there."

Her boyfriend appeared at her table. "Do you mind if I have another game, babe?"

"Please yourself."

"Ta, babe."

"Don't know why I put up with him," she said.

"When you say stables, is that like racehorses?"

"Yeah. It's one of the most successful stables in the country."

"Wow! I love horses. Not that I can ride, but I keep saying I'll take lessons one day. Do they do lessons at your stables?"

"No, nothing like that. We just look after racehorses."

"Do you get to ride them?"

"Yeah, I take them on the gallops."

"That must be amazing. Aren't you scared? Some of those racehorses look enormous."

"No, I love it."

"Have any of the horses you look after won any big races?"

"Sure. A lot of them. Like I said, Ease Stables is one of the best in the country."

"Any horses that I might have heard of?"

"Maybe. Rose Garland? Three Jesters?"

"They don't ring any bells. We had a sweepstake at work some time ago and I won a few quid on a horse. I'm trying to remember what it was called. Something *tears*."

Her face fell.

"What was that horse's name?" I scratched my chin. "Majestic, that's it. Majestic Tears. I won twenty quid."

"Ray!" She shouted at her boyfriend. "I want to go."

"We're halfway through this game."

"I don't care." She stood up. "I don't feel well. I want to go."

"Sorry, lads," he apologised to his friends and then followed Maxine who was already headed for the door.

I had hoped that when I mentioned Majestic Tears, Maxine would take the bait, and at least acknowledge that he was one of the horses stabled at Ease Stables. I hadn't expected her to reveal that the horse was missing, but nor had I expected such an extreme reaction. On a hunch, I hurried out of the pub, just in time to see Maxine and her boyfriend having a blazing row.

"Sod off back to your mates, then!" she screamed at him.

He had clearly had enough because he took her at her

word, and turned back to the pub, while she stormed off in the direction of her house.

I quickly cast the 'invisible' spell and hurried after her. I caught up with her just as she reached her house. Instead of going inside, as I'd expected her to do, she took out her phone and made a call from the front doorstep.

"It's me, Max. No, nothing's wrong. At least, I don't think so. I was in the pub just now when this woman came over and started talking to me. I thought it was a bit weird because she was getting on a bit."

Getting on a bit? Cheek.

She continued, "Anyway, she told me that her husband had stood her up, so she was having a drink by herself. Next thing, she asked me what I do for a living. When I told her, she asked about the horses we look after. No, of course I didn't, but that's the weird part. She was the one who mentioned Majestic. What? No, she just said something about winning money on him in an office sweepstake. It was all getting weird, so I walked out of the pub. Yeah, okay. I'll see you tomorrow at the stables."

Unfortunately, I could only hear Maxine's side of the conversation, but it was clear she was talking to someone at Ease Stables, and it was also clear that my mention of Majestic had freaked her out.

Chapter 25

What a weekend! It had been so stressful that I was actually looking forward to getting back to work. I'd barely seen Jack over the last couple of days because he'd been working at the store most of the time.

"We need a holiday," I said.

"Easier said than done with the store." He sighed.

"We haven't had a proper one for years. There must be some way of organising it so that we can get away for at least a week sometime."

"I guess I could sort something out. What about Florence?" Jack said.

"We'll take the holiday in between terms, so she can come with us, obviously."

"That's assuming she wants to."

"What do you mean? Why wouldn't she?"

"I'm not saying she won't. We just shouldn't take it for granted. By the way, did your grandmother take the bait of the cupcake competition?"

"I haven't mentioned it to her yet."

"I assumed you'd do it while you were helping her with the move."

"I thought about it, but the twins would have overheard, and I don't trust them not to give the game away. I'm going to try and catch her sometime today."

***

"Sylvia's here already." Jules gestured towards my office. "I let her go through. I hope that's okay."

"Yeah. What time did she get here?"

"She was waiting outside the door when I arrived; that was about twenty-five minutes ago."

"Have you made her a drink?"

"She said she'd have one when you got here."

"Okay, I'll have a tea, please."

Sylvia was seated at my desk, which was covered in all manner of paperwork. And, in other bad news, Winky was sitting on the sofa. I had hoped he might decide to stay in GT permanently.

What? Of course I meant it.

Sylvia looked up when I walked into the office. "Good morning, Jill. I hope you don't mind me sitting here, but I needed space to be able to spread out all the papers. I can move if you like?"

"No, you're fine. I'll probably be out for much of the day, anyway."

"I already have a few questions for you."

"Oh?"

"There's a bill here for cat food. It seems to have been charged to general expenses. I assume that's a mistake?"

"Err—I—"

"Cat food can't possibly be a business expense. Do you even have a cat?"

"Me? No. I can't stand them."

"Then why would you have a bill for so much cat food?"

"I've no idea."

"Okay, I'll take that one out, then. There's another one that has me confused too: Under entertainment, there's a charge of one-hundred and sixty pounds for custard creams." She gave me a puzzled look. "Aren't they biscuits?"

"I can see how that might have you confused. Custard Cream is also a small restaurant in—err—Wolverhampton."

"That's a very strange name for a restaurant."

"It is, isn't it?"

"And it's in Wolverhampton?"

"I had to go there while working on a case about—err—wolves."

"A case about wolves in Wolverhampton?"

"That's right. It was a very unusual case."

"Right, well that's all I have for you at the moment."

"Great."

While I'd been talking to Sylvia, Winky had been waving his paw around, obviously in an attempt to catch my attention. He clearly wanted to tell me something, but if I spoke to him while Sylvia was in the office, she would think I'd lost my mind. Instead, I gestured for him to follow me.

"Are you going out, Jill?" Jules asked, as I walked past her desk.

"I'm just nipping to the loo."

Winky followed me out into the corridor.

"What do you want?" I snapped.

"I'm starving."

"I can't feed you while the accountant is in my office."

"Why not? It's the least you can do after what you did on Saturday."

"After *what I did*? I almost killed myself, carrying you all around GT. That's what I did."

"You cost us the competition."

"How do you work that out?"

"We came second to the GT Dogs' Barbershop Choir.

Do you have any idea how embarrassing it was to lose to them?"

"I neither know nor care. And I don't see how I had anything to do with you losing."

"After all the shouting I had to do to get you moving, my voice was hoarse. I let my troupe down and it was all your fault."

"You ungrateful little—"

"It's okay, I've decided to forgive you."

"You've decided to—"

"Yes, I realise it's magnanimous of me, but that's just the kind of guy I am. So, how about that food?"

"I can't feed you while the accountant is in the office. She'll think I've lost my mind if I start to put cat food into a bowl."

"She's probably already reached that conclusion. *Custard cream*, the restaurant? Really?"

"It's all I could come up with. She caught me off guard."

"You'll have to do something, or I'll pass out. I'm already feeling faint."

"You're just being melodramatic."

"Oh no!" He put a paw on his forehead and started to stagger around. "I feel quite dizzy."

"Okay, okay. I'll get you some food. Stay here. Don't move an inch!"

"Are you sure you're alright, Jill?" Jules said.

"I'm fine."

Fortunately, Sylvia had her head down, sifting through the papers, and she didn't look up when I re-entered the room. I edged to the far side of the office and slowly opened the cupboard, where I kept the tins of cat food. I dare not take my eyes off Sylvia in case she looked up, so I had to open the cupboard by feel alone. So far, so good. She was so engrossed in her work that she hadn't noticed me. With my eyes fixed on her, I managed to get the cupboard open. All I had to do now was grab one of the cans, and then—

"What the—?" Sylvia almost jumped out of the chair at the sound of the cans of cat food crashing to the floor.

"Sorry about that," I said.

She stared at the cans of cat food that were spread across the floor. Only a few minutes ago, I'd told her I didn't have a cat and that I'd never ordered any cat food. How was I supposed to talk my way out of this? I just couldn't do it, so I did the only thing I could, I cast the 'forget' spell. Next, I used the 'sleep' spell to make her doze long enough for me to clear up the cans and feed Winky. Once I'd done all that, I returned to my office, and reversed the 'sleep' spell.

Sylvia had slept with her head on the desk. When she stirred, she looked around a little confused.

"Jill, I'm so sorry. I think I must have dozed off for a moment."

"Don't worry about it. That stuff must be pretty boring."

"I'm mortified. It's so unprofessional. I hope you can forgive me."

"Don't give it another thought. Is there anything else you need to ask me before I go out?"

"Nothing else at the moment."

"Great. I'll see you later then."

I was just about to tell Jules that I was going out when she held up her hand.

"Look what someone left outside our door."

She held up the empty cat food can that I'd intended to collect on my way out.

"What is that?" I said, all innocent-like. "A soup can?"

"No, it's a cat food tin. Look."

"That's weird."

"It's against the rules to have animals in this building. Do you think we should report it to the management company?"

"No, I wouldn't bother. Best not to get involved. Anyway, I'm off out now. Keep Sylvia supplied with drinks, will you?"

"Sure. Shall I give her some of your custard creams?"

"No!" I snapped.

"Sorry, I just thought—"

"Sylvia is diabetic; she can't eat sweet stuff."

"Oh, okay. It's just as well you told me."

***

Somehow, I had to find a way to spin the story about the cupcake competition to Grandma. I deliberately hadn't mentioned it in front of the twins, for fear they would give the game away, but I couldn't afford to leave it any longer in case Grandma made some other arrangement for Sunday.

Although we'd finished all the heavy lifting yesterday, Grandma had said she would be at Candlefield Science Park most of the week, making sure everything was just so. If I was going to pull this off, I would need to come up with another Oscar-worthy performance. Anything less, and Grandma would sense a ruse, and that would be fatal.

After taking a few moments to compose myself, I strode

confidently into the building and headed straight for the basement. At the bottom of the stairs, in front of the double-doors, was a large sign that Grandma must have put up after the twins and I left the previous day. The sign read:

The new home of the Witch Heritage Society - Opening Soon.

I thought the doors might be locked, but when I pushed one of them, it swung open. Grandma had moved a few of the exhibits around, but for the most part, it was pretty much as we'd left it yesterday. There was no sign of the woman herself, and I was beginning to think that she wasn't there when I heard her call out.

"Those stupid girls!"

"Grandma?"

I still couldn't see her, and I was about to call out her name again when she appeared from behind the large display of broomsticks. She was hopping around and appeared to be in some pain.

"Are you alright, Grandma?"

"Do I look alright?"

She didn't, but she managed to hop over to one of the sofas.

"What's the matter?"

"Which one of you three dimwits decided to put a cannonball on top of that chest back there?"

I had a flashback to the previous day.

"Where shall we put it?" Amber said.

"How should I know?" I shrugged.

"Hurry up and decide," Pearl said. "I'm going to drop it."

"Just put it on top of that chest for now. We can ask Grandma later."

"I've no idea," I lied. "It must have been one of the twins."

"Those two don't have a braincell between them."

"Why is there a cannonball in the exhibition, anyway?"

"Haven't you heard of the great witch wars?"

"No."

"I despair of the youth of today."

"Are you alright now?"

"I'm just peachy. I love having a cannonball drop on my toe." She pulled off her shoe and sock, to reveal an angry looking big toe.

"Is there anything I can get for you?"

"Go and run some cold water in a bowl."

"Okay, where will I get the water?"

"Try a tap."

"Right. Sure." I went upstairs and found a small kitchen.

"You took long enough," Grandma snapped when I returned with the bowl of water.

"Sorry, I had to—"

"Never mind. Put it down."

She put her foot into the water.

"Do you think you should go to hospital?"

"Are you kidding? Those idiots will probably take my leg off. It'll be okay in a minute. What are you doing here, anyway? You couldn't wait to get away yesterday."

I was beginning to doubt if this was the right time to spin my story about the cupcake competition, and the only reason I did was because I couldn't come up with another explanation for my being there.

"The twins have decided to hold a competition to see who can bake the best cupcake in Candlefield."

"That's the kind of ridiculous thing that only those two could come up with."

That wasn't the response I'd been expecting.

"I thought it was a good idea."

"You would because you have about as much business acumen as those two."

"I don't understand."

"What is the name of the twins' shop?"

"Pearl and Amber's."

"Not the stupid new name. The original one."

"Cuppy C."

"Right, and what does the C stand for?"

"Cake."

"Exactly. So basically, the thing they're best known for is cupcakes. Why then would they want to hold a competition which will result in someone else being awarded the title of best cupcake baker?"

"I—err—"

"What if one of their competitors enters the competition and wins?" Grandma had a point. Jack and his stupid ideas. This whole plan was a bust and I was just about to say so when she continued, "I'll have to judge the competition."

"You?"

"Yes, that way, I can make sure that the twins win."

"Win their own competition? Won't that look suspicious?"

"Of course it will, but do you really think anyone will step forward and accuse me of not being impartial?"

"Definitely not."

"That's decided, then. When is the ridiculous competition?"

"Next Sunday."

"I might have known." She sighed.

"Is that a problem?" I played dumb, so as not to let on that I knew it was her birthday on that day.

"It won't have to be, will it? Just make sure to tell those two airheads that they have to enter the competition, and they'll need to let me know which are their cupcakes, so I can pronounce them the winners."

"Okay, will do. Thanks, Grandma. Do you need anything else before I go?"

"Not unless you have a spare big toe."

That had actually worked out much better than I could have hoped. In the end, I didn't have to ask her to be the judge because she'd volunteered.

Result!

Hopefully, Grandma would have forgotten about the cannonball before Sunday, otherwise the twins would be sure to grass on me.

Chapter 26

I'd just magicked myself back from Candlefield when I got a phone call from Jules.

"Jill, thank goodness I managed to get hold of you."

"What's wrong?"

"There's nothing *wrong* exactly."

"Then why are you in such a tizz?"

"Sorry. You know how you asked me to contact Rhonda Elpme."

"Yeah, did you manage to get hold of her?"

"I did, and I told her that I was calling from Washbridge Business First. She was really keen to do an interview."

"That's great."

"The thing is she was like *really* keen."

"So, what's the problem?"

"She kind of caught me off guard."

"What do you mean?"

"She said she was free now and asked if that would work."

"What did you tell her?"

"I said yes. Sorry."

"It's okay. It won't take me long to get back to the office."

"I didn't think you'd want her to come here because she'd see what you really do."

"Good point. Where am I supposed to meet her?"

"She suggested a coffee shop."

"That works. Which one?"

"I was in a bit of a panic, and the only one I could think of was the one on the high street. The one you go to sometimes."

"Mad's place?"

"No, the other one. The one with the animals."

"Coffee Animal?"

"Yeah. She said she'd be there in fifteen minutes."

Not the ideal location for an interview, but I couldn't be too hard on Jules. She'd done well to set something up so quickly.

"Okay, thanks, Jules. I'll go straight over there."

"Hang on, Jill. There's just one more thing."

"Yeah?"

"You know you said I should make up a name for you?"

"Yeah. What did you tell her my name was?"

"Penny."

"That's not so bad."

"Penny Punch."

"*Punch*?"

"I should have thought of a name before I called her, but I didn't, so when she asked me your name, I just looked at the stuff on my desk and saw the pen and the hole punch. Sorry."

***

I hightailed it over to Coffee Animal and, despite my new diet and fitness regime, I was struggling for breath by the time I got there. A young woman, with hair the colour of a plum, was standing by the door.

"Are you okay?" she asked.

"Yeah, I'm fine." I gasped.

"Are you sure?"

"Yeah, I've just got a bit of a chest cold."

"You wouldn't happen to be Penny Punch, would you?"

"Who? Err, I mean, yes. Rhonda?"

"That's right." She offered her hand. "I was so excited when your assistant called me."

"Shall we go inside?" I desperately needed to sit down.

"Sure. I've been looking through the window while I was waiting for you. Everyone seems to have a guinea pig on their table. Is that usual?"

"It's not always guinea pigs. It's a different animal every day. I'm just grateful it isn't snakes today."

"Right. What are we supposed to do with the guinea pigs?"

"Nothing, although if past experience is anything to go by, they'll probably expect some of your cake if you have some."

"I had no idea that guinea pigs liked cake."

"Oh yes. Particularly Victoria sponge. Why don't you grab a table and I'll get us some drinks? What would you like?"

"Could I have a Cappuccino, please? With plenty of chocolate sprinkles."

"Anything to eat?"

"You mentioned Victoria sponge. A slice of that would go down a treat. Thank you."

I hadn't intended having any cake, but I thought it might look rude if I didn't join her, so I forced myself to have a piece of Black Forest gateau. I had to make two trips to the table: the first to deliver the drinks and cake; the second to carry the cages containing the guinea pigs.

"Victoria sponge, yummy," said the brown and white guinea pig, as I walked back to the table. "Can I have some?"

"Judging by the size of you, you've had far too many cakes already."

"So rude."

"What's that other cake?" his black and white companion enquired.

"Black Forest gateau."

"Are those cherries?"

"They are."

"I love cherries."

"There's no cake for you two," I said without thinking.

"Sorry?" Rhonda had overheard me and was understandably confused.

"I—err—said there's no cake-yoohoo, so I had the Black Forest gateau."

"*Yoohoo*?"

"Don't tell me you've never tried cake-yoohoo? It's amazing." I handed her the cage containing the brown and white guinea pig.

"He's a little cutie, isn't he?" She put her face up to the bars.

"He's a bit on the fat side if you ask me."

"Kettle. Black," the cheeky guinea pig retorted.

"I think he wants a bit of my cake," Rhonda said, and before I could stop her, she'd cut off a piece and pushed it through the bars.

"What about me?" His friend gave me a pathetic look.

"I think your little guy wants some too," Rhonda said.

"They don't like cherries."

"Yes, I do. I love cherries," my guinea pig insisted.

"Are you sure?" Rhonda said. "He can't take his little eyes off them."

"Okay, but just a small piece." I cut him some and passed it through the bars.

"There aren't any cherries in this piece," the ungrateful guinea pig complained.

Ignoring his whinging, I suggested to Rhonda that we get started on the interview.

"I believe my assistant told you about the publication I work for?"

"She said it's called Washbridge Business First."

"That's right. The owners identified a gap in the market: a business-oriented magazine that covers local markets. Their long-term plan is to launch Business First magazines throughout the country. You could say this is the pilot."

"Is it an online magazine?"

"Print and digital."

"Interesting."

"A lot rides on the success of the Washbridge edition, as you can imagine. It's very important that the first edition makes an impact. As they say, you only get one chance to make a first impression."

"That's true."

"We have a number of exciting articles planned. One of those will be titled Washbridge's Movers and Shakers, in which we plan to feature a number of leading businessmen and women who have made an impact on the local scene."

"And you want to feature me?"

"I must be candid with you, Rhonda. Is it okay to call you Rhonda?"

"Of course."

"What about a cherry?" said the guinea pig, who was starting to do my head in.

Ignoring him, I continued. "As I was saying, I want to be candid. I'll be interviewing half a dozen people for possible inclusion, but only three will make the cut. Are you happy to proceed on that basis?"

"Absolutely, I consider it an honour just to be shortlisted."

"Great, let's get right down to it, then."

For the next twenty minutes, I spouted more BS than you could shake a stick at.

What do you mean: *nothing new there*? Cheek.

I used every buzzword I could think of, and Rhonda lapped it up. She was clearly so far down the corporate rabbit hole that she bought into the lot. It soon became clear that her favourite subject was herself, and that she didn't suffer from a modesty complex.

"I was nominated twice for Marketing Executive Of The Year while I was working for Jade Holdings," she said.

"Very impressive."

"I should have won, but—you know—politics."

"Right, and I understand that you recently changed jobs?"

"That's right. I was headhunted, actually."

"Remind me again who by."

"Slade Marketing."

"Slade?" I hesitated. "Haven't they been in the news recently?"

"Err, I—"

"Oh yes, I remember now. That awful incident where someone threw themself off the roof. How terrible. Were you there at the time?"

"No, I hadn't joined Slade then. In fact, I almost turned down the job because of what happened to Marcy

Bowkoo."

"Really?"

"I had already agreed to join Slade before Marcy's unfortunate death, but I knew how it would look. I actually called Victor Slade and said I thought I should give back word, but he wouldn't hear of it. As he pointed out, they had an even greater need of my services because of what happened to Marcy."

"Hang on. Let me make sure I understand this correctly. Had you been recruited to replace Marcy Bowkoo?"

"No, the intention was that we'd work together. The workload had become too much for one person."

"I see."

"There are still people who think I jumped into Marcy's job while she was still warm in her grave, but that's simply not true."

If Rhonda was spinning me a line, she was an even better actor than I was. Her explanation that she'd been recruited to join Slade Marketing before Marcy's death certainly had a ring of truth about it.

I spun the interview out for a few more minutes and then thanked Rhonda for her time.

"What do you think, Penny?" she said. "Will I make the cut?"

"I can't make any promises. We'll make a decision only after we've completed all the interviews, but I have been very impressed by what you've had to say."

"Brilliant. When will you make your decision?"

"The first issue comes out in three months' time. To meet that deadline, we'll have to have the article completed within a month. I'll let you know then."

"I look forward to hearing from you."

So excited was Rhonda, at the prospect of appearing in the first edition of a non-existent magazine, that she practically floated out of the coffee shop. As I returned the two cages to the counter, the black and white guinea pig was still giving me grief about the cherries.

***

Jack was working late in the store, so like the good wife I was, I had dinner waiting for him when he got home.

"What's that?" he said.

"Chicken casserole. What does it look like?"

"Definitely *not* chicken casserole."

"Is that all the thanks I get for slaving over this for the last hour?"

He walked over to the kitchen bin and pressed the pedal. "Just as I thought: microwave."

I picked up some on my fork and popped it into my mouth. "Mmm, delicious."

"Why are you pulling that face, then?"

"I'm not—" I jumped up, ran over to the bin, and spat out what was left.

"Fish and chips?"

"Yes, please."

The wait for Jack to go and get the fish and chips was well worth it.

"I'll say it again, Jack. You should change the store into a fish and chip shop. We'd make a killing."

"Sorry, never happening. Did your new accountant turn up?"

"She did. She was there before me. Why are all accountants so pedantic?"

"Explain."

"She was nitpicking at some of the expenses I'd put through the business."

"Such as?"

"Cat food. Custard creams."

He said nothing; he just shook his head.

"What?"

"Nothing. Did you get in touch with your grandmother?"

"I did, but I didn't pick a very good time; she'd just dropped a cannonball on her toe." I laughed.

"You shouldn't laugh. Is she okay?"

"She'll live."

"And did she fall for the cupcake competition wheeze?"

"I didn't think she was going to because she was very quick to point out one fundamental flaw with your plan."

"What's that?"

"She pointed out that the twins hosting a cupcake competition was akin to turkeys voting for Christmas."

"I don't understand."

"The twins' business was built upon their cupcakes. If they host a cupcake competition and it's won by someone else, that's like saying the twins' cupcakes aren't the best."

"I hadn't considered that."

"To be honest, neither had I, but Grandma spotted the problem straight away."

"Does that mean the surprise party is a bust?"

"No. Luckily, Grandma came up with the idea that she should be the judge, without me even having to suggest it. She said that way she can make sure the twins win."

"That's cheating. She can't do that."

"Hello! The competition isn't real."

"Oh yeah, I got carried away."

"The bottom-line is that Grandma is going to Pamber on Sunday, and that's all that matters."

Chapter 27

The next morning, at breakfast, I'd just poured myself some Strawberrycandy pops, and was about to put the box back into the cupboard when Jack spoke up.

"Could I have some of those?"

"Are you serious?"

"Of course I'm not. I wouldn't eat that rubbish if you paid me. Would you pass me the muesli?"

"Get it yourself."

"Come on. I came up with that plan to get your grandmother to the party, didn't I?"

"The flawed plan, you mean." I handed him the muesli.

Jack was one of the few people I knew who still insisted on reading a printed newspaper.

"Why don't you just read the news on your phone?" I said.

"I prefer a good old-fashioned newspaper. And besides, I'm mainly interested in the local news, which has better coverage in here."

"If you say so."

We sat in silence for the next few minutes, but then he made me jump.

"What a surprise!" he yelled. "Who would have seen that coming."

"What are you getting so excited about?"

"Do you remember about a month ago when I told you they'd released Hursty."

"Who's that?"

"I told you all about him at the time."

"I probably wasn't listening."

"Nothing new there, then."

"So, who is he?"

"He's a one-man crimewave: theft, burglary, GBH. You name it, he's done it. He should still be behind bars but he somehow managed to convince those idiots on the parole board that he'd turned over a new leaf. I hope they're feeling good about themselves now."

"Why, what's happened?"

Jack picked up the paper and began to read from the article that had so raised his hackles, "Washbridge police have today arrested Doug Hurst on suspicion of robbing Green's Jewellers. Hurst, who had only been released on probation a couple of months ago, will appear in court on Friday morning."

"Read it again."

"All of it?"

"No, just the first bit."

"Washbridge police have today arrested Doug Hurst on suspicion—"

"That's it!" I punched the air.

"What is?"

"I'll explain later." I walked around the table and gave him a kiss. "See you tonight."

As soon as I was out of the house, I called Kevin Wright.

"Kevin, it's Jill."

"Hi. Do you have any news for me?"

"I'm getting closer, I believe, but right now I need your help."

"What do you want me to do?"

"I need to get Bernt Toste and Gordon Sandwich in the same room."

"Why?"

"I can't go into detail but suffice to say that it's crucial to proving your innocence. Do you think you could persuade them to meet you somewhere?"

"I'm not sure. We haven't spoken since I was kicked out of F-O-F."

"There must be some way that you can pique their interest."

The line went silent, and I could almost hear the cogs turning in his head, then eventually he said, "There is one way, I guess."

"Go on."

"They've both long been jealous of my collection of cages."

"The ferret cages, you mean? Surely, they already have some?"

"They do, but they aren't the same quality as mine. I spent a small fortune on state-of-the-art cages. I could tell them that I'm thinking of getting out of the business of keeping ferrets, and that I want to get shut of the cages."

"Will they go for it, do you think?"

"They might if I tell them I'm letting the cages go at rock-bottom prices."

"Brilliant. Let's go with that. Give them a call and get them both to come to your house as soon as possible. Tonight if they will."

"Then what?"

"Once you've spoken to them, let me know, and I'll take it from there. Okay?"

"Okay."

***

Even though I arrived at the office earlier than usual, Sylvia Silver was already seated at my desk.

"Good morning, Sylvia. Everything okay?"

"Do they allow animals in this building?" she said.

"Animals? No, it's against the terms of the lease."

"That's what I thought, and yet I could have sworn I smelled cat food outside the door to your office."

"It probably belongs to the solicitor just down the corridor. He's always wearing socks with cats on them."

"You should report him."

"I'll keep my eyes peeled and if I see him with a cat, I'll be sure to do that."

It was all I could do to keep a straight face because, unseen by Sylvia, Winky was standing on the desk, pulling silly faces at her.

"Do you need your desk, Jill?"

"No, it's okay. I'll be shooting off again in a minute."

"I should be done here today. I'll be able to finish things off back at my office."

"Okay, I'll leave you to it."

When I went through to the outer office, Jules was on the phone.

"Jill, it's Sonny Ease. Can you speak to him?"

"Sure." I took the phone from her.

"Hi, Sonny."

"I tried to call you on your mobile earlier, Jill."

"Sorry, I forgot to charge it last night," I lied.

"Any news for us?"

"Actually, I'd like to speak to you, Honey and your father, face to face, if that's possible."

"Have you found Majestic? Has something happened to him?"

"No, nothing like that. I just need to acquaint you all with my findings so far."

"When would you like to do it?"

"The sooner, the better."

"Hang on. Let me check when they're available." The line went dead for a couple of minutes, then he said, "We're all available this morning if you can come over about ten."

"Great. I'll be there then."

Ever since I'd overheard Maxine Westlake talking to someone at Ease Stables, I'd become convinced that Majestic Tears' disappearance had been an inside job. If my theory was correct, this meeting would hopefully set off a series of events that would smoke out those responsible.

Honey Ease met me at the door and took me through to the boardroom where Sonny and Dez were waiting for us.

"Thank you all for seeing me at such short notice. I didn't want to discuss what I have to tell you over the phone."

"Take a seat, Jill," Dez said. "Do you have news about Majestic?"

"Not exactly, but I have made some progress."

"Excellent. Tell us what you've discovered."

"Okay, but I should warn you that you aren't going to like what I'm about to tell you."

"Majestic isn't dead, is he?" Sonny blurted out.

"No. At least, I have no reason to believe so."

"What then?"

"Following my inquiries so far, I've concluded that Majestic Tears' disappearance is an inside job."

"What do you mean?" Dez was clearly stunned.

"I mean that Majestic was taken by one or more people who work at these stables."

"I don't believe it," Honey said. "How can you know that?"

"I can't get into it right now, but I believe I'm getting closer to finding out who is behind it."

"I really find it hard to believe that anyone who works for us would do such a thing," Sonny said.

"I think you're wrong about this, Jill," Honey said.

"Maybe, but ask yourself this: Why haven't you received a ransom note? What other reason could there be for taking the horse?"

"Let's say you're right," Dez said. "And I'm not saying you are. But if it was someone who works here at the stables, what's their motivation for taking Majestic?"

"Once we know that, we'll know who took him. And I believe I'm very close to answering that question." I stood up, mainly for dramatic effect. "In fact, I'm very hopeful that I'll be able to furnish you with all the answers by the end of this week."

"Is there anything we can do?" Dez said.

"Just make sure you keep this conversation between the four of us."

And with that, I made my exit.

With the trap set, all I could do was hope that the bait would be taken.

***

When I'd interviewed Rhonda Elpme for a non-existent magazine, she'd told me that she'd been offered the job at

Slade Marketing *before* Marcy had died. Was that true? If so, I wanted to know why Victor Slade had said nothing about Rhonda's appointment when I'd asked him about Marcy's untimely death.

Instead of going to my office, I took the lift and punched the button for the top floor. The same young man was seated behind reception, and judging by the apprehensive look on his face, he remembered me from my previous visit.

"Is he in?"

"Yes, but—"

As I strolled past him, he reached for the phone. No doubt he was going to warn Slade that I was on my way. I didn't bother to knock on the door; instead, I just burst into his office.

Slade stood up when I entered the room. "Jill? I wasn't expecting—"

"Why didn't you tell me that you'd offered Rhonda Elpme a job?"

"I didn't think it was important."

"I don't believe you."

"Okay, the truth is that I didn't tell you because I knew how it would look."

"It looks like you told Marcy that she was being replaced, so she killed herself."

"That's not what happened."

"How can you be so sure?"

"First off, Rhonda wasn't going to replace Marcy. The idea was that they would work alongside one another."

"Maybe Marcy didn't see it that way. Maybe she thought you were trying to push her out."

"That's not what happened."

"How can you be so sure?"

"Because at the time Marcy killed herself, she didn't even know about Rhonda's appointment."

"Do you really expect me to believe that?"

"It's true. I'd been putting off telling her because I knew how she'd react. Marcy would have seen it as a sign that I'd lost faith in her, but that wasn't true at all. I was actually trying to make her life easier."

"If you didn't tell her about Rhonda's appointment, is it possible that she heard about it from someone else?"

"No. Rhonda and I were the only two people who knew about the appointment, and I had sworn Rhonda to secrecy. Look, Jill, you may not believe it, but I'm as devastated about what happened to Marcy as you are. If I thought that anything I'd done had led to her death, I would never forgive myself, but nothing I did can explain why Marcy took her life."

After leaving Slade's office, I took the stairs back to my place. When I was halfway there, I (literally) bumped into Scotty, the head of security.

"Steady on, Jill. Are you okay?"

"Yeah, sorry, Scotty, I was miles away."

"Are you still looking into your friend's death?"

"Yeah, I've just been to talk to her ex-boss again. Not that it did me any good."

"I know you're finding this difficult to accept, but fate can be a cruel thing."

"What does fate have to do with anything?"

"If the lift guy had arrived an hour later to carry out the maintenance, or if he'd taken an hour longer, Marcy wouldn't have been able to take the lift, and then maybe she wouldn't have—"

"Maintenance? I thought the lift was broken that morning?"

"No, it was closed for routine maintenance."

"In the daytime? Isn't the maintenance usually carried out in the evenings when the offices are mostly empty?"

"That's what normally happens, but this guy showed up with an order to do it in the morning. Like I said, if he hadn't finished when he did, Marcy wouldn't have been able to take the lift."

"What's the name of the company that services the lift?"

"Washbridge Ace Lifts. Why?"

"No reason. Thanks, Scotty."

Chapter 28

Back at the office, Sylvia was packing up her laptop computer.

"Finished already?" I said.

"Far from finished, but as I said this morning, I'll be able to do the rest at my office. I may need to call you from time to time if I have any more queries, though."

"No problem."

"Thank goodness she's gone," Winky said, after Sylvia had left. "Why are all accountants so boring?"

"That's a terrible generalisation. Luther Stone wasn't boring."

"You're only saying that because you had a thing for him."

"Rubbish."

An image of Luther popped into my head; that man was hot.

"Earth to planet Jill!"

"What?"

"Now that Little Miss Boring has gone, can I put my trophy out?"

"What trophy?"

"The one we won at the barbershop choir competition."

"You told me that you came second."

"We did. The first three placed teams all got a trophy."

"How many teams took part altogether?"

"Five. Well, four, actually. The GT Fire Service got a call out just as they were about to perform." He took out the world's tiniest cup and placed it on the windowsill.

"That tiny thing is pathetic." I laughed.

"How many cups have *you* won recently?"

Before I could respond, I got a call from the twins.

"We have a bone to pick with you, Jill," Pearl said.

"Yeah, you dropped us right in it," Amber shouted in the background.

"What did I do now?"

"You know what you did."

"Sorry, girls, but I have no idea what you're talking about."

"The cannonball," Amber said.

"Oh. That."

"You told Grandma that it was our idea to put it on top of that chest."

"I don't think I used those exact words."

"That's what she told us."

"I think she must have misunderstood. Anyway, I have good news. Grandma has agreed to come to Pamber on Sunday."

"Don't call it that!" they both yelled down the phone.

"Sorry. Didn't she mention it to you?"

"No, she was too busy giving us a hard time about the cannonball. How did you manage to persuade her to come?"

I told them about the imaginary cupcake competition. Everything apart from the fact that it had been Jack's idea.

"That's actually not a bad plan," Pearl said.

"Thanks. Does that mean I'm forgiven for the cannonball?"

"Only if you actually manage to get Grandma here on Sunday."

I made a call to the lift company who maintained and serviced the lift in our building.

"Washbridge Ace Lifts. How can I help you today?"

"Hi, my name is Jill Maxwell. I work at Washbridge Central Point. I believe your company provides the servicing for our lift."

"That's correct. Do you need to report a fault?"

"No, everything is working fine as far as I know. I'm a private investigator and I'm working on a case involving an unexplained death."

"I don't see how—"

"It's okay. It has nothing to do with your lift, but I believe that one of your engineers might have information that would help with my enquiries."

"I see. Which engineer would that be?"

"I was hoping you could tell me. The guy I need to talk to was carrying out routine maintenance on the lift on the day in question."

"What date was that?"

I gave her the date that Marcy had died. "He was here in the morning."

"Carrying out routine maintenance, you said?"

"That's right."

"Can you hold on for a minute while I check our records?"

"Sure. Thank you."

The line went silent for a couple of minutes, then she said, ""I've checked and double-checked our records. None of our engineers were at Washbridge Central Point on that day."

"Are you sure?"

"One hundred percent."

"Right, thanks."

"Will there be anything else?"

"No, thanks. I appreciate your help."

Hmm, very interesting.

I'd not long finished speaking to the lift company when I got a call from Kevin Wright.

"It's all set for tonight, Jill."

"That was quick. Have they both said they'll come to your house?"

"Yeah, they were both a little cool at first, but when I said I was looking to offload my cages, their attitude soon changed."

"What time are they coming over?"

"Seven-thirty. Is that okay?"

"Perfect."

"What will I say to them if they arrive before you do?"

"They won't. I'll be there before seven, just to be on the safe side."

"And what do you want me to do while you're talking to them?"

"You won't be there."

"Sorry?"

"As soon as I arrive, I'll need you to make yourself scarce."

"Oh, I thought—"

"Let me do the thinking, Kevin. You just have to make sure you don't bump into them on your way out."

I love it when a plan comes together.

Scotty was clearly surprised to see me again so soon.

"Back again, Jill?" He grinned. "People will start talking about us."

"Can I view the CCTV footage of Marcy in the lift

again?"

This time he didn't bother going through the pretence of refusing me access.

"Sure."

A couple of minutes later, I was watching the same footage I'd viewed previously. After entering the lift, and pressing the button, Marcy leaned against the wall, and adjusted her hair while looking at the full-length mirror. When the doors opened, Marcy hesitated for a moment and then stepped out.

"What are you looking for, Jill?" Scotty said.

"Hold on a minute." I pressed rewind and replayed the footage several times.

It was only on the fourth viewing that I noticed it.

"There!"

"What?" Scotty moved closer to the screen. "I don't see anything."

"Try again." I rewound the footage. "Watch her closely when she presses the button."

After he had viewed it again, he said, "I don't know what I'm supposed to be looking at."

I rewound it again. "Which button does she press?"

I played it again.

"Number 12. That's her floor."

"Now watch the illuminated display when the doors open.

"It shows an 'R'."

"Correct."

"I don't understand." Scotty scratched his head.

"Marcy pressed the button for her floor, but the lift actually went up to the roof. Don't you see what that means? If she had intended to kill herself, she would have pressed the button for the roof, but she didn't. She pressed the number 12 button."

"What does that mean?"

"That's what I need to find out. Can I see the footage from earlier that day?"

"Sure. From when?"

"What time did the guy come to service the lift?"

"It would have been about nine-thirty, I guess."

"Okay, let's start an hour before that."

Scotty received a call from someone on the sixth floor with a belligerent client who was refusing to leave the building.

"Will you be okay here by yourself while I see to this, Jill?"

"Sure."

Before he left, Scotty cued the footage to start an hour before the guy arrived to service the lift. Nothing out of the ordinary happened during the next fifty minutes of the footage. People got in and out of the lift and travelled up and down the floors, seemingly without incident. Then, with the display showing that the lift was on the ground floor, the doors opened, and a man, wearing a red uniform and matching cap, stepped into the lift. A woman tried to follow him inside, but he put out a hand to stop her. He spoke to her for a minute and then she stepped back out of the lift. Once alone, the man opened the control panel to reveal a small computer touchscreen.

Scotty returned at that moment, so I paused the footage.

"Is that the guy who came to carry out the maintenance on the lift?"

"I think so, but I can't really see his face on here. It's

definitely the uniform he was wearing, though."

"Any idea what he's doing with that control panel."

"Not a clue. We don't have access to that."

We continued to watch the man who was tapping away on the touchscreen.

"What do you reckon he's doing?" Scotty asked.

"I've no idea."

After he'd finished whatever it was he was doing, he pushed the control panel closed. Then, for the first time, he turned his head slightly towards the camera. Throughout the footage, his cap had hidden most of his face, but just as he exited the lift, I did get the briefest of glances at him. Fortunately, it was long enough for me to recognise him as Marcy's ex, Leonard. He had sworn to me that he was at the dentist, undergoing root canal treatment, on the day that Marcy had died. Clearly, he had lied, so why had the dental receptionist confirmed his alibi? More importantly, what had Leonard been doing in that lift?

***

When I walked into the kitchen, Jack was standing next to the table, making weird gestures with his hands. He was clearly trying to tell me something, but I wasn't in the mood for a game of charades.

"What?"

He pointed towards the garden and mouthed, "Kathy."

Before I could respond, the door opened, and my sister stepped in from the garden.

"Kathy." I forced a smile. "To what do we owe this pleasant surprise?"

"Why do you have a weasel in the garden?"

"He isn't a weasel. He's a ferret and his name is Sandy."

"And why, pray tell, does Sandy have a mini-TV in his cage?"

"I'm not sure if I locked the store," Jack said. "I'll just go and check."

Before I could stop him, the coward had made a break for it.

"Cup of tea, Kathy?"

"That would be lovely. Do you have any Earl Grey?"

"Of course I don't. It's PG Tips, take it or leave it."

"That'll be fine, I suppose."

I made the tea and we both took a seat at the table.

"No custard creams?"

"I'm all out."

"Liar." She stood up and went straight to the cupboard where I kept my stash. "Oh, look what I've found."

"Jack must have brought them back from the store."

"Including the half-eaten packet?" She grinned, and then helped herself to three of the biscuits.

"Did you want something or is this just *another* social call?"

"Before I get into that, you haven't told me why your weasel has a TV."

"*Ferret*."

"Whatever. Why is there a TV in its cage?"

"I didn't like to say anything while Jack was here, but I think he's having a midlife crisis."

"What?"

"Out of the blue, he suddenly announced that he wanted a ferret."

"I thought men bought motorcycles when they had a

midlife crisis."

"Jack's always been a bit different. You know that."

"That still doesn't explain the TV."

"Jack used to keep ferrets when he was a kid. He insists that they need a TV for company. I know what you're thinking: that's insane. I agree, but what can I do?"

"Pete has his weird ways, but nothing on this scale."

"You were going to tell me why you're here."

"I've decided that it's time I came out of retirement."

"Okay."

"Aren't you going to ask me what I'm going to do?"

"If I must. What are you going to do?"

"I'm going to open an art gallery."

"You don't know anything about art."

"Yes, I do. I've always had an eye for the finer things in life."

"If you say so. Where will this gallery be?"

"In Washbridge of course. I've been on the lookout for suitable premises for some time now, and the perfect location has just come on the market. It's in the creative quarter of town, obviously."

I laughed. "Since when does Washbridge have a creative quarter?"

"Since several years. Not that I'd expect you to know."

"What does that mean?"

"Let's be honest, Jill, I have always been the classy one between us."

"The snob, you mean? What's in this *creative quarter*?"

"Lots of local artisans: artists, designers, musicians, that kind of thing."

"It sounds like you'll fit right in. What are you going to call this gallery of yours?"

"Gallery K. Catchy, eh?"

"Great."

"I'd better be making tracks." She drank the last few drops of tea. "I've got a ton of stuff to sort out prior to the big opening day."

"When is that?"

"In about three weeks. Don't worry, you'll get an invitation."

A few minutes after Kathy had left, Jack reappeared.

"Thanks, pal," I said.

"The ferret and TV were your idea. I wasn't getting involved. How did you manage to explain it away?" He grinned.

"I told her it was all part of your midlife crisis."

That wiped the grin off his face.

"My what?"

"Don't worry about it. She came over to tell me that she's coming out of retirement to open an art gallery."

"Kathy? What does she know about art?"

"Nothing, but that won't stop her."

"Where is it?"

"In Washbridge's creative quarter."

"That makes sense."

"Hang on. Did you know there was a creative quarter?"

"Of course I did. It's full of quaint little shops and studios. Kathy's art gallery should do okay there."

"How come I've never heard of the creative quarter?"

"You always were a philistine, Jill."

***

Kevin Wright was watching through the window when

I turned up at his house at seven o'clock.

"What are you going to do, Jill?" he said, as soon as he opened the door.

"There isn't time to get into that now. I just need you to make yourself scarce before those two arrive."

"But won't they scarper the moment they see you're the one waiting for them?"

"Just get your coat on and leave. I'll call you as soon as there's something to tell you."

"Okay."

Somewhat reluctantly, he left me alone in the house. Only when I was sure that he wasn't going to turn around and come back did I cast the 'doppelganger' spell, to make myself look like him. Now, all I had to do was to await the arrival of Bernt Toste and Gordon Sandwich. And pray that my hunch paid off.

I didn't have long to wait because just after seven-twenty, a car pulled up outside the house. Gordon got out of the driver's seat, and Bernt climbed out of the passenger's side. I hadn't expected them to arrive together, but that wouldn't have any effect on my plan.

I didn't answer the door on the first knock. Instead, I waited until they tried a second time. This time, I opened the door and welcomed them with a smile.

"Thanks for coming, guys. Come in." I led the way into the lounge.

Both of them hesitated when they caught sight of the cages that were still occupied by Kevin's ferrets.

"I thought you'd decided to get out of the game?" Bernt said.

"I have. I just haven't got around to rehoming these guys yet. I take it you're both still interested in the cages, though?"

"Absolutely," Gordon said. "It's very magnanimous of you to offer us this opportunity. After—you know."

"There's no point in holding grudges," I (AKA Kevin) said. "I have to nip upstairs for a moment. Why don't you take a closer look at the cages? Then we can discuss prices."

"Okay, great."

I stepped out of the lounge but listened at the door.

"These cages are as good as they get," Bernt said.

"He always did buy the best."

"What do you think he'll want for them?"

"Not much if he's quitting the game like he said he was."

I reversed the 'doppelganger' spell and then walked back into the lounge where both men were too busy studying the cages to notice me.

"Hello, gentlemen."

That got their attention.

"What are you doing here?" Bernt said.

"Are you here about the cages too?" Gordon asked. "If so, you're too late. Kevin is going to sell them to us."

"I'm sorry to be the bearer of bad news, but Kevin won't be selling the cages to anyone."

"Yes, he will. He's getting out of the game. That's why he asked us to come over."

"I'm afraid that was a lie. I told him to tell you that."

"Why? Who are you?"

"I'm the only thing that's standing between you two and a prison cell."

"What are you talking about?" Gordon started towards the door. "I'm leaving."

"You're not going anywhere." I blocked his way. "Not until you tell me about Doug Hurst."

Sandy had told me that he'd overheard Bernt and Gordon talking about someone called *Dugger*, but in fact he'd misheard them. It was only when Jack told me about the article in the newspaper that I'd realised they must have been talking about *Doug Hurst*.

Hearing me say that man's name had the same effect on both men, who now looked terrified. After the longest moment of silence, it was Gordon who managed to regain his composure first.

"Never heard of him. Now let me get past."

"Sorry, I can't do that. I had hoped to avoid involving the police, but you leave me no choice." I took out my phone.

"No!" Bernt Toste said. "What do you want to know?"

"Shut up, Bernt!" Gordon yelled at him.

"What good will that do? She already knows."

"He's right, Gordon," I said. "I do know."

"You don't know anything." It was clear Gordon intended to try and brazen it out.

"I know that you colluded with Doug Hurst to steal the money from Kevin's safe. How am I doing so far?"

"Don't tell her anything," Gordon snapped.

"You do what you want. I'm not going down for this," Bernt said. "We didn't collude with anyone. All we did was to tell Hurst that Kevin kept a safe in his shed."

"Whoa, let's take a step back. How did Hurst know about the F-O-F funds in the safe at Kevin's house, anyway?"

"Do you really think he was interested in that paltry amount?" Gordon scoffed. "He was after Kevin's inheritance. He must have read about it in the press. It was splashed across all the papers at the time. The papers also mentioned he was the treasurer of F-O-F, so he turned up at one of our meetings, looking for Kevin. As chance would have it, Kevin was ill that day, so he wasn't there."

Bernt chipped in, "We assumed that Hurst was interested in becoming a member, so we went to talk to him, much like we did when you showed up. But it became clear that he had no interest in the club, when he threatened us and our families if we didn't tell him where Kevin lived."

"We had no choice in the matter." Gordon sighed. "Hurst said that if we told anyone about our conversation, he'd come looking for us."

"You should have gone to the police there and then."

"That's easy for you to say. The man is a psycho."

"Even if all that is true, why didn't you come clean after the money had been taken? Why kick Kevin out of F-O-F?"

"We should never have done that to Kevin." Bernt glared at Gordon. "It wasn't my idea."

"We had to keep up the charade," Gordon said. "Hurst had told us that he'd be watching, and that if the finger of blame was pointed at him, he'd come and find us. We couldn't take that risk."

"I assume you heard that Hurst has been arrested for robbing a jeweller, and is back behind bars?"

"Yeah, I saw it in the Bugle," Bernt said.

"And yet here you both are, prepared to buy Kevin's cages at a knockdown price. Have you no shame?"

Neither of them spoke for the longest moment, then

Bernt said, "What are you going to do?"

"Shortly after I leave, Kevin will return, and you're going to do exactly what I tell you."

I spent the next few minutes giving them their instructions, and then I went outside and called Kevin.

"How did it go, Jill?"

"Fine. I need you to get back here as quickly as you can. Gordon and Bernt are waiting for you."

"What do I say to them? What do I do?"

"Just let them do the talking, and I'd like you to call me in the morning with an update. Got it?"

"Yeah, I'm on my way."

Chapter 29

The next morning, when I arrived at the office, Jules' coat was on the stand, but she wasn't at her desk. I found her in my office, looking rather bemused by something.

"Are you okay, Jules?"

"I just noticed this." She was holding Winky's tiny trophy in her hand. "I had no idea you were in a barbershop choir, Jill."

"I—err—" I glanced around, to find Winky rolling around on the floor; he clearly found this situation hilarious. "It's just a hobby."

"You must be good if you won the second prize. What does GT stand for?"

"GT?"

"I think that's what it says on here." She squinted. "The writing is so small."

I took the trophy from her. "Ah yes. GT. It stands for Greater Todmorden. That's where the competition was held."

"I'm well impressed, Jill. What did you sing?"

"*Sing*?"

"For the competition. What songs did you sing?"

Fortunately, my phone rang with a call from Kevin Wright, so I was able to gesture to Jules that I wanted to take the call in private. Once she was out of the room, and before I began to talk to Kevin, I said to Winky, "I want that trophy gone yesterday."

"But it—"

"If it's still here when I finish on this call, it's going out of the window."

Without another word, he snatched the trophy and

went off in a huff.

"Sorry about that, Kevin, there was someone in the office with me."

"Are you okay to talk now?"

"Yes. How did it go after I left yesterday?"

"It was a bit weird at first. They seemed to think I'd spoken to them earlier, then disappeared. Anyway, Bernt and Gordon admitted that they'd been a party to the theft of the money. I was livid at first, but then they explained that they'd been forced to do it by that Hurst character. They made it sound like he had them over a barrel."

"They did a terrible thing, but I do believe that they were terrified of the consequences if they had refused."

"I got the same impression, that's why I accepted their apologies."

"That was very magnanimous of you, Kevin. Not everyone would have done that."

"They even asked me to return to my position of treasurer at F-O-F."

"That's great."

"I said no."

"Really?"

"Yes. I will start attending the meetings again, but I would prefer not to have the responsibility of being one of the officers."

"I'm glad to hear you intend to return to F-O-F, at least."

"I really do appreciate everything you've done, Jill. You'll let me have your bill, I assume."

"It'll be in tonight's post."

"And if there's anything I can ever do for you, please let me know."

"Actually, Kevin, there is one small thing you could do for me."

"Where's your trophy gone?" Jules asked when she brought me my mid-morning cup of tea.

"It's in my bag. I'm taking it home."

"I bet Jack is very proud of you. Did he watch the competition?"

"No, he had to work in the store."

"What a shame."

My phone rang and I could see from the caller ID that it was Edna.

"Sorry, Jules, I need to take this."

I waited until she was out of the office before accepting the call.

"Oh, you are still alive, then," Edna said.

"What do you mean?"

"I was beginning to wonder, seeing as how I haven't heard from you since you asked me to follow this weird little guy."

"Sorry, Edna. I've been really busy."

"It's no skin off my feathers, but your final bill is going to be a real doozy."

"I suppose you ought to send me what you've got so far and then I can decide if I want you to continue to follow him."

"Okay. I'll email them to you now."

"How many photos do you have?"

"Not many. The guy is a bit of a Johnny No-Mates. Let me just check." The line went silent for a moment. "I only have about ten photos altogether."

"Okay, send them over."

I ended the call, and less than a minute later, the email arrived with the photos attached. I scrolled through them quickly. Edna was right about Leonard: most of the photos showed him interacting with the person behind the counter in a shop or coffee shop. I was just beginning to think the whole exercise had been futile (to say nothing of expensive) when I came to the final photograph. Clearly, Leonard wasn't quite the Johnny no-mates Edna had suggested he was because this image showed him kissing a young woman.

It was a young woman I recognised.

"Jules, do you think you could make me an appointment here, please?" I handed her the address I'd just scribbled down.

"Do you have a toothache, Jill?"

"No, my teeth are fine; it's related to a case I'm working on. I'd like you to tell them it's an emergency, and that I'm in agony. See if you can get me an appointment today if possible."

"Okay, I'll do my best."

Once again, we were interrupted by my phone ringing. This time it was a call from Honey Ease.

"Hi, Honey."

"Jill, you'll never guess what just happened." I was pretty sure I could guess exactly what had happened. "We've received a ransom demand for Majestic."

"No! Really?" I did my best to sound astonished. "When?"

"It was in the letterbox next to the main gate when Sonny checked it this morning."

"Who else has touched it?"

"Just Sonny and me."

"Put the letter and the envelope it came in somewhere where no one else will touch them."

"Okay. Do you think there'll be fingerprints on them?"

"Possibly. Or DNA. I'll come straight over."

***

I was halfway to Ease Stables when I got a call from my office, so I pulled into the side of the road.

"Jill, the dentist couldn't fit you in today, but they said they can see you first thing in the morning. Shall I make you an appointment?"

"Yes, please, Jules, and text me with the time."

"Will do."

For the second time in twenty-four hours, I joined Honey, Sonny and Dez Ease in the dining room. Lying in the centre of the table was a letter and an opened envelope.

"That's it, I assume." I took out a pair of tweezers from my bag, in order to examine the letter, which had been put together from words cut from magazines or newspapers. "Thirty million?" I gasped - rather convincingly, even if I do say so myself.

"You told us yesterday that you thought this was an inside job," Dez snapped.

"That's true, and the reason I believed that was the lack of a ransom demand. This letter changes everything. Thirty million sounds like an awful lot of money."

"It's a ridiculous amount," Sonny said. "We don't have that kind of money."

"I want to know what you intend doing about it." Dez glared at me. "You seemed so convinced it was an inside job."

"I was, but now that I have this note, I'll obviously change the focus of my investigation. As soon as I leave here, I'll get this letter and envelope analysed."

"Do you have the facilities to do that?"

"I have access to them."

"Do you believe Majestic is still alive?" Sonny asked, somewhat out of the blue.

"Yes, but of course I will ask for proof of life before—"

"Before what?" Dez interrupted. "We don't have the money to pay them, and we wouldn't give in to scum like this, even if we did."

"Don't worry about any of that. Let me see what the letter and envelope reveal, and we'll take it from there." I took out a small, clear plastic bag, and used the tweezers to place the letter and envelope inside. "I'd better get going so that I can catch the laboratory before they close." I turned towards the door.

"I'll walk you out, Jill." Honey offered.

We talked as we walked back to my car.

"I think your father may be losing faith in me," I said.

"He's just stressed out about Majestic."

"I wouldn't blame him if he had. After all, I was convinced that someone here at the stables was responsible for taking Majestic."

"You weren't to know we'd get the ransom demand the next day."

"That's true. You must have been shocked when Sonny showed you the letter."

"Yes, I was. Absolutely gobsmacked."

We'd reached my car. "Thanks for walking me out, Honey. I'll be in touch as soon as I hear back from the lab."

"Thanks, Jill."

I drove out of the stables and parked the car up a sideroad, out of sight of the house. After casting the 'invisible' spell, I used the 'faster' spell to enable me to get back to the house just ahead of Honey. Instead of going into the house, she walked around the side. After checking no one else was around (or so she thought), she took out her phone.

"It's me. Yes, she's just left. It worked like a dream. She's taken the letter away to test for fingerprints and DNA. Good luck with that." She laughed. "Yeah, I think so. How is he? Great. Okay, I'll call you later. Bye, Max."

Bingo! Am I a genius or am I a genius?

And before you start with the wisecracks, that's a rhetorical question.

***

Jack must have finished early at the store because he'd already started dinner when I got home.

"You look like the cat that got the cream," he said.

"Have I ever told you that I may be the world's best PI?"

"I seem to recall you mentioning it a few times. I take it you've had a good day?"

"The best. I've put the ferret case to bed and I'm close to putting the other two to bed as well."

"Good for you. What happened with ferret man?"

"Kevin's name has been cleared, and he was even

invited to return to his post as treasurer of F-O-F."

"He must be thrilled."

"He is, but he doesn't want to be the treasurer again. He's just happy to be back with his ferret buddies."

"Another happy client, then?"

"Very. In fact, he was so pleased, he agreed to do us a favour."

"Oh? What's that?"

"I take it you haven't looked in the garden since you got back home."

"No. Why?"

"Take a look."

He walked over to the door and peered out. "What am I supposed to be looking at?"

"You must be the world's most unobservant man."

"I don't know what—hang on—the cage has gone."

"I got Kevin to agree to take Sandy. After all, he's better equipped to look after him than we are."

"Yes!" Jack gave a fist-pump. "What about the TV?"

"That was a bit awkward. I had to make him agree to take the mini-TV too. And to keep it on at all times."

"He must have thought you were crazy. What did you say to explain the TV?"

"Just that we'd discovered that Sandy found watching it very comforting."

"Did he buy that?"

"Probably not, but he agreed to let Sandy keep it, so that's all that matters." I took out my phone and discovered that I had a text from Jules. It must have come through while I was driving back from Ease Stables. "Looks like you'll have to eat breakfast alone in the morning because I have an appointment with the dentist."

Chapter 30

The next morning, I was up before Jack.

"I'm leaving, Jack," I shouted upstairs.

"Already?"

"My dentist appointment is at eight-fifteen."

"That's early."

"I told them it was an emergency. See you tonight."

Before I could get into the car, Goldie called to me. I didn't really have time to hang around, but I could tell by her expression that something was wrong.

"What's up, Goldie?"

"It's happened again, Jill. Last night."

"What happened this time?"

"When I got up this morning, I noticed the door to the spare bedroom was ajar. I looked inside, and it was obvious the bed had been slept in."

"Are you sure?"

"Positive. The covers had been pulled back and there was an indentation in the pillow."

"Have you checked to make sure there's no one in the house now?"

"Yes, from top to bottom. There's no one inside. But you haven't heard it all yet. When I checked the second bedroom, both beds in there looked like they'd been slept in too."

"Both?"

"There are twin beds in that room."

"Right. Did you speak to Liam after the last incident?"

"I did, and I'm one-hundred percent certain he isn't the one doing this. Do you think I should call the police?"

"I don't think you have any other choice."

"I'm worried they'll think I'm making it up."

"There's no reason for them to do that. You have to call them, Goldie. Whoever is doing this could be dangerous."

"You're right, Jill. I'll give them a call now."

"I have to dash because I have a dental appointment."

"Oh. I'm sorry I've delayed you. Are you in pain?"

"No, I'm fine. Give the police a call."

"I will. I promise."

I arrived at the dental surgery twenty minutes before my appointment, only to find the door was locked. I tried the doorbell but there was no response.

"You're early," someone behind me said.

I turned around to find Sarah, the receptionist I'd spoken to on my previous visit when I'd posed as a policewoman.

"My appointment is at eight-fifteen." I held my jaw. "I've been in agony all night."

"I was the one your assistant spoke to. As I explained to her, the first appointment of the day is usually at nine o'clock, but I told Mr Avity about your situation, and he agreed to start a little earlier today."

"I really do appreciate that."

"Colin is a great dentist. He always goes out of his way to help anyone in acute pain." She unlocked the door and reset the alarm. "Why don't you come in and I'll take your details while we wait for Colin to arrive."

Once inside, Sarah switched on her computer, and she was about to take my details when I cast the 'sleep' spell, causing her to slump onto her desk. There were very few icons on the desktop, so I was easily able to identify the one for the appointment system. I clicked on it and a calendar appeared on-screen. It defaulted to today's appointments, with my name appearing at the top of the list. I clicked on the small calendar and selected the date on which Marcy had died. I quickly scanned the names of the patients listed for that day, but one name was conspicuous by its absence.

Having confirmed my suspicions, I reversed the 'sleep' spell. Sarah sat up and looked around, clearly still a little dazed.

"What happened?" she said.

"Will you take a look at this, please." I held up my phone, which was displaying one of the photos that Edna had sent to me.

"How did you get that?" she snapped.

"Never mind how I got it. Judging by the way you're kissing one another, I assume you and Leonard are an item."

"Who are you? What's this all about?"

"I'm a private investigator and I'm looking into Leonard's ex-wife's death. Why did you tell the police that Leonard was undergoing a root canal on the fifth?"

"Do you even have toothache?"

"Not really."

"I'd like you to leave."

"I can, but if I do, my next stop will be at the police station. I'm sure they'll be interested to hear that you lied to them in order to protect a murderer."

"Leonard isn't a murderer. He's done nothing wrong."

"You admit you know him, then?"

"We've been seeing each other for a while. Not that it's any of your business."

"If he has nothing to hide, why did he ask you to lie for

him about the root canal?"

"Because he knew that people would try to blame him for his ex's death. And that's just what's happening, isn't it?"

"What if I was to tell you that Leonard was at Marcy's place of work on the day that she's supposed to have committed suicide."

"That can't be right."

"Why do you say that?"

"He told me he'd gone fishing, but that there were no witnesses who could back up his story."

"So, you lied for him?"

"I—err—"

"There's CCTV footage of Leonard at Marcy's offices just before she died."

"That still doesn't mean he killed her."

"True, but you have to ask yourself this: if he was prepared to lie to you about where he was on that day, what else might he be lying about? Let me spell it out for you, Sarah. You're already in a whole world of trouble for lying to the police. Unless you get out in front of this thing quickly, you could find yourself charged with obstruction of justice. If not worse."

"I didn't know, honestly." She began to well up.

"I believe you and I'd like to help, but you'll have to do everything I tell you."

"I'll do whatever you say."

"Excellent."

I spent the next few minutes telling Sarah what I wanted her to do, and she agreed readily. I'd just finished when the door behind me opened and in walked a man with teeth so perfect they could only belong to a dentist.

"Good morning, Sarah," he said.

"Good morning, Colin."

He glanced at me. "And you must be my emergency. I understand you've been having a lot of pain?"

"Actually, the tooth feels much better now." I made a beeline for the door. "The pain has completely gone."

"There really is nothing to be afraid of," he called after me. "You won't feel a thing."

***

I don't need to tell you that I am a woman of many talents. One of which, is my ability to do a near-perfect impression of anyone's voice. Okay, yes, I do use magic, but that doesn't detract from the sheer genius involved. I mention that only to explain how I was able to fool Honey Ease into thinking she was speaking to Maxine Westlake.

"Honey, it's me. Max."

"Why aren't you calling from your usual number?"

"I dropped my phone in the bath yesterday. Listen, Majestic isn't well."

"What's wrong with him?"

"I don't know. He's listless and he won't eat or drink anything. Should I call the vet?"

"You can't do that."

"But I'm really worried."

"Don't do anything. I'll come straight over."

"Okay, but hurry. Please."

What did I tell you? A masterful impression if I do say so myself.

I'd made the call from a burner phone while sitting in

my car, which was parked just down the road from Ease Stables. Just as I'd hoped, Honey's car came thundering out of the driveway and headed west. I wasn't concerned that she might realise that I was tailing her because she had other things on her mind.

Honey's driving was a little erratic, and she was only paying lip-service to the speed limits. I had no idea where she was headed, but very soon the roads became narrower, as we went deeper into the countryside. I started to get worried when the roads became single track, and I felt sure that it was only a matter of time before she spotted me in her rearview mirror.

Then, without indicating, she turned sharp right through a pair of open gates, so I pulled onto the grass verge a little further down the road. I jumped out, cast the 'faster' spell, and sprinted through the gates. On the way in, I noticed a sign: **Westlake Farm**.

Honey's car wasn't in front of the farmhouse, so I headed around the back. I reached the rear of the building just in time to see Honey get out of her car and head towards the row of outbuildings. I followed her inside and heard Maxine call out, "Honey?"

"How is he?"

"Who?"

"Majestic of course. Has he got any worse?"

"What do you mean?"

"You said he was ill."

"I don't know what you're talking about."

"Stop messing around, Max. This isn't funny."

"Honestly, Honey, I don't—"

"I might be able to throw some light on your confusion, ladies." I stepped forward.

Honey spun around to face me. "Jill? What are you doing here?"

"I've heard so much about the amazing Majestic Tears that I thought it was time for me to actually meet him."

Honey turned to Max who shook her head. "I didn't tell her."

"She didn't need to," I said. "I've known for some time that it was one or both of you that took Majestic. I just can't work out why you did it."

"What about the ransom demand we received?" Honey said.

I laughed. "Sorry, but that wasn't fooling anyone."

"Was it you who phoned me just now?"

"Guilty as charged. I'm sorry if I had you worried, but I needed you to lead me here."

"I suppose you're going to tell my father."

"I'm not sure what I'm going to do yet, but I really would like to see the horse, to make sure he's okay."

They didn't put up any objections. Instead, the two of them led me to a stall at the far side of the building.

Majestic was a fitting name for the magnificent horse who was clearly enjoying the fuss Max was making of him.

"He's a beauty," I said.

"He's the best." Honey gave him a sugar cube. "What happens now?"

"Is there any chance of a cup of tea?" I said.

"Sure." Max nodded. "Let's go into the house."

"Sounds good. I noticed this place is called Westlake Farm."

"It belongs to my parents," Max said. "But they don't actually farm any longer. They're both retired. In fact, they're visiting my sister in New Zealand at the moment."

"Which is why you were able to keep Majestic here, I assume?"

"Correct."

Once Max had made the tea, we all took a seat at the oak kitchen table. It was clear that they were both waiting for me to lead the discussion, so I started with the obvious question.

"Why?"

"You've seen Ease Stables, Jill," Honey said. "They're stuck in the last century. Our training facilities haven't been kept up to date and our security is non-existent. Sonny and I have been trying to persuade Dad to invest in the place, but he doesn't see the need."

"I thought Ease was one of the top stables in the country?"

"It used to be, but right now we're living off our past reputation. And it's not just Sonny and I who are saying this. A lot of owners have pulled their horses out of Ease over the last couple of years. If that carries on, very soon, Ease will be history."

"Even if all that is true, how does removing Majestic help?"

"I've tried everything I know to get Dad to listen, but he won't. He still thinks of Sonny and me as kids. I thought this might actually shock him into taking action."

"I assume Sonny is in on this too?"

"No. He would never have gone along with it if I'd told him my plan. He's terrified of upsetting Dad."

"What's your part in all this, Max?" I asked.

"Honey and I have been friends since we were kids. I love working with the horses at Ease. There's nothing I'd rather do. My parents wanted me to take over this farm, but I have no interest in it. Horses are my life."

"What did you think when Honey told you of her plan?"

She looked at Honey and hesitated before saying, "I thought it was a crazy idea, but I could see how desperate she was, so I agreed to help."

"It was you who took Majestic from Ease, I assume?"

"Yeah, I did. He'll go anywhere with me."

"What are you going to do, Jill?" Honey said.

"That's up to you."

"What do you mean?"

"Obviously, I'll have to tell your father that I've found Majestic—"

"You can't do—"

"Hold on. Let me finish. I have no choice but to tell him, but I don't have to do it immediately. I'd prefer to wait until you've told him yourself. And returned Majestic of course."

"He'll kill me."

"No, he won't. You did this to shock him into making changes. Well, one thing is for certain, you gave him the shock of his life. Hopefully, it will be the catalyst needed for him to accept changes are needed."

"But what if he doesn't?"

"If he doesn't, then there's nothing more you can do because it will be clear he never will. In which case, you'll have to decide if you want to stay at Ease or leave and make a fresh start somewhere else."

"But Ease is all I've ever known."

"I realise that, but there really is no alternative. I'll give you until tomorrow to return Majestic and to speak to your father. Whether you do or not is obviously up to you, but either way, I intend to tell him everything I know on the following day." I stood up. "I believe you two have a lot to discuss."

Chapter 31

Although I was never going to be Kiki's biggest fan, I did appreciate the fact that, with two assistants, Jack and I would be able to eat breakfast and dinner together more often.

"Penny for them," he said in between spoonsful of muesli.

"I was just wondering what Honey Ease has decided to do."

"From what you told me last night, it didn't sound like she had many options. If she doesn't come clean to her father, you're going to tell him anyway. She's between a rock and a hard place. What do you think she'll do?"

"I hope she tells her father, but more importantly, I hope he listens to her reasons for doing what she did."

"Do you think he will?"

"I'm not sure. From what little I've seen of him he strikes me as a man who is set in his ways."

"The horse is safe, though. That's the main thing, surely."

"Definitely, and a fine specimen he is too."

"Have you prepared your lesson plan for CASS today?"

"There's no need. It's an inset day."

"I didn't realise they had those in the paranormal world too. Do you remember when Florence used to call them *insect* days?" He grinned.

"I do. Why do they have to grow up so quickly?" I sighed.

"Cheer up. It's the weekend tomorrow."

"Which means it's Aunt Lucy's gameshow and Grandma's surprise birthday party. Big whoop!"

Just then, there was a knock at the door.

"Who's that?" Jack said but didn't make a move to answer it.

"I'll get it, then, shall I?" I huffed.

"You're the nearest."

"And you're a lazy so and so."

It was Goldie Barr.

"I'm really sorry to disturb you so early, Jill, but I—err—" She burst into tears.

"Come inside."

I led her into the kitchen and gestured to Jack that he should make himself scarce.

"I ought to be going to the store." He took one last mouthful of muesli and then headed out.

"Take a seat, Goldie, and I'll make some tea."

"Thanks, Jill," she sobbed.

By the time we had our drinks, she'd just about managed to compose herself.

"Feeling better?" I asked.

"A bit."

"Why don't you tell me what's happened?"

"After I spoke to you yesterday morning, I rang the police like you suggested."

"Good. What did they say?"

"They sent someone to my house: a young woman police constable. I told her about the beds, and she asked to see them, so I took her into both bedrooms."

"Right."

"Then I told her about the other incidents."

"The milk bottles and the bowls?"

"Yeah."

"What did she say?"

"Not much really, but I got the impression that she wasn't taking it very seriously."

"Why not? Someone has been entering your house. I'd say that's very serious."

"So would I, but judging by the questions she asked me, I don't think she believed anyone else was involved."

"What do you mean?"

"I got the distinct impression that she thought I was making it all up, just to get attention. I could be wrong, but that's how it felt."

"How did she leave it? Did she promise to follow up with you?"

"Not really. She just gave me an incident number."

"That's outrageous. What are you going to do now?"

"What can I do? Maybe she was right. Maybe I did those things but can't remember doing them."

"No. That's rubbish. I saw how upset you were each time. There's no way you would have done that to yourself. Would you like me to speak to the police for you?"

"No, it's okay. I think I might go and stay with my parents for a while. Maybe a short break away from Middle Tweaking will do me good."

"Are you sure?"

"Yeah, I'm sure." She stood up. "I really do appreciate you putting up with all my nonsense."

I had no idea what to make of that. Had the policewoman been right? Was Goldie doing these things herself? At the time she'd told me about them, such a thought hadn't even entered my head. I'd simply taken her claims at face value. Maybe a complete break was what she needed.

***

Instead of heading into the office, I drove to a flat in Wash Side where Sarah, the dental receptionist lived. She had telephoned me late the previous night to confirm that she'd carried out my instructions to the letter. She opened the door before I had the chance to ring the doorbell.

"Quick, come in." She practically dragged me inside. "He might turn up early."

"Relax, Sarah, it's going to be okay."

"That's easy for you to say. If he did what you say he did to his ex, what's to stop him doing the same to me?"

"Because he'll be behind bars before the day is over."

"Do you promise?"

"I promise."

"What about me? They won't lock me up as well, will they?"

"Provided you're prepared to stand up in court and testify to what you've already told me, you won't have anything to worry about. Now, get your coat on and get out of here before Leonard arrives."

"Okay."

She was all fingers and thumbs, but she did eventually manage to fasten her coat and leave the flat. As soon as I was sure she wasn't coming back, I cast the 'doppelganger' spell to make myself look like Sarah. All I had to do now was to wait until Leonard arrived.

It was just as well that Sarah had left when she did because, less than ten minutes later, there was a hammering on the door.

"Sarah! Let me in!"

Clearly, Leonard was not a man blessed with patience.

I opened the door, but before I had the chance to greet him, he'd pushed past me and was headed for the kitchen.

"What's going on?" he demanded.

"I told you last night on the phone."

"But who was she?"

"She didn't tell me her name, but she said she was investigating Marcy's death."

"Police?"

"No. Some kind of private investigator, I think."

"I bet it's the same woman who caught me at Marcy's place."

"What were you doing there?"

"Nothing!" he snapped. "Why was she talking to you?"

"She knew I'd lied about your appointment."

"She was probably just bluffing. You didn't admit to it, did you?"

"I didn't have any choice."

"Great."

"I was scared. She said I might go to prison."

"You stupid cow!"

"Don't call me that."

"What else did she say?"

"That she had CCTV of you doing something to the lift at Marcy's offices on the morning that you were supposed to be having your root canal work. You told me that you'd gone fishing that morning."

"Be quiet. I need to think."

"Why were you at her offices?"

"I just wanted to talk to her. That's all."

"About what? I thought you and her were history."

"We were."

"Did you kill Marcy, Leonard? I'm not going to prison for you. She said if I told the police what I know that they won't charge me. What were you doing to the lift?"

"I just gave it a bit of a tweak so that when Marcy pressed the button for the top floor, it would take her up to the roof instead. You should have seen her face when the lift doors opened up on the roof and I was standing there." He grinned.

"You lied to me, Leonard. You told me that you and Marcy were over."

"We were. I just wanted her to apologise for the way she treated me."

"You were divorced. What did any of that matter?"

"It mattered to me. I wanted her to admit she was the reason we split up."

"And did she?"

"Of course not. She just laughed at me. I told her to stop, but she wouldn't."

"What did you do, Leonard?"

"I made her stop. You should have seen her face when I pushed her. She wasn't laughing then."

"You killed her."

"She let me down, just like you have. You women are all the same." He lunged for me, but I sidestepped and tripped him. He hit the floor with a thud, and before he could get back up, I reversed the 'doppelganger' spell, then used magic to tie his arms and legs.

Somewhat confused by this turn of events, he screamed at me.

"Where did you come from? Where's Sarah?"

"She had to leave."

"Let me go."

"Sorry, no can do, Leonard."

Leaving him bound on the kitchen floor, I went outside to call the police.

Inevitably, it was my old friend, Big Mac, who responded to my phone call. Accompanied by two uniformed officers, he knocked at the door less than twenty minutes later. I showed him into the kitchen where Leonard was rolling around, groaning into the gag I'd placed over his mouth to stop his constant moaning.

"You can't go around tying up random people, Maxwell," Big Mac said.

"I had no choice. He attacked me, so I was just acting in self-defence."

"I was told that you said something about apprehending a murderer."

"This is him. He murdered Marcy Bowkoo."

"Isn't that the woman who committed suicide?"

"Yes, except that she didn't. Leonard here pushed her off the building, as you'll hear if you listen to this." I handed him the recorder that I'd had in my pocket all along.

"Take that tape off his mouth," Big Mac ordered one of the uniformed officers.

"She was Sarah a minute ago!" Leonard blurted out as soon as the gag had been removed. "Then she transformed into her."

"He hit his head when he fell," I said by way of explanation. "You might want to get the doctor to take a look at it."

"There's nothing wrong with my head. She changed bodies."

Big Mac had clearly heard enough. "Untie this man and take him down to the station. And ask the doc to take a look at him before I question him."

The uniformed officers untied Leonard and led him away.

"You're saying this guy killed Marcy Bowkoo?" Big Mac said.

"I'm not the one saying it. He says it himself. It's all on the recording."

"My understanding was that he had a cast iron alibi, something about a dental appointment."

"This house belongs to a young woman called Sarah. She works at the dental surgery in question. Leonard persuaded her to lie for him."

"Where is she?"

"I told her to leave before Leonard got here. She knows she shouldn't have lied, but she had no idea that he'd murdered his ex. I told her you'd probably go easy on her if she testifies that she lied about the dental appointment."

"You had no right to promise her anything."

"I know, but I'm sure you'll do the right thing."

***

As usual, Big Mac was in no hurry to allow me to leave the police station. Even though, as I pointed out to him more than once, he should actually have been thanking me for helping him catch a murderer. When I was allowed to leave, and handed back my phone, I noticed that I had a missed call from the landline at Ease Stables.

As soon as I was clear of the police station, I returned the call, and it was Dez Ease who answered the phone.

"Sorry, I wasn't able to take your call earlier. I was—err—rather tied up on another case."

"That's okay, Jill. Are you free now, by any chance?"

"Yeah."

"Great. Would you mind popping over? I believe we need to have a talk, don't you?"

"Sure, I'll be over there as soon as I can."

Although Dez hadn't said as much, I concluded from that phone call that Honey had come clean about the Majestic Tears incident. I tried to call her, in the hope that I might find out what had transpired, and what I could expect when I got to the stables, but she didn't pick up.

It felt a little like walking into the lions' den when I arrived at Ease Stables, where Sonny greeted me at the door.

"Thanks for coming over so quickly, Jill."

"No problem. Is Honey here?"

"We'd best go through to the boardroom. Dad's waiting for you in there."

"Okay."

Dez was seated at the head of the table as usual, but for once, he didn't greet me with a smile. He simply shook my hand and asked me to take a seat. Honey was nowhere to be seen, which I took to be a bad sign.

"Jill, you probably know why I asked you to come over."

"I can guess. Is Majestic Tears back?"

"He is." Now Dez managed a smile. "And looking none the worse for his little adventure, I'm pleased to report."

"That's good."

"The last time you were here, you told us that you believed this was an inside job, and you were proven to be correct. I have to be honest with you. When Majestic was taken, the last person I suspected was my own daughter."

"I'm sure she—"

"Please, let me finish."

"Sorry."

"I understand that you gave Honey an ultimatum that either she told me what she'd done, or you would."

"That's right."

"When she brought Majestic home yesterday and told me what she'd done, I—err—well, let's just say that I'm not often lost for words, but I was struck dumb. I couldn't believe my own flesh and blood would do something like this."

"Dez, I know you don't—"

"Jill, please."

"I was just going to—"

"Apart from these stables, my family is my world, and since I lost my darling wife, that means my children. Can you begin to imagine how much it hurt to discover what had happened?"

"No, I can't, but I'm sure it was never Honey's intention to hurt you."

"I don't think you quite understand what I'm saying. It hurt to think that my stubbornness and stupidity had driven her to the point where she felt the need to do what she did."

"Oh? I—err—"

Suddenly, out of the blue, he shouted, "Come in."

The door opened behind me, and in walked Honey, who was all smiles. Before I could say anything, she took the seat next to mine.

"Dad has decided to hand over the reins of the business

to Sonny and me."

I must have looked as gobsmacked as I felt because Dez said, "Sorry for the subterfuge, Jill. I just wanted to see your reaction."

"I'd be lying if I said I wasn't surprised. I wasn't sure how you'd react when Honey told you what she'd done, but I didn't expect this."

"Neither did I," Honey said.

"Nor me." Sonny was smiling too now.

These two are the future of Ease Stables," Dez said. "I've always known that, but I guess I just didn't realise that I was standing in their way."

"It was never like that, Dad," Sonny said.

"Yes, it was. You two have been telling me things needed to change for years, but I've never listened. Even when we started to haemorrhage clients. Well, you were right, and if we're to stop the decline, we—sorry, I meant to say *you* need to take action now."

"What do you plan to do, Dez?" I asked.

"I'll still be around if they need advice, but I've promised only to offer it when asked. In the short term, though, I plan to take myself off on a holiday in the sun. We have a small villa in the south of France that I've barely seen for the last three years."

"Sounds like a good idea."

"So, Jill," Dez stood up. "This was hardly the outcome that I expected when we hired you. To be perfectly honest, I wasn't confident that you'd even manage to find Majestic. But you did, and you have helped to breathe new life into these stables. I can't thank you enough."

"It was my pleasure. I'm just glad things have turned out as well as they have."

"Now, before you go, I understand that you're something of an accomplished horse rider yourself."

"Well, I—err—"

"Why don't the four of us go over to the gallops and put some of those beautiful horses through their paces?"

"I really don't—"

"I won't take no for an answer."

Oh bum!

Chapter 32

Jack had had the same stupid grin on his face ever since he'd poured out his bowl of sawdust.

"Aren't you going to sit down to eat your cereal?" he said, while obviously trying to stifle a laugh.

"You're enjoying this, aren't you?"

"Come on, Jill, you have to admit it's funny."

"I'm glad you think so. I'm in agony here."

Despite my best efforts, I'd been unable to talk my way out of joining the Ease family on the gallops. Amazingly, the horse-riding spell I'd found had worked as advertised, and even Dez had complimented me on my riding style. When I'd got back home, I'd made the mistake of bragging to Jack about my newfound riding ability. What I hadn't anticipated was the effect it would have on the muscles in my legs and bum. When I woke up this morning, I'd struggled to get out of bed, and I certainly couldn't contemplate sitting down.

"How are you going to drive if you can't even sit down?" he said.

"I won't have to. I can magic myself over to Aunt Lucy's this morning for the gameshow, and then the same again for Grandma's birthday party."

"Won't you have to sit down for the gameshow?"

"I don't think so. The contestants were all standing in the program that Aunt Lucy showed me."

Jack rinsed his bowl and then put it in the dishwasher.

"Do you need anything from the store today?"

"No, I don't think so."

"A couple of soft cushions, maybe?" He laughed, but then only just managed to duck out of the way of the spoon that I hurled at him.

***

I'd arranged to meet Aunt Lucy at her house because I had no idea where the gameshow studios were located.

"You're very punctual, Jill." Aunt Lucy gave me a hug. "Are you excited?"

"Yeah," I lied.

"Are you okay? You seem to be walking rather strangely."

"I'm fine. What time do we need to leave?"

"We probably should set off now. As it's such a lovely day, I thought we'd walk over there."

"*Walk*?"

"It's only a couple of miles. That's alright, isn't it?"

"Yeah, fine."

The muscles in my upper legs burned with every step, and I could tell Aunt Lucy was wondering why I was walking so slowly.

"Are you sure you're okay, Jill?"

"I'm fine. Is it much further?"

"No, it's just around the next corner."

Candlefield Central Studios was a small, unremarkable building, which was obviously in need of serious renovation. Aunt Lucy practically skipped up the steps to the main entrance. I took them somewhat slower.

ID badges, attached to lanyards, were waiting for us at the reception desk, and the eager young man gave us directions to studio 3B. After a false start, when we inadvertently ended up on the set of a daytime soap, we eventually found our studio.

"Come in, ladies." A woman, with a surplus of red curls, checked our IDs and ticked our names off on her clipboard. "The studio audience are just arriving. As soon as they're seated, Lucius will come and collect you. Until then, would you mind going and standing over there with your opponents for today's show?" She pointed to two wizards, one much older than the other.

"Studio audience?" I whispered to Aunt Lucy, as we made our way to join the others.

"Didn't you know?"

"I thought it was just canned laughter and applause on the soundtrack."

"No, it goes out live in front of a studio audience."

"Live?"

"Exciting, isn't it?"

Exciting wasn't the word I would have used to describe it. I'd assumed that if I messed up they would simply be able to do another take.

"Hello, ladies." The older of the two wizards greeted us with one of the most insincere smiles it had ever been my misfortune to see. "I'm Reid. I hope you're on good form. Terence and I have been practising for several months and I'm confident that we can spot fake magic a million miles away."

"So have we," Aunt Lucy said. "So, I wouldn't count your chickens just yet."

Reid and Aunt Lucy were clearly taking this gameshow much more seriously than me or Terence, who looked as uninterested as I was.

"Here you all are." Lucius Wonderheart appeared wearing another gaudy, sequinned suit; this one was a sickly shade of green. "I hope you haven't been coming to blows."

"It's such an honour to finally meet you, Mr Wonderheart," Reid said.

"You're one of my favourite celebrities," Aunt Lucy gushed.

The two of them were trying to outdo each other to see who could do the most bootlicking.

"You must all call me Lucius." He checked his watch. "It's almost time to roll, so I'll go and welcome the audience, then I'll call you onto the set." He pointed to the two desks that were now illuminated on the stage behind him.

"There are seats," I blurted out, causing everyone to look at me as though I'd lost my mind. "Sorry, it's just that when I watched the show on TV, the contestants were standing at the desks."

"We made that change for this season," Lucius said. "It was my idea. It stops people shuffling around."

"Right."

"Okay, I'll go and get things started." He disappeared through the huge red curtains, and moments later the place exploded with applause and cheering. Once the audience had settled down, he said, "I know you're all eager to meet this week's contestants, so without further delay, here they are."

The curtains opened and I found myself looking out into a sea of eyes. Until then, I'd managed to keep my nerves in check, but now they really kicked in.

"I feel sick," I whispered to Aunt Lucy.

"You'll be fine. We'll beat these two, no problem."

Lucius took to the mic again. "Our first team is Reid and his son, Terence. Come and take your seats, gentlemen."

Reid beamed as he led his unsmiling offspring across the floor to the desk, where they took their seats.

"Our second team is aunt and niece: Lucy and Jill. Please go and take your seats, ladies."

Aunt Lucy floated across the floor and mounted the high stool with ease. It was the first time I'd sat down since I got out of bed that morning, and it felt like sitting on hot coals.

"Are you alright, Jill?" Lucius must have seen my pained expression.

"Fine. Just a little nervous."

"There's no need to be. We're all friends here. But then, there is the little matter of one thousand pounds for the winning team." He turned to face the audience. "And what does the losing team get?"

"Nothing!" the members of the audience all replied as one.

"That's right. Magic Or Not is an all or nothing game, which is what makes it so exciting."

Aunt Lucy had never mentioned that there was prize money to be won. Knowing that, heaped even more pressure onto me.

"Okay," Lucius said. "I'm sure everyone here knows the rules, which are as simple as simple can be. The teams will be shown clips of magic, which may or may not be *real* magic. Some of the clips will be illusions carried out by human magicians. Each competitor must decide whether what they have seen is magic or not."

***

"How did it go?" Jack said when I reappeared in the

lounge.

"Don't ask."

"That bad, eh?"

"It wasn't my fault we lost. Not really."

"Come and sit next to me and tell me all about it."

"I'd rather stay standing."

"Still suffering?"

"Yes, that's the reason we lost."

"You're going to have to explain that."

"In the recording that Aunt Lucy showed me, all the gameshow contestants were standing, but they'd changed that for this season, and we all had to sit on high stools."

"I bet that was painful."

"Extremely. I just couldn't get comfortable, which made it practically impossible to concentrate. Anyway, we were holding our own right up to the final round. The scores were level, and it was all to play for. Whoever won that final round took home the one thousand pounds."

"What did the losing team get?"

"Zilch."

"Ouch."

"The format was actually quite simple. We had to watch clips of someone, supposedly performing real magic, and buzz in as soon as we thought we knew if it was real or just an illusion. For the most part, it was quite easy to determine."

"How?"

"It's hard to describe. I guess you'd have to be a sup to understand. Anyway, the game was really close. They took the first round. We took the next two. After they'd won the fourth round, it was all on the last one. The final clip had only been playing for a matter of seconds when I buzzed."

"And you guessed wrong?"

"I hadn't intended to buzz at all. It was much too soon to make a judgement."

"So how come you buzzed?"

"I was in so much discomfort on the stool that I shuffled around and in doing so I inadvertently pressed the buzzer. I told the compere that it was an accident, but the rules state that once you've buzzed, you have to give an answer. I said I thought it was magic. It was a pure guess and I got it wrong, so we went home emptyhanded."

"Oh dear. How did your Aunt Lucy take it?"

"That was the worst part. She was really understanding, which somehow made it even worse. I'd have felt better if she'd laid into me for being such a klutz."

"You need a drink."

"You're right about that, but I'd better only have one because I don't want a hangover for Grandma's birthday party tomorrow."

Chapter 33

"Are you sure you don't want any breakfast?" Jack said.

"I couldn't face anything." I groaned. "I feel like death warmed up."

"I did try to warn you not to have that third glass of wine last night. Still, look on the bright side."

"What bright side?"

"Your hangover seems to have taken your mind off your other problem. You seem to be sitting okay."

"That's slim consolation."

"Do you know what you need?"

"What?"

"A birthday party to cheer you up." He laughed.

"I know what *you* need: My foot up your backside."

"What time have you got to go?"

"Grandma is coming around at midday, so make sure you're not here."

"No worries. I'll be at the store. In fact, I'd better get over there now." He gave me a peck on the cheek. "Have a *great* day."

"Some chance."

It wasn't just the hangover and the thought of a rowdy birthday party that was bothering me. I was dreading seeing Aunt Lucy again so soon after letting her down in the gameshow.

After Jack had left, I managed to sleep for a couple of hours on the sofa. When I woke, I still felt grim, but I did manage a couple of slices of toast and a cup of tea.

Punctual as ever, Grandma turned up a few minutes before midday. She didn't bother with any of the niceties, like knocking on the door. Instead, she just appeared in the lounge.

"You look awful." Was her opening gambit.

"Thanks."

"Were you drinking last night?"

"No, of course not. I think I might be coming down with flu. Shall we get going?"

"Before we do, I have a question."

"Okay?"

"Who's made the cake? I hope it wasn't the twins."

"What do you mean? It's a cupcake competition that you'll be judging."

"Let's cut the pretence. You and I both know this is my birthday party. All I want to know is who made my cake. I hope it was Lucy and not you or the twins."

"When did you find out?"

"That it was my birthday party you were planning? I've always known. You didn't actually think I'd fallen for that cupcake competition nonsense, did you? So, who has made the cake?"

"Aunt Lucy, but you mustn't let on that you knew about the party."

"Why not?"

"Because they'll think I let it slip. You have to pretend you're expecting to judge a competition."

"If I must. Come on. Let's go."

We magicked ourselves over to the function room where Aunt Lucy and the twins were awaiting our arrival. The birthday cake at the head of the table was nothing short of amazing.

"Surprise!" everyone shouted.

"Happy birthday, Mother." Aunt Lucy handed

Grandma a card.

"Happy birthday, Grandma," the twins echoed.

"Wow, what a surprise." Grandma couldn't have sounded any less convincing if she'd tried.

"We really fooled you, didn't we?" Amber said.

"There is no cupcake competition." Pearl laughed.

"Colour me gobsmacked," Grandma said, then looked around the room. "When do the other guests arrive?"

I waited for someone to respond, but it soon became obvious that everyone else was waiting for someone to speak up too.

"Jill?" Amber said.

"What? I was in charge of getting Grandma here. You two were supposed to send out the invitations."

"Not us." Pearl turned to Aunt Lucy. "You said you'd do it."

"I said no such thing. I don't even remember the invitations being discussed."

Grandma cleared her throat to get everyone's attention. "Let me see if I've got this right. You arranged this *surprise* birthday party for me, but you failed to invite even one of my friends."

I almost expressed my incredulity that she had any friends, but my sense of self-preservation kicked in just in time.

"What does it matter?" Aunt Lucy said. "The four of us can have our own little party. It will be lovely."

"Do you really expect me to celebrate my one-thousandth birthday with just the three of you?" Grandma snapped.

I said, "Maybe we could still—"

"Shush!" Grandma held up her hand to silence me.

"Fortunately, I had the foresight to anticipate a problem such as this. That's why I sent out my own invitations. One for every year of my life." She checked her watch. "My guests should be arriving in about fifteen minutes, so I hope you have plenty of food prepared."

And sure enough, thirty minutes later, the room was packed with dozens of Grandma's friends, most of whom had arrived bearing gifts. Watching the twins running around in ever decreasing circles, as they tried to find enough food and drink for everyone, was quite hilarious. Aunt Lucy's cake was a hit, and thanks to a little magic, there was enough for everyone to have a slice.

"I'm really sorry about yesterday, Aunt Lucy," I said when I managed to grab a quiet word with her.

"Don't be silly, Jill, I had a blast."

"Yeah, but I lost us the money."

"I was never in it for the prize money. I just wanted to experience the gameshow, and I had a ball."

"You seemed to be a little down afterwards yesterday."

"It would have been nice to win, but honestly, that's not what was important. I really do appreciate you taking part. I know you didn't really want to."

"Grandma looks like she's having a good time. I can't believe she knew about the party all along."

"It's just as well she did, otherwise there wouldn't have been any guests here."

The twins came rushing over, clearly excited about something.

"It's nearly time," Pearl said.

"Time for what?" I had no idea what they were talking about.

"I'm not sure this was a good idea," Aunt Lucy said.

I still had no clue what they were going on about, but then Pearl pointed. I looked around just in time to see three little fairies land on Grandma's nose. It was the same three greetings fairies who had come to my address by mistake.

"Happy birthday to you. Happy—"

That was as far as they got because Grandma swatted them away.

"Annoying little things."

I almost felt sorry for the three fairies, as they picked themselves off the floor and made their exit.

"I did warn you, girls." Aunt Lucy chuckled.

When, eventually, things started to wind down and the guests began to leave, I managed to catch up with the twins again. By then, they both looked dead on their feet.

"Well done, girls. You've worked wonders."

"I hope it was worth it," Amber said.

"It definitely was." I gestured to Grandma. "She's loved every minute of it. Well, apart from the greetings fairies."

"Did you know she knew about the party, Jill?" Pearl said.

"Not until just before we came here."

"I can't believe none of us thought about the invitations."

We all laughed.

"Amber and I have some big news," Pearl said.

"No more surprise parties, I hope. I don't think I could stand it."

"No. We've made a big decision about this place," Amber said.

"Surely not more changes?"

"Just one."

"What's that?"

"We've decided to change the name."

"Again? You've not long since changed it."

"That's just it. We've realised it was a big mistake. Everyone hates the new name and lots of people, including you, are calling it Pamber."

"That's only a joke."

"I know, but we've decided to change the name anyway."

"To what?"

"Cuppy C."

"You're going back to the old name?"

"Yeah. We were crazy to ever change it. What do you think?"

"I think that's probably the best idea you two have ever had."

***

"I can't believe your grandmother knew about the party all along," Jack said.

"It's just as well she did, otherwise there would have been no guests there."

"You look much better than you did when I left this morning."

"I feel much better. It was a great party. It was nice to see Grandma having such a good time with all her friends."

"I'm amazed she has any. Friends, that is."

"Be careful. She might hear."

"From what you told me about how much she drank,

she's probably going to sleep for a week."

"I haven't told you the twins' big news."

"They're not both pregnant again, are they?"

"What? No. I think they've both decided one kid is enough for them. They're changing the name of the tea room back to Cuppy C."

"Not before time."

Chapter 34

It was Monday morning, the start of a new week, and I was feeling more positive than I'd felt in ages.

"What are you looking so pleased about?" Jack said.

"Just life. The weather is gorgeous, and the day is full of possibilities."

"Have you been reading one of Kathy's self-help books?"

"No, I've just decided to adopt a positive attitude."

"That won't last."

"Why so cynical?"

"Because I've seen this before. If past experience is anything to go by, your new positivity won't last the day."

"You're wrong. Nothing that could happen today will dampen my mood."

Just then, there was a knock at the door.

"How about a cold caller?" Jack grinned. "I know how much you love those guys."

"Everyone has a job to do. I'll hear them out and then respectfully decline whatever it is they're selling."

"This I have to see."

Jack was looking over my shoulder as I answered the door, but it wasn't a cold seller who was standing there; it was Big Mac.

"Detective?"

"Mrs Maxwell. I was hoping I'd catch you in."

"Is it about Marcy Bowkoo?"

"No, actually it's about one of your neighbours: a Ms Goldie Barr."

"Ah right. You've decided to follow up her report then,

have you?"

"Which report would that be?"

"She thought someone had been in her house. She spoke to one of your constables."

"I see. No, that's not why I'm here."

"I don't understand."

"Ms Barr was murdered last night."

ALSO BY ADELE ABBOTT

The Not-A-Date (a sweet romantic comedy)

I'd just been fired, so the last thing I needed was some guy hitting on me, and I told him so in no uncertain terms. Then he goes and offers me the job of my dreams.

Pushing All My Buttons (a sweet romantic comedy)

I got stuck in a lift with this guy who then tried to hit on me, so I told him he was a jerk. A few days later, I started a new job and discovered he was my boss.

So Not The One (A sweet romantic comedy)

I was devastated when my old boss had to take early retirement. But that was nothing compared to how I felt when I discovered who his replacement was.

The Witch P.I. Mysteries (A Candlefield/Washbridge Series)

Witch Is When... (Season #1)
Witch Is When It All Began
Witch Is When Life Got Complicated
Witch Is When Everything Went Crazy
Witch Is When Things Fell Apart
Witch Is When The Bubble Burst
Witch Is When The Penny Dropped
Witch Is When The Floodgates Opened
Witch Is When The Hammer Fell

Witch Is When My Heart Broke
Witch Is When I Said Goodbye
Witch Is When Stuff Got Serious
Witch Is When All Was Revealed

Witch Is Why... (Season #2)
Witch Is Why Time Stood Still
Witch is Why The Laughter Stopped
Witch is Why Another Door Opened
Witch is Why Two Became One
Witch is Why The Moon Disappeared
Witch is Why The Wolf Howled
Witch is Why The Music Stopped
Witch is Why A Pin Dropped
Witch is Why The Owl Returned
Witch is Why The Search Began
Witch is Why Promises Were Broken
Witch is Why It Was Over

Witch Is How... (Season #3)
Witch is How Things Had Changed
Witch is How Berries Tasted Good
Witch is How The Mirror Lied
Witch is How The Tables Turned
Witch is How The Drought Ended
Witch is How The Dice Fell
Witch is How The Biscuits Disappeared
Witch is How Dreams Became Reality
Witch is How Bells Were Saved
Witch is How To Fool Cats
Witch is How To Lose Big
Witch is How Life Changed Forever

Witch Is Where... (Season #4)
Witch is Where Magic Lives Now
Witch Is Where Clowns Go To Die
Witch Is Where Squirrels Go Nuts
Witch Is Where Rainbows End
Witch Is Where Unicorns Cry
Witch Is Where The Lights Went Out
Witch Is Where Fairies Wing It
Witch Is Where Roses Bloom Early
Witch Is Where Decisions Are Made
Witch Is Where Gnomes Rules
Witch Is Where Cats Always Win
Witch Is Where Chickens Go To Roost

Witch Is The... (Season #5)
Witch is The Nest Now Empty

Susan Hall Investigates (A Candlefield/Washbridge Series)

Whoops! Our New Flatmate Is A Human.
Whoops! All The Money Went Missing.
Whoops! Someone Is On Our Case.
Whoops! We're In Big Trouble Now.

Murder On Account (A Kat Royle Novel)

Her boss has been murdered. Now she must find his killer. Smart, sassy and kickass tough, private investigator, Kat Royle, is nobody's fool, but does she have what it takes to keep the agency afloat, and find the murderer?

Web site: AdeleAbbott.com
Facebook: facebook.com/AdeleAbbottAuthor

Printed in Dunstable, United Kingdom

65057450R00191